DEADLIER THAN THE PEN

Other books by Kathy Lynn Emerson

The Face Down Mystery Series:
Face Down in the Marrow-Bone Pie
Face Down Upon an Herbal
Face Down Among the Winchester Geese
Face Down Beneath the Eleanor Cross
Face Down Under the Wych Elm
Face Down Before Rebel Hooves
Face Down Across the Western Sea
Murders & Other Confusions (short stories)

Nonfiction:
Wives and Daughters: The Women of Sixteenth-Century
England
Making Headlines: A Biography of Nellie Bly
The Writer's Guide to Everyday Life in Renaissance England

Novels for Ages 8-12:
The Mystery of Hilliard's Castle
Julia's Mending
The Mystery of the Missing Bagpipes

DEADLIER THAN THE PEN

A Diana Spaulding Mystery

by

KATHY LYNN EMERSON

PEMBERLEY

Published by
P E M B E R L E Y   P R E S S
P O Box 1027
Corona del Mar, CA 92625
www.pemberleypress.com

A member of The Authors Studio
www.theauthorsstudio.org

Cover art by Linda Weatherly
Cover design by kat & dog studios

Publisher's Cataloging-in-Publication

Emerson, Kathy Lynn.
    Deadlier than the pen : a Diana Spaulding mystery /
by Kathy Lynn Emerson.
    p. cm. -- (Diana Spaulding mystery series)
    ISBN 0-9702727-8-2
    LCCN 2003109449

    1. Women detectives--United States--Fiction. 2. New
York (N.Y.)--Fiction. 3. Bangor (Me.)--Fiction.
4. Detective and mystery stories. 5. Historical fiction.
I. Title.

PS3555.M414D43 2003   813'.54
                          QBI03-700459

To Miss C.J. Smith

on the occasion of
her birth day

CHAPTER ONE

ഇൗരു

March, 1888 ~ New York City

Unable to see for the darkness, Diana Spaulding paused just inside the entrance to Heritage Hall, waiting for the curtain to rise before she tried to find her way to a seat. In anticipation of the start of Damon Bathory's performance, all lights had been extinguished, leaving the auditorium as black as the inside of an abandoned coal mine.

After a moment, a faint green glow appeared at the front of the proscenium. An eerie silence permeated the entire theater . . . until it was broken by a sepulchral voice reading the first lines of a selection from *Tales of Terror*.

As an effect at the start of an evening of horror stories, that disembodied sound was nicely theatrical, but Diana deplored the icy chill that raced along her spine. She did not like being tricked into an emotional response.

Limelight came up slowly, brightening until the man in front of a black backdrop was clearly visible. Even in that intense glare, he retained an aura of mystery. The dark curtains billowed behind him as he moved, now revealing, now concealing a form attired entirely in ebony hues. An obsidian-colored mane framed his face.

For a long moment, Diana simply stood at the back of the hall and stared, mesmerized by her first good look at the writer she'd been ordered to interview. He was not what she'd expected. She'd been certain anyone whose mind could spawn such ghastly, unforgettable images, who could create such horrible, evil, memorable characters, would be equally repulsive in person. The late Edgar Allan Poe, in the likenesses Diana had seen of him, looked as if he suffered the torment of the damned in order to create his nightmare tales.

The twisted, tortured soul of Damon Bathory, however, resided in a vital, superbly conditioned body, at least six feet tall, with a muscular chest and perfectly proportioned arms and legs. His facial features were difficult to discern but were certainly not deformed. The paleness of forehead and nose stood out in contrast to jet black waves of hair above and a neatly trimmed mustache and beard below.

What struck Diana most forcibly was that he moved with leonine grace, holding a copy of his book in one strong, long-fingered hand while he used the other to gesture. Each movement was subtle but compelling. Choreographed. He rarely glanced at the text.

Tearing her gaze away from the stage, Diana located an empty seat and slid in from the aisle. As she sank gratefully into a comfortable plush-velvet chair, she wondered if being surrounded by other people would diminish the impact of Bathory's performance. One glance around her answered that question. The deep pitch and hypnotic cadence of his voice held the entire audience spellbound.

Read aloud, Bathory's words possessed even more power than they'd had on the page, and they'd been evocative enough in print to give Diana nightmares. As she listened, he reached the climax of the story, the death of his hero. There was a moment of stunned silence in the crowd, followed by a smattering of shocked gasps and nervous, hastily muffled titters. Into that highly charged atmosphere Damon Bathory spoke the last line of his text in a voice calculated to make the strongest man's blood run cold.

Since the spectators consisted primarily of young women, the effect was particularly successful, eliciting first horrified shrieks and then tumultuous applause. In the seat next to Diana, a girl of no more than sixteen sighed in ecstasy.

How many in the audience, Diana wondered, had come here solely to gawk at the man himself? This was the last night of the six he'd been scheduled to appear. Had word spread that it was worth the fifty-cent price of admission to sit in blackness and weave forbidden fantasies about a darkly handsome and charismatic artist?

Diana tugged off her suede gloves, shrugged out of her warm wool Ulster, and fumbled at her flat, beaded bag for one of the small notebooks she always carried. At the bottom, beneath her handkerchief, sufficient cab fare for a hansom, and an essence bottle, she unearthed a pencil. By the time Bathory launched into his second selection, her eyes had adjusted to the dimness of the auditorium. Long practice enabled her to write without much light.

"Smooth, cultured voice," she scribbled, then paused to listen for any trace of regional accent. It was there, she decided, but never quite strong enough for her to place.

Setting that small puzzle aside, she concentrated on the text of his presentation. He wove a powerful spell with words and voice. She was no more immune to it than the other women in the audience.

As the evening wore on, Diana despaired of ever being able to convey to her readers even a fraction of the primordial feelings Bathory's words evoked. His use of metaphor and symbolism made her think her own writing style pallid in comparison. And how could she possibly do justice to a description of the atmosphere of subtle, sensual menace emanating from the stage?

As a performer he was very good. With his voice alone he made her believe in eternal hellfire. Many an actor would envy him its resonance. They'd kill for his consummate skill at evoking a mood.

Diana had never enjoyed grim and distressing subject matter, but when Damon Bathory began his last selection, "The Tale of the Blood Countess," she could not help herself. There was an undeniable attraction about the thrill of being safely frightened. A delicious, anticipatory shudder raced through her.

When Damon Bathory reached the end of the story, the lights came up in the hall. Some members of the audience departed at once, struggling into coats and chattering among themselves as they headed for the doors at the back. But several of the sweet young things who'd flocked to the reading, and a few who were neither sweet nor young, surged forward to accost the performer before he could escape backstage.

Noting the strained smile on Bathory's face, Diana felt a moment's sympathy. He played the role of famous writer well, answering all but the most inane of questions. He evaded those while modestly acknowledging the praise the women wished to heap upon him. Once, he politely, but firmly, dislodged the clinging hand of a particularly eager young female from his forearm.

Her head bent to hide a smile, Diana scribbled a few final comments into her notebook while he dealt with the remaining fans. When all but the last two had left, she stood, collected her coat and gloves, and started towards the stage.

At first, Ben Northcote gleaned only a general impression of the woman moving gracefully down the aisle. She wore a pleasing costume in navy blue trimmed with embroidery and cut-work. The small bustle on her round skirt bounced as she walked, lending a certain jauntiness to her progress.

As she came closer, Ben's gaze slid upward. Her hat, a spot of color in red felt trimmed with red velvet, sported several feathers that drooped low enough to conceal her features until she was right in front of him. At last she looked at him, and he discerned wide-spaced, bright blue eyes and a pert little nose. The slightly square shape of her face gave it character, rendering her handsome rather than pretty. What little he could see of her thick, mahogany-colored hair—a strand had come loose from confinement beneath her hat—softened the effect and brought out the likeness to gardenia petals in her complexion.

She waited until they were alone before she stepped onto the stage and addressed him. She'd clearly been taking his measure while he had taken hers. When she gave him a tentative smile and thrust out a hand, he took it and shook it without hesitation, just as if she were a man.

"Good evening, Mr. Bathory. My name is Mrs. Evan Spaulding. I write a column called 'Today's Tidbits' for the *Independent Intelligencer.*"

Ben dropped her hand as if he had been burnt. He made it his practice to read all the local newspapers. "Today's Tidbits" was written in epistle style and enlivened by personal asides. The previous Friday, the columnist had skewered *Tales of Terror,* but it was not that unsigned review alone which made Ben wary. Monday's column had left a sour taste in his mouth. In that one she'd not only dissected a new production of an old play but the private business of the actresses in the cast as well.

"I realize this was the last of your public readings here in New York," Mrs. Spaulding went on, the deepening pink stain in her cheeks the only indication that she might have guessed his thoughts, "but I am sure you can have no objection to more publicity. Booksellers still stock your titles. You—"

"Sales are quite brisk, Mrs. Spaulding, and I've no desire to answer impertinent questions about my personal life."

Although she winced at his curt tone, she did not give up. "Would you rather I speculate?" She was nothing if not persistent. "Be assured, Mr. Bathory, your name will appear in my column again whether you agree to an interview or not."

"Indeed? Do you mean to drop hints to the public about my bedroom scenes?"

This second, more pointed reference to Monday's column brought another, darker rush of color to her cheeks. "I have read *The Curse of Hannah Sussep, or The Indian Witch* and I mean to evaluate it for the benefit of my readers." An involuntary *moue* of distaste accompanied this announcement.

Her critique would not be favorable, Ben concluded. The lady did not care for horror stories. Truthfully, he could not blame her, although he had no intention of voicing that opinion. Some of the Damon Bathory tales made even him queasy, and he was no stranger to spilled blood or grievous wounds.

"You surprise me, madam," he said instead. "What need have you to write this review when less than a week ago you gave yourself free rein to criticize other works by Damon Bathory?"

"It is my job to comment on all current books and plays." Stiff of speech, standing erect, her chin stuck out at a belligerent angle, she was an irresistible target.

"Will my reading tonight be covered in your critique?"

"Why else should I have come?"

He met that response with a sardonic lift of one brow, a gesture that produced another frown from his attractive adversary.

"I will write about what I saw and heard," she said, but he noted that her voice was not completely steady.

He knew the effect Damon Bathory had on women. During a performance he could not see his audience, and he had decided early in his four-month tour that this was a good thing. It was disconcerting enough afterwards, when the harpies descended upon him, clamoring for attention, craving a word, a smile . . . a fright to tell their friends about. Doing readings in every major city in America had become more of a burden than he'd ever anticipated when he'd agreed to the endeavor. That his readings were so popular with females of all ages never failed to amaze him.

"Far be it from me to stand in the way of freedom of the press," he said now, to this one. "I am merely curious when I ask this: do you mean to be equally fair-minded this time?"

Already defensive, she went rigid at his sarcastic tone. "I will be honest," she said through clenched teeth, "as I always strive to be. It is not only my right but my duty to express a negative opinion if I have one."

Ben watched her, reluctantly fascinated, as she visibly fought for control of her temper. He wondered if she was counting to ten. More likely to twenty, he decided as the silence lengthened between them. Both her tone and her words surprised him when she finally spoke.

"The books are not badly written."

"How gratifying to be damned with faint praise."

"You write too well. The images you evoke are dreadful to contemplate. All else aside, was it necessary to end with a bloodbath? In spite of myself, I came to like your half-mad heroine. I sympathized with her plight and hoped for her recovery. There was no warning before she and most of her family were brutally slaughtered. How can you expect me to recommend such a terrible story to my readers?"

Ben smiled slowly. She stood up for herself, a trait he'd always admired in a woman. He realized he was enjoying this exchange more than any conversation he'd had in months. Her dislike of the tales did not bother him at all. In fact, it had been his experience that bad reviews produced better sales than raves.

"You were moved by the story." He could hazard a guess as to the real reason behind her reaction. "I understand why you wouldn't want to confess to that in print."

Her frown created twin furrows on either side of the bridge of her nose. "I cannot recommend that any gently reared young lady peruse your book, but I will tell my readers that the story has a moral, and that the images are brilliantly crafted."

"Admit the truth, Mrs. Spaulding," he coaxed. "Just to me.

These stories wreak havoc with your emotions. That is why you dislike them so much."

His perception plainly startled her, but after a moment she rewarded him with an appealingly rueful smile and a nod of agreement. "I cannot help but admire your skill in managing it so seamlessly."

"So, you applaud Damon Bathory's ability as a writer?"

"But despise the subject matter, and that opinion will not alter." The smile vanished and she was all business again. "Won't you reconsider granting me an interview?"

"I think not."

The idea of spending more time with this charmingly contradictory woman tempted Ben, but not strongly enough to offset the risk. One slip of the tongue and all his efforts would have been for naught. He could not trust her. That Monday column was proof she had no regard for privacy. She'd print anything and everything she learned about him. While it was unlikely someone from home would read this particular newspaper and make a connection, he did not want to take any chances.

"It would give you the opportunity to explain yourself, to express your views on the merits of telling such dark tales."

Ben shook his head. Her forthcoming review would generate sales without additional revelations from him.

"Such an arrangement could benefit us both," she persisted. "If only you—"

"There will be no interview, Mrs. Spaulding."

With that final, curt dismissal, Ben started to leave the stage. A sharp tug stopped him. She'd caught hold of the high-swirling hem of the long, black cloak he wore as part of his costume.

"Mr. Bathory, I—"

He held up one hand as he turned, forestalling further argument, but she did not release her hold on the fabric. They stood disturbingly close to each other, a mere step away from an intimate embrace.

Mrs. Spaulding, he reminded himself. And a woman who wielded that most dangerous weapon, the pen. Few arms in any arsenal were deadlier.

With a little gasp, she dropped the cloth and backed away, eyes wide as she stared at his uplifted fingers. Her focus was on the ornate ring he wore. It was jade, carved in intaglio with a crest that showed a dragon biting its own tail. The beast encircled three wolf's teeth surmounted by a crown.

With a wicked smile, Ben lifted his right hand a little higher, until the stage lights fully illuminated the stone. There was no doubt in his mind that Mrs. Spaulding recognized the coat of arms. It was the one he'd earlier described, in loving detail, as belonging to Elizabeth Bathory, the evil heroine of "The Tale of the Blood Countess." He gave her a moment longer to recall that "Damon Bathory" claimed descent from this 16th century noblewoman, a fiend who had murdered hundreds of young peasant girls in the belief that bathing in their blood would keep her eternally youthful.

He spoke in the soft, ominous tone he'd perfected for the stage. "It is not wise to try to strike a deal with the devil, Mrs. Spaulding." Then, before she could do more than catch her breath in alarm, he made a swift, smooth exit. This time she made no attempt to stop him.

The moment he vanished from sight, Diana recovered her courage. He'd been toying with her, she realized, deliberately playing on the imaginary terrors he himself had instilled in her.

He was mysterious, threateningly virile, and wickedly attractive. But he was neither a monster, nor one of his characters. There was no fire and brimstone in the air.

She frowned. An elusive odor had been teasing her nostrils ever since she'd stepped onto the stage. A slow smile enveloped her face as she belatedly identified it. The dark and dangerous Damon

Bathory smelled of Ivory soap.

She considered continuing her pursuit backstage but decided against it. Clean, fresh scent or not, the man affected her strangely and the fact that not all her reactions were negative seemed an excellent reason to keep a distance between them.

A young widow could not afford to fall prey to such feelings—either unfounded fear or lustful thoughts.

To prove to herself that she was not afraid, and that she had control of other emotions as well, Diana forced herself to stay right where she was and make a few more notes in her little cloth-covered notebook. When she'd recorded the impressions she thought might be helpful in her account of the reading, including a detailed description of that ring, she closed the book and returned it to her bag, buttoned up her coat, and made her way, at a dignified pace, through the empty theater.

Although she heard nothing, and was careful not to look back over her shoulder, she could not quite shake the feeling that Damon Bathory was watching her. He might have stayed nearby easily enough, hidden backstage, expecting to witness a hasty retreat. She felt a rush of relief when she reached the well-lit street without being accosted.

He was just an ordinary man, she told herself, as she walked back to 10th Street and her tiny rented room. He was a writer, not a ghoul. He'd probably run the other way if he ever came upon a real dead body.

She almost managed to convince herself that she'd have talked him into an interview if she hadn't reacted so foolishly to the sight of that ring.

She'd let the power of his performance stimulate fancies. That was all.

Unfortunately, her subconscious mind continued to be influenced by what she'd seen and heard in that darkened theater. Damon Bathory haunted her dreams throughout the night, appearing in guises she was embarrassed to recall in the light of day.

When Diana arrived at the city room of the *Independent Intelligencer* the next morning she still suffered vestiges of uneasiness. Cheerful greetings from the other reporters, delivered in accents as diverse as brash Brooklynese and a Charleston drawl, helped dissipate them. Diana returned the salutations with a smile as she hung her coat on a convenient rack and made her way across a carpet of fresh newspapers to her desk.

Before she'd come to work in the city room, her friend Rowena had warned Diana that she'd need only inhale to know that the place was as much a male enclave as the most exclusive gentleman's club. She'd answered that she liked the smell of printer's ink and had refused either to acknowledge or to be put off by the other ever-present odors. These days she barely noticed the miasma of stale cigar smoke. As for the reeking spittoons, lately they were cleaned and polished at least once a week. Only a faint stench rose up to greet Diana if she ventured too close.

With a determined expression on her face, Diana tugged off her kid gloves and put them inside the small, leather bag she carried during the day. Then she unpinned and removed her small, high-crowned blue hat and set it carefully on top of the bag. She wished she could dispense with her restrictive corset and bustle as well, but she was already skirting the limits of propriety by going about the office with her head bare.

Arranging herself as comfortably as she could on her hard, wooden chair, Diana wound a sheet of paper into the typewriter she'd spent the last few weeks learning to use. Most of the men she worked with refused to have anything to do with this newfangled device, but Diana felt it had potential and was committed to mastering it.

She hadn't really been frightened by Damon Bathory, she assured herself as she pecked at the keys, referring now and again to her notes. She certainly wasn't afraid of him this morning, just relieved that she would never have to cross paths with him again. As soon as she finished writing this column, she could permanently banish Bathory's disturbing presence from her mind.

Normally, Diana had no trouble concentrating in the midst of chaos. She found most of the sounds in the noisy city room soothing—voices murmuring, pens scratching, the steady but muffled clank of the expensive new Lin-o-type machine on the floor below. Once in a while she could even hear the distant rumble of the presses in the basement. It was rare that she let anything distract her.

Today was different.

For some peculiar reason, the keys of the typewriter refused to cooperate. Worse, the review she was trying to compose seemed to have a mind of its own. Her irritation increased when she stopped typing to skim what she'd written. The words in front of her made her as vexed with herself as she was with Bathory. How could she have wasted so much space describing the man's appearance, something that had nothing to do with the quality of his stories?

Ripping the page from the machine, she went over the text again, appalled not only by the number of mistakes but by the fawning, almost admiring tone that had somehow crept into her account. She'd set out to describe a dangerous-looking man reading horrifying material and had ended up making Bathory sound like an appealing rogue.

A wave of heat swept into her face at the sudden clear memory of one particular passage in a night full of vivid dreams. She'd been back on the stage at Heritage Hall, trying to stop Damon Bathory from walking out on her. In her nightmare his swirling cloak had completely enveloped her in its dark folds when he turned.

Unable to see, Diana had let other senses take over. She'd felt warm hands on her body, building both excitement and terror. Then the cloak had no longer held her prisoner, but she'd still been in darkness. She'd heard a heart beating loudly, rapidly. His? Her own? She hadn't been able to tell.

Next, scents had begun to impinge on her consciousness. First fire and brimstone. Then grease paint and gas lights. Theater smells. And suddenly she'd been awash with confusion. Was the man caressing her Damon Bathory? Or her late husband, Evan Spaulding?

With a jolt, Diana came out of her reverie. She had not noticed any smell of grease paint when she'd accosted Bathory on stage. There had only been that contradictory whiff of Ivory soap, its clean, pure connotations at odds with the dark images she associated with a writer of horror stories. That must mean that she'd dreamt of Evan, who had made his living as an actor.

Darting a self-conscious glance at the other reporters, she saw that no one had noticed she'd been staring off into space. Only she knew that she'd folded and refolded the page in her hands to make accordion pleats of the draft of her story.

Uttering a muttered expletive, Diana crumpled the mangled paper into a ball, barely controlling the urge to fling it across the city room. Instead, on her way to confront her editor, she dropped it gently into the wicker basket beside her desk.

CHAPTER TWO

ഇൽ

Did you get the Bathory interview?" Horatio Foxe demanded the moment Diana entered his office.

"No, I did not." She dearly wished she'd never heard of the wretched man. She'd proven herself a good journalist in the last year and a half, but so far her successes had not convinced her editor to listen to even one of her ideas.

With a sound that was almost a growl, Foxe chomped down so hard on the end of his cigar that he bit clean through it. He tossed the pieces aside in disgust, heedless of where they landed.

Diana chose not to respond to his display of temper. With studied calm, she seated herself opposite him and met his glare head-on across the piles of paper and newsprint that littered the top of an oak double desk. At the same female seminary where she'd met Foxe's younger sister Rowena, Diana had been taught that a lady must always conceal her emotions. The previous evening's encounter with Damon Bathory had been all the more irritating because she'd failed so miserably to hide her reactions to him. Determined to hold onto her temper this morning, she kept her hands demurely folded in her lap and studied her employer, trying to discern his mood. Although he was a small, wiry man, when he was in a temper he displayed the fierceness of a bantam rooster.

"Well?" Foxe demanded. "What happened?"

"I talked to Mr. Bathory briefly and he declined my invitation to discuss either his writing or his life. In fact, he seemed to prefer that he not be mentioned in my column at all."

Foxe reached for a fresh cigar and gnawed one end of it as it drooped, unlit, from the corner of his mouth. "Odd attitude for a writer. Most go out of their way to get their names into print. I can think of only one reason why Damon Bathory would refuse to be interviewed. He must have something to hide."

He drummed thin, ink-stained fingers on the only bare spot on the scarred wooden surface in front of him. A moment later he lifted them to tunnel through his sand-colored hair, leaving an unkempt topknot behind.

Diana fought a smile at the familiar gesture. Her acquaintance with Foxe went back eight years, to a time when she'd still been in school and he'd been no more than her friend Rowena's older brother. Without Rowena's help, Diana doubted she'd have been able to persuade Foxe to hire her after Evan's sudden death, let alone allow her to come to the office every day to work. The other female columnists employed by New York's *Independent Intelligencer* sent their stories in from home.

Why, then, was she so nervous about talking to him? She'd won that skirmish. Moreover, she suspected Horatio Foxe was the one who'd ordered old newspapers put down on the floor of the city room and changed every morning before she arrived. This considerate gesture saved her from soiling the hems of her skirts in stray puddles of tobacco juice. Several of her male co-workers were notorious for their poor aim. No matter how many brass cuspidors were set out, the surface underfoot tended to be pockmarked with stinking, standing pools.

"I see no point in badgering the man," she ventured. "Mr. Bathory has a right to his privacy."

"Balderdash! He's famous. That makes him fair game." An avaricious gleam came into Foxe's narrowed eyes. "I want you to follow up on this, Diana."

Diana felt a frisson of alarm. She tried to ignore it, telling herself she wasn't afraid to face Bathory again. She simply did not wish to pursue this particular story. "I have enough copy for my column without the addition of Mr. Bathory's comments or opinions."

"Who cares about his opinions? I want scandal. What about women in his life? I suppose it's too much to hope that he'll turn out to be another Bluebeard, but that's the sort of thing that pulls in readers."

Diana was glad of the reprieve when a knock sounded at Foxe's door, sparing her the necessity of an immediate reply. The last thing she wanted was to spend more time with Damon Bathory. A strong instinct for self-preservation warned her to stay away from any man who could leave her feeling so unsettled.

Women in his life? She had seen the mesmerizing effect he had on the opposite sex. And she had already wasted far too much time remembering the way he'd swept her off her feet in that dream. Throughout her marriage, Diana had experienced quite enough excitement and danger, with sufficient emotional highs and lows to last a lifetime. She wanted nothing more to do with creative, driven men like her late husband or Damon Bathory. And she wished, in particular, to avoid men who kept secrets.

By the time Foxe had dealt with the interruption, Diana was braced for another round. "The readers of my column want and expect only my review, which I will most assuredly give them. If, however, you feel I must also conduct interviews, then I can think of several people more interesting than Damon Bathory."

His expression skeptical, Foxe resumed his seat. "Who do you have in mind? Some leader of the Woman Suffrage Alliance?"

Annoyed by his snide tone, Diana made her own voice sugar sweet. "You're the one who always says that controversy improves circulation. Think of all the publicity you'd generate by having the *Independent Intelligencer* come out in favor of votes for women."

"That, my dear, would be as suicidal as backing those blasted anarchists who preach free love on street corners and advocate abolishing all forms of government."

"What if I do an entire series of interviews and promise that none of their subjects will be suffragettes or anarchists?" Or horror writers, she added silently. She shifted position in a futile attempt to avoid the acrid cloud steadily enveloping everything in the room.

Worrying both the cigar and his pet project with the dedication of a hound with a bone, Foxe made a counter-proposal. "Talk to Damon Bathory first. Then I might be more inclined to consider your suggestions."

"Anyone but Bathory." She put as much firmness as she could manage into the words. "I've already told you—"

"What you've already done is promise your readers a profile of Damon Bathory, including never-before-published facts about his personal life. It's to run next week."

Diana felt her eyes widen. "I never made any such promise!"

Even as she spoke, she knew what had happened. *Again.* Anger replaced disbelief as Foxe confirmed her suspicion.

"Indeed you did, in your column in this afternoon's paper, which is even now being printed." His voice oozed self-congratulation. "Your assignment is simple enough. You contact Bathory, and this time you find out all you can about his past. You won't have to lie. All you need do is write up everything you learn in a way that will titillate our readers."

In her lap, Diana's hands clenched so tightly that her knuckles turned white. Foxe had neatly boxed her in. Now not only her job was at stake, but also her reputation as a journalist.

When she finally spoke, she did not sound upset, but just beneath the surface her temper was simmering close to the boiling point. "You have no notion, do you, of how much trouble you caused for me with your additions to Monday's column?"

"I am the editor of this newspaper." A meaningful look

accompanied the haughty words. "That gives me the authority to make any changes I deem necessary to any part of it."

"Necessary?" Surely he could not mean that. "I shared certain details in confidence. I never intended to include them in my column. And don't try to tell me you misunderstood. Or that using initials instead of names made the item any less hurtful to those concerned."

Diana had been appalled to open the newspaper on Monday afternoon and discover that the review she'd written of a play had been followed by sordid hints that the company's ingenue had won her part in a bedroom audition and stolen the affection of the troupe's manager away from the leading lady. That the tale was true in no way lessened her dismay.

"That story, my dear, increased this newspaper's circulation for two days afterward. Your readers obviously approve and hope for more like it. From now on that is exactly what you are going to give them." Foxe's grin showed a row of small, straight, tobacco-stained teeth.

"No." The word came out in a whisper as Diana stared at him in disbelief. The idea of deliberately exploiting someone's personal life for the benefit of the newspaper made her skin crawl.

Bad enough, she thought, that she'd already gone beyond what she was comfortable with to write unflattering comments about the acting abilities of the newest members of Todd's Touring Thespians. It did not matter that their performances had been lackluster, the delivery of Mr. Charles Underly all bombast when simple enthusiasm would have served him better. Until six months ago, she had not been in the habit of voicing negative comments at all. Why pan a production when she could find some redeeming grace to write about instead? She'd tried to live by the rule that when one could not say something nice, one should not say anything at all.

Foxe had changed all that. He'd taken her aside to explain that she would mislead readers if she had nothing but praise for every subject. It was her duty, he'd said, to express her honest opinion, even if it was wholly negative. Diana had reluctantly accepted this edict, had even seen the logic of his argument, but she hoped she would never reach the point when it became easy to say hurtful things.

"I have told you before that scandal sells newspapers," Foxe said now. "We're in a war, Diana."

He swiveled in his chair to gesture at the bank of windows behind his desk. They overlooked New York's Newspaper Row. Foxe's panoramic view encompassed the headquarters of the *Independent Intelligencer's* greatest rivals, the *Times,* the *Sun,* the *Tribune,* and Joseph Pulitzer's *World.*

"Whichever publisher captures the greatest number of readers wins. The one with the lowest distribution faces almost certain bankruptcy. Make no mistake, Diana, the more scandalous the revelations, the more secure our future will be. That is why I want an interview with Damon Bathory. Find out why he writes the sort of thing he does. Does he have personal experience with murder and mayhem? What ghoulish habits does he practice in private?"

Involuntarily, Diana's hands tightened in her lap. Reading his stories in the safety of her own home had been bad enough before she'd come face to face with him and heard the words in his unforgettably compelling baritone. Damon Bathory's powerful prose left her uneasy, looking over her shoulder at the smallest sound and checking under the bed at night when she knew perfectly well that nothing evil lurked there. The man himself had a presence that disturbed her deeply on a very personal level. She was quite certain she did not want to investigate what might have inspired him.

"I have already reviewed his *Tales of Terror.*" She'd assigned to it, in print, a status lower than the worst penny dreadful, a sincere opinion, if unflattering. "Why give further publicity to Mr. Bathory or the sort of literature he creates?"

"Why? Because this newspaper will reap the benefits of a first-hand encounter." Foxe looked smug. "Those stories of his are clearly the outpourings of a tortured soul, full of torment, but no one knows anything about their author, not even if Bathory is his real name. Go after the scandal, m'dear. Find out who he is and where he's from and what secrets he's keeping. That is your assignment."

"If he wants his personal life kept private, he's hardly likely to share its details with me."

"I have confidence in you, Diana. You will worm information out of him. People talk to you. They trust you."

"They will soon cease to if you have your way."

She was already being shunned by some of her oldest friends. It did not matter that her column was unsigned. New York's theater community was small and close-knit. Actors and managers alike knew that Evan Spaulding's widow wrote "Today's Tidbits." Until Monday, they had accepted her occasional reviews of dramatic productions with good grace, certain she would avoid unnecessary vitriol even if she did give her honest opinion of performances and staging. On a number of occasions, they had provided her with advance information on new ventures.

Foxe occupied himself with relighting his cigar and allowed an uncomfortable silence to lengthen. Diana drew in a deep, steadying breath. She must reason with him, make him see she simply could not do as he asked.

"Isn't it possible that Mr. Bathory has no deep, dark secrets? Perhaps he merely desires privacy."

"If you can discover nothing scandalous, then you will have to rely on innuendo." Foxe blew a cloud of smoke at the ceiling and stared up at it as it dissipated. "There is, of course, one other choice. You could invent something. Make up a juicy scandal out of whole cloth. Who's going to know the difference?"

"I will." Outraged, Diana surged to her feet, her hands fisted at her sides.

"Sit down, Diana."

She obeyed only because he rose from his chair and circled the desk so swiftly that she had nowhere else to go. The moment she was down, he placed one hand on each arm of her chair and leaned in until the tip of his glowing cigar threatened the end of her nose.

By a supreme effort of will, Diana managed not to cringe. In her lap, hidden by her tightly clasped hands, her fingernails bit into the soft pads of her palms until they broke the skin. She was not physically afraid of Horatio Foxe, but even a small man could be daunting at such close quarters.

"Those are your only options, Diana. Choose."

"I will not lie to my readers." Although the additions to Monday's column had upset her, they had, at least, been true.

"Then you must be diligent in your pursuit of Bathory's past. There's scandal in it somewhere. There has to be." The cigar glowed brighter as he sucked on it.

Diana's nose wrinkled when she was forced to breathe in the noxious smoke he exhaled. Her eyes teared. Grinning at her discomfort, Foxe finally straightened, setting her free.

"Make no mistake, Diana. I gave you your job and I can take it away. If you want to keep your column, and your position on this newspaper, you will do all you can to uncover Damon Bathory's secrets."

He was serious. His attempt to dominate her by hovering and breathing fire had not unnerved Diana half so much as the prospect of unemployment. Scruples were all very well, but she had painful personal experience with what it meant to be without work, without money, even without food. The details of those difficult days were etched in her memory. She had no desire to repeat the experience.

The consequences of fighting for her principles loomed before her, daunting and more than a little frightening. There were no jobs at other newspapers. All of them already had their quota of female journalists. Even if they had not, she knew that Foxe's rivals were no more liberal than he was when it came to giving out assignments. Men were sent after news stories. Women wrote society gossip or household hints columns, or risked their necks as "stunt girls" like the *World's* Nellie Bly.

A pity she had no talent for the stage. "Respectable" occupations for females were limited. Most businesses preferred to hire men. Domestic service paid poorly, as did factory work, and conditions in factories were so deplorable that employment there meant risking one's health.

With a sigh, Diana capitulated. As much as she wanted to take a stand in the face of Horatio Foxe's ultimatum, she could not afford the luxury. If she intended to go on eating and have a roof over her head, she had no choice but to do whatever she had to in order to keep her job.

"How am I supposed to discover where Bathory has hidden himself? He has no more readings scheduled. For all we know, he may already have left the city."

Foxe's wide grin dashed the faint hope that this might prove to be the case. "This is your lucky day, Diana. The messenger who interrupted us a little while ago brought word from one of the newsboys. On my orders all the street arabs have been on the lookout for Damon Bathory. They report that he has a suite at the Palace Hotel."

❧❧❧

Damon Bathory answered her knock so quickly that she could only assume he'd been on his way out, though he wore neither topcoat nor hat. "What did you do?" he demanded irritably. "Bribe a desk clerk for my room number?"

The quick rise of heat in her cheeks betrayed the accuracy of his guess, but she slipped into the parlor of his three-room suite before he realized her intent. "It was either that or skulk behind the pillars in the lobby, waiting for you to appear."

"This is not a convenient time for a visit," he said to her back. "I was just leaving."

"I would be happy to wait here until you return."

"No doubt you would love a chance to search my possessions, but I've no intention of leaving you in my rooms. Exactly what do you want, Mrs. Spaulding?"

"To interview you, Mr. Bathory." She favored him with an insincere smile as she faced him. He was no less formidable in a dark gray worsted suit than he had been all in black.

"In spite of the fact that I've already declined to be interrogated?" His answering smile had a wolfish quality as he closed the door to the corridor and stalked towards her. "Tell me, Mrs. Spaulding, does your husband know the lengths to which you'll go for a story?"

Recoiling from the lash of his words, she retreated a few steps. "My husband is dead, Mr. Bathory."

Turning her back to him once more, she tried to focus on her surroundings. The Palace's much publicized luxury accommodations struck her as pretentious. A marble fireplace provided heat. Velvet and brocade upholstery cushioned the furniture. The wallpaper was flocked. In the adjoining bedroom, just visible through the open door, sun shining through a velvet-hung bay window picked out the muted blues, reds, and greens of the room's flowered carpet and highlighted the gilded grooves in the footboard of a heavily carved walnut bed.

The sight of that decadent piece of furniture unnerved Diana. In a flurry of skirts, she changed direction, appropriating the chair drawn up to the writing desk in the parlor. She forced another smile. "All I want are the answers to a few simple questions. And I needed to see you in daylight," she added candidly, "when you haven't the advantage of darkness to enhance your appearance of menace and evil."

His eyes on her, he removed an ornate gold watch from his pocket. "I think you want much more than that, Mrs. Spaulding." He glanced at the time. "You have five minutes."

"Scarcely long enough for you to tell me your life story."

"You don't want to write biography, Mrs. Spaulding. You are only after scandal."

Diana lowered her gaze to her hands, which were primly folded in her lap, and did not reply.

"Can you promise me an account free of speculation and innuendo?" he taunted her.

"Scandal sells newspapers." She heard the hint of desperation in her own whispered words and didn't dare meet his eyes.

"Yes, it does. People read your column for the same reason they read Damon Bathory's books, for the little thrill they get from a vicarious glimpse at things that shock and horrify. There is one difference, though. Fiction doesn't ruin anyone's life by making private matters public."

Her head shot up, followed by the rest of her. Indignant, she opened her mouth to deny his charges, but before she could speak he got close enough to place one finger on her lips. She pursed them tight.

"You know it's true."

His fingertip traced the line of her jaw and flowed over the curve of one cheek to caress a strand of hair that had tumbled out from beneath her hat. When he bent his head, she backed away so rapidly that she came up against a wall.

"You could try to seduce my secrets out of me." Cool and appraising, his gaze raked over her from head to toe, sweeping back up again to stop at her mouth.

"You are misnamed." She glared at him but her voice was thick and none-too-steady. "It should be Demon, not Damon."

"I am told that fear is a potent aphrodisiac. You are not the first reporter who's wanted to . . . interview me. There was a particularly annoying one near the start of this tour." He sent a chilling smile in her direction. "I dealt with her in a most satisfactory manner. Some women hanker after the thrill of going to bed with a man who frightens them. Did you come here, Widow Spaulding, in the hope of being seduced by Damon Bathory? It seems a pity to disappoint you, especially when a part of me clamors for just such an encounter." He moved forward, closing the minuscule distance between them.

Diana kicked him in the shin and darted out of reach, but she stopped halfway to the door to face him with shoulders squared. She could feel her cheeks flaming, but temper renewed her resolve and steadied her nerves.

"You have reached an entirely erroneous conclusion."

"Indeed?" With a rueful grimace, he rubbed the spot where the toe of her boot had connected with his leg.

"Indeed. I want an interview. Nothing more."

"Odd. You gave the impression you'd be willing to do almost anything to get your story." It seemed to amuse him to see how flustered she'd become. "Are you such an innocent then, in spite of having been married?"

"I would do *almost* anything for a story, Mr. Bathory. You have no call to insult me."

"My apologies."

Her eyes narrowed. She doubted he meant it, but she was not yet ready to abandon her quest for an interview. "What harm in giving me a few crumbs, Mr. Bathory? As no one knows anything about you, everything is news. For example, is Bathory your real name or a pseudonym?"

With a shrug, he answered her. "Bathory is a real name."

She rewarded him with a tentative smile and felt her tension ease. "You see how easy it is to please me? A few minutes is all I ask."

"To please you properly would be the work of hours, not minutes. A pity I cannot afford to spend any more time with you." He consulted his watch again and clicked it closed with an air of finality.

"Wait! You said Bathory is a real name, but is it *your* real name?"

Abruptly, he lost patience. "No more crumbs, Mrs. Spaulding."

Over her protests and a barrage of new questions, none of which he answered, he ushered her through the door, down the corridor, and into one of the hotel's mirror-lined elevators.

"Take this woman to the lobby," he instructed the operator, "and see that she's escorted out of the building."

CHAPTER THREE

ಐ)ೞ

The satisfied smirk on Damon Bathory's face as the elevator door closed was enough to spur Diana on. She returned to the hotel by another door within a minute after being escorted out the front. She had no difficulty eluding the elevator operator or any other hotel staff, but once she was back in the lobby she hesitated.

Still shaken by what had happened in Bathory's room, Diana curbed her impatience. That dreadful man obviously thought she was little better than a whore, and yet she'd responded to him. He was a menace in every sense of the word.

She had not yet steeled herself to return to the fourth floor when the object of her interest exited the elevator and passed not two feet in front of the spot where she stood, fortuitously concealed by a potted palm. Oblivious to her presence, he headed towards the nearest exit. From the intent look on his face, he was on important business.

Before she could think better of it, Diana followed him.

Damon Bathory did not deserve any consideration, she told herself. He had insulted her with his casual assumption that she'd crawl into his bed in order to get her story.

Spying on anyone wasn't to her taste, but Diana rationalized that Bathory had only himself to blame. She'd given him two opportunities to contribute to what she meant to write about him. Now she was free to get the details for her story any way she could.

Horatio Foxe wanted scandal. Dark secrets. She couldn't be certain that Bathory was guarding anything more than his right to privacy, or that she would learn anything significant by dogging his footsteps for the rest of the day, but all of a sudden she was very tired of being told what to do. Although she could sympathize with Bathory's natural desire to keep his past, jaded or otherwise, from becoming public knowledge, her frustration over Foxe's demands fueled her irritation at the other man's behavior. She'd have liked to tell both of them to go to the devil.

Instead, when Bathory stepped off the curb outside the hotel and hailed a Hansom cab, Diana flagged down an olive-green Gurney.

"Where to, miss?" the driver asked in a raspy voice.

All Diana could see of his face over a bright plaid muffler were two bloodshot eyes. She hesitated only an instant. If she waited, she'd lose sight of her quarry.

"Follow that cab," she ordered, and was relieved when the driver sneezed, indicating that he was suffering from a head cold rather than keeping himself warm with drink.

Committed to the chase, Diana unlatched the rear-facing door of the vehicle, scrambled onto one of the two lengthwise seats, and pulled the curtains across the side windows. She was left with a narrow opening through which she could see without being seen. If her luck was in, Bathory would never know she was behind him. She might just get her sensational story, after all.

The bubble of excitement that danced in her veins at the start of the chase popped only moments later. As the two cabs sped north and then east, Diana realized that she might not have enough money with her to pay for the ride.

A cab was the most expensive way to travel in Manhattan, fifty cents for the first mile and twenty-five cents for every mile thereafter. Although she did not often use it, it was Diana's custom to carry the necessary cab fare to get home when she ventured out at night. In the daytime, however, she went about on foot—which cost nothing—or at most paid her ten cents and took a horse car. She could not afford to chase Damon Bathory far if he insisted on this means of transportation.

Diana's Gurney stayed close behind the Hansom all the way to 1st Avenue, but she never even saw the speeding ambulance until it cut between them. There was no time to brace herself. The sudden stop jounced her right off the seat. Her elbow struck the door.

"Close one." The hackman cracked his whip to start the horse moving again.

Diana swallowed hard as she righted herself and rubbed her funny bone. Less than three weeks earlier, on the night of the fire at the Union Square Theater, another ambulance had taken the corner at 6th Avenue and 14th Street too sharply and overturned. The injured men in the back had been thrown into the street.

Such traffic accidents were far too common of late. She ought to write an article exposing the situation. A rueful smile tugged at the corners of her mouth. Foxe would probably expect her to claim she'd been injured near to death before he'd approve the idea.

Moments later, the Gurney stopped again. An empty Hansom, heading the other way, clattered past. With a sinking sensation in her stomach, Diana recognized the yellow topcoat and shiny silk hat of Bathory's driver. "Where could he have gone?"

"Not much here but Bellevue," her cabman mumbled into his muffling scarf. "Ambulance came out of the hospital yard by the 26th Street gate."

Bellevue?

Diana stared up at the high, bleak walls. The facility was a respected medical school and hospital these days, but when it had first been built it had also housed a penitentiary. There were still bars across some of the windows.

It was a perfectly logical destination for someone in Damon

Bathory's profession. Diana's imagination could conjure up any number of ghoulish reasons for him to pay the place a visit. Was he there to tour the operating theater? The morgue? The insane pavilion?

The cab driver cleared his throat, reminding Diana that she could not afford to have him wait until Bathory decided to leave. Getting out, she paid her fare. When she counted the change, she knew she'd not be taking any more cabs, not with only fifteen cents to her name.

A stiff breeze off the East River made Diana shiver, even though she knew the temperature was above freezing. The days had been mild for weeks now. Crocuses were already pushing their way out of the earth and a few trees had started to bud. That morning, she'd been tempted to trade her Ulster for a lighter-weight coat. Thank goodness she had not! The warmth of the heavy woolen garment was very welcome now. She wished she'd also thought to carry a muff.

And more money.

Most of all, she thought as she shivered again, she wished she'd never heard of Damon Bathory.

Propelled by the cold wind and her own curiosity, Diana entered the hospital. Once inside, she sought out those women wearing distinctive blue and white striped seersucker dresses and starched white caps, collars, cuffs, and aprons. Their costumes marked them as students at Bellevue's Training School for Nurses. Diana hoped they would prove the most approachable members of the hospital staff.

No one recognized the name Damon Bathory, but the fifth young woman Diana accosted remembered seeing a man who fit his description.

"He's a handsome devil," she confirmed. "Dark haired. I saw him walking with Dr. Braisted, head of the insane pavilion. He must be a physician himself if he's been allowed in there. That area is off-limits to visitors."

More likely he was impersonating a doctor, Diana thought. She'd seen for herself what a talented performer he was.

She also knew far more than she wanted to about what went on inside the insane pavilion. The previous fall a fellow journalist had made headlines by feigning madness in order to reveal the abuses at Bellevue and conditions in the madhouse on Blackwell's Island. Nellie Bly's story had appeared first in the New York *World* and then, in December, in a book called *Ten Days in a Mad-House.*

According to Miss Bly, inmates were kept in cheerless surroundings, sleeping on iron cots furnished with straw-stuffed pillows and wool blankets, but the latter were worn thin by hundreds of washings and there was no heat. Cold air eddied into stark, dimly-lit rooms through windows which had bars but no glass, further adding to the torment of patients wearing hospital gowns made of cotton-flannel that barely reached their knees.

Most patients were classified as hysterics, Diana recalled, a catch-all term applied indiscriminately to those who suffered from symptoms as varied as muscular twitching and loss of memory. The restless, the apathetic, the delusional, all might be labeled hysterics. Standard practice after that diagnosis was to do little more than keep the sufferer institutionalized.

Yes, Diana thought, she could imagine Damon Bathory in that setting. As a doctor . . . or as a patient.

The relative warmth of the hospital no longer held any appeal for her. Retreating outside, she found a secluded spot from which to keep an eye on the entrance to the wing with the barred windows. For the best part of the next hour, she waited for Bathory to come out, unable to stop herself from wondering if the mind of a horror writer differed all that much from that of a madman.

By the time he reappeared—head down and looking neither right nor left as he turned south down 1st Avenue—Diana had recalled more than she wished to of the content of Nellie Bly's articles and had also revisited all the tales in both of Bathory's books. As she began to follow her quarry once more, myriad possibilities lingered in her mind, all of them dreadful to contemplate.

She trailed Bathory on foot, all the way back to his hotel. By the time they reached it, the only things she still worried about were the blisters rising on her feet. He was remarkably fit. She'd been hard put to keep pace with him. Although she was grateful he'd not taken another expensive cab, she was sadly footsore when she once more stood in Union Square.

She waited there, watching the Palace, until he reappeared a short time later. Diana followed him to an art gallery near 34th Street, her reward for diligence a new blister on one heel.

Through the display window she saw two men, Bathory and a dapper little gentleman who appeared to be the gallery manager. A sign on the door indicated there had been an auction on the premises the previous evening—landscape paintings by an assortment of contemporary artists—but today the place was quiet. Too quiet for her to enter and eavesdrop on their conversation without being noticed.

Bathory made no purchases. After a few minutes, he cut short the little man's chatter, exited the gallery, and returned to his hotel. Trailing after him, tired and discouraged, she considered her situation. Should she have remained at the art gallery to ask questions of the proprietor? If she had, she'd have lost sight of Bathory. She could go back. But what if he went out again?

As if in answer to her prayers, she spotted one of the street arabs Horatio Foxe employed to run errands. She felt sorry for the urchin, one of so many homeless lads who ran wild in the city. They earned a pittance by selling newspapers on the street corners and lived in whatever shelter they could find. The "newsboys' lodging house" was Printing House Square, in the open. She'd seen dozens of them there late at night, fighting for the warm spots around the grated vent holes that let out heat and steam from the underground press rooms.

"You, lad," she called to the lanky, sullen-faced boy. "What's your name?"

"Poke, missus." He pulled off a filthy cap and looked hopefully up at her.

"Did you see the man who just went into the hotel?"

"De bloke wit no hat?"

"Er, yes. I want to hire you to watch for him to come out again and follow him if he does."

"On de level?"

She produced a few pennies, nearly all the money she had left, to persuade young Poke to take over surveillance of Bathory's hotel.

"My eyes, ain't it nice!" The pennies disappeared into a grubby hand.

After giving the boy further instructions, Diana left him lurking in front of the Palace Hotel.

&)G&

What was she up to now? Ben watched from the small balcony attached to his hotel room as Mrs. Spaulding carried on an intense conversation with a rough-looking lad with unkempt hair and clothes that hung loosely on his thin frame.

Posting a guard, Ben decided when he saw money change hands. His nemesis went back the way she had come, limping slightly. The lad remained behind.

She'd return to the art gallery, he had no doubt. Ben had caught sight of her there, peering at him through the huge plate glass windows that fronted the place, and had abruptly taken his leave.

Mentally damning the woman to perdition, Ben had to admire her tenacity. He doubted she would learn much from the manager. The authorization Ben had shown him in order to collect Aaron's bank draft had not borne his name and he did not think the fellow would give out any information about Aaron, either, not when Ben had taken the precaution of warning him he'd lose future commissions if he did so.

Because he was thinking about his brother, Ben did not at first credit his identification of the man standing in the shadow of the iron fence surrounding Union Square Park. Then the figure moved, and there was no mistaking that habitual slump. Instead of being almost five hundred miles away, Aaron Northcote was here in New York City.

Cursing even more creatively than he had when he'd noticed Mrs. Spaulding on his trail, Ben headed back towards the lobby at a run. He ignored the elevator and took the stairs. He didn't worry about being seen by the young watchdog Mrs. Spaulding had posted. He'd deal with the boy later. He exited the hotel at top speed and snagged Aaron's arm just as his brother was about to set out in the same direction Mrs. Spaulding had taken. All but dragging the younger man back into the three-acre park, he held his temper until he was sure they were out of earshot of the urchin.

"What are you doing here?" Ben demanded.

To his relief, Aaron did not try to get away. "Following you."

It did no good to get angry with Aaron. Taking a deep breath, Ben willed himself to calm down. He shoved his brother onto a bench and sat beside him. With luck, and the aid of a healthy bribe, the boy watching them would not report any of what he saw to Mrs. Spaulding.

"You went to the art gallery," Aaron said. "I could have done that."

"Yes, but you agreed after what happened in Philadelphia that I'd take care of business matters for you. Remember?"

Aaron didn't answer.

"I have the bank draft. Do you want it?"

"No. You know I lose things like that."

"That's why I collected it, Aaron. You do what you do best and I do what I do best."

"There was a woman following you," Aaron said with one of the abrupt changes of subject for which he was notorious. "She's trouble, Ben."

"Why do you think that?"

He tapped his forehead. "I just know."

"Do me a favor? Stay away from her. There's no need for you to speak to her." The thought of Mrs. Spaulding interviewing Aaron chilled Ben's blood.

"I know where she lives."

For a moment Ben felt as if he'd been struck. He had to breathe deeply before he could ask the next question. "How do you know that, Aaron?"

"I followed her last night after the reading. She was the last one to leave the theater."

"Why didn't you stay and talk to me, Aaron?" And just how long had his brother been in New York?

But when Aaron only shrugged his shoulders, Ben knew it was no use asking him more questions. Aaron never remembered details.

"You let me deal with her, Aaron."

"You'll take care of her?"

"I'll take care of her."

He gave a nod. "Good. Can't let people follow you, you know."

He seemed unaware of the irony of that statement.

"I want you to go home," Ben said. "Will you do that for me? Today?"

"Are you coming, too?"

"I need to stay a little longer. I wish I could leave now. My business in New York is finished. I'd planned to head home first thing tomorrow morning. But there is that woman."

His eyes bright, Aaron listened closely to Ben's suggestion that he travel in a private compartment.

"I'll follow along just as soon as I can. Believe me, I don't want to spend any more time than I have to in the city."

"You've been gone a long time."

"Yes. I have."

Aaron nodded sagely. "Mother's fault."

Silently, Ben had to agree with his assessment. Much of this was Maggie Northcote's fault, but it was pointless to assign blame.

"I'm hungry," Aaron complained.

Most likely, he'd forgotten to eat. Ben thought a moment, then hailed a horse-drawn jitney, instructing the driver to take Aaron to the Park Avenue Oyster House. It had the advantage of being located just past the entrance to the Murray Hill Tunnel, on the south side of Grand Central Station. "I'll meet you there in an hour," he told his brother, and gave Aaron sufficient money to buy a hot meal.

As soon as Aaron's cab was out of sight, Ben turned to the scruffy lad leaning against a nearby lamppost. "I'll double what the lady paid you," he said.

∞)(∞

On her arrival back at the art gallery, Diana immediately approached the manager, a nattily dressed little man with thinning hair that smelled of too much oil.

"I do not know his name," she said disingenuously after she'd described Damon Bathory.

"I cannot give you any information about the gentleman, madam."

"Can you tell me why he came here? What interested him?"

"That's privileged information. I do not discuss my clients' tastes."

"If he is a client, then you must know his name."

"No, madam, I do not. He did not give it." Looking down his nose at her, he inquired, "Is there something you would like to buy?"

"I'll look around," she told him, and she did so, hoping for inspiration. If she only asked the right question, she felt certain she could learn something. The manager must have more information than he'd volunteered.

Most of the landscapes on display were well executed, but none compelled her complete attention until she came upon a canvas towards the back of the gallery. It was a large seascape, featuring ships, brightly colored birds, and scantily clad maidens. The artist had signed it with the initials A. N.

"Excellent work, is it not?" Inexplicably, the manager sounded nervous.

"Interesting work. How has it been received by the critics?"

"Oh, them!" He waved a dismissive hand.

"Fit only to line a parrot's cage?" she guessed.

"Madam!"

"Perhaps a reference to Section 317 of the Penal Code."

He drew himself up to his full height—which made him only an inch taller than Diana—and huffed out a breath. "I assure you, madam, that neither this painting nor any of Mr. North—" He broke off, annoyed with himself for giving away the artist's name. "That is to say, I can assure you that none of the work painted by this artist and handled by this gallery violates any city statute."

Section 317 prohibited the showing or selling of prints, figures, or images that were "obscene, lewd, lascivious, filthy, indecent, or disgusting." The mere mention in her column of a painting that skirted the bounds of decency would no doubt lead to its immediate sale. Damon Bathory was right about that. The scandalous always had appeal for the masses.

Diana's amusement faded when she realized she was no closer to learning anything about Damon Bathory. Whoever "A.N." was, he did not seem likely to have any connection to her assignment. There was, it appeared, no clue here to explain Bathory's visit.

"The gentleman you spoke with earlier calls himself Damon Bathory. He's prominent in his field," she said. "He is a writer and lecturer."

"Never heard of him."

"Perhaps he'll come back and buy something."

"Perhaps he will, madam, but many people simply stop in to

have a look around."

The gallery manager gave her a pointed look.

By the time Diana retraced her steps to Union Square, she felt as if her feet were on fire. Nearly an hour had passed since she'd left Poke on watch. He bounded towards her the moment he saw her coming, all but dancing up and down with excitement.

"He come right out again after you went," Poke said.

"Did you follow him?"

"No need, missus." Poke launched into a colorfully worded account of how Damon Bathory had rushed out of the hotel, entered Union Square Park, and accosted a man. "Caught right ahold of him and give him a shake. My eyes, I thought he'd sock it to him."

Diana blinked. It took her a moment to translate the slang. "You thought he meant to rob the man and beat him up?"

Poke nodded. "On de level."

"This other man—what did he look like?"

"One of doze guys wot gits lost in a crowd."

Diana persisted, eliciting a bit more description. Like Bathory himself, the mystery man had been dark-haired, but he'd been clean-shaven save for a mustache.

"Taller or shorter than Mr. Bathory?"

"Hard to tell, missus. De bloke, he slumped."

Puzzled, Diana urged Poke to go on with his tale, but there was not much more to it. The two men had argued a bit, although Poke had not been close enough to hear what they said to each other. Then Bathory had given the other fellow some money and hailed a cab for him. He'd watched it drive away, then gone back into his hotel.

Had the mysterious stranger been following Bathory, too? A creditor? A blackmailer? Whoever he was, it was too late to catch up with him now and Diana was glad of it. She'd had enough confrontations for one day.

"Are you certain Mr. Bathory didn't come out again?"

Poke assured her he had not.

Thoroughly confused by what she'd just heard, exhausted by the long hours she'd spent in a futile effort to learn something useful about the personal life of this man who wrote horror stories, Diana was reluctant to risk coming face to face with Bathory again. When Poke volunteered himself and two of his friends to keep an eye on the hotel for the rest of the night, she accepted with gratitude.

"Mr. Horatio Foxe from the *Independent Intelligencer* will pay you," she told him.

Poke's eyes lit up at that. The street arabs knew Foxe was good for the money.

"If anything interesting happens," Diana continued, "send word to me at Mrs. Curran's boarding house on 10th Street."

She hoped the boy would not have reason to contact her. In dire need of a hot bath and a good night's sleep, she didn't even want to think about Damon Bathory again until tomorrow.

∽◯◇

Seated at the breakfast table the next morning, Diana looked up as her landlady pushed aside a lace curtain to peer into the areaway used as a servants' entrance. "And who would that be, knocking at my door at such an hour?" she said.

Abandoning her breakfast, Diana joined Mrs. Curran at the small window. They were the only occupants of the house who were up this early. The others, who kept late hours, were accustomed to sleep in. Diana blinked in surprise when she recognized a familiar face. "Why, it's Horatio Foxe. My editor."

"Whatever is he doing here?" Without waiting for a reply, Mrs. Curran threw open the door and invited him in.

Diana wondered the same thing. Foxe had never visited her at home before. Somehow, she did not think he'd come in person to deliver the expense money she'd requested.

A few minutes later, his ever-present cigar clamped firmly between his teeth, he sat across from Diana at the recently scrubbed pine table. She resumed eating her usual morning fare, slicing a bite out of a tender beefsteak and chewing slowly as he watched her. In the quiet kitchen of Mrs. Curran's small house on 10th Street, with the cast iron cookstove warming the chill out of the morning air and the pleasant, familiar scent of yeast enveloping them, Foxe seemed as out of place as mourning dress at a wedding.

"You've seen the column?" He gestured at the pile of newspapers she'd been reading as she ate. She'd set aside the previous day's *Evening Telegram* and that morning's *Times, Tribune,* and *World* in favor of the latest *Independent Intelligencer.*

She nodded and dug into a mound of fried potatoes. As he'd warned, Foxe had tinkered with her text.

"What did he do this time?" Mrs. Curran asked, turning from the stove with the coffee pot in hand.

She was a small, birdlike woman, her exact age anybody's guess. When she'd given up the stage, she'd bought this house and announced that she had bedrooms to let to other women of a theatrical bent. At present, two actresses, a dresser, and a seamstress lived under her roof. And Diana. Because her late husband had been an actor, she had been welcomed into the fold. She'd come close to being evicted over Monday's column and been obliged to explain herself to her landlady.

"Mr. Foxe has committed me, in print, to getting a story on Damon Bathory," Diana said.

"And is that bad?" Mrs. Curran had already brought a plate overflowing with fresh rolls to the table. She refilled Diana's cup with strong black coffee, poured out cups for herself and Foxe, and sat down with them.

Foxe shifted uneasily in his chair. It was obvious his hostess did not intend to be driven out of her own kitchen. If he'd hoped for privacy to speak with Diana, he was doomed to disappointment.

Hiding her amusement at Foxe's frustration, Diana answered Mrs. Curran's question. "It is impossible!"

She gave a brief account of the previous day's adventures for the benefit of her landlady and her editor.

"In other words, you learned nothing." Foxe glowered at her.

"Why are you here?" she asked, giving him a suspicious look. "Have you discovered something new?"

He glanced at Mrs. Curran. The older woman beamed back at him and did not budge.

"Mrs. Curran is unlikely to leak our secrets to a rival newspaper."

Diana's curiosity had been aroused by Foxe's unprecedented visit, but she was not yet fully awake and felt out of sorts besides. If he wanted to speak with her alone, he could wait until she'd finished her breakfast. She lifted her cup, inhaled the rising steam with something akin to bliss, and took a long, satisfying swallow of the reviving brew.

Foxe buttered a roll and ate it in three bites. He drank some coffee. Then the need to gloat got the better of him. Reaching into his pocket, he withdrew two telegrams.

"Take a gander at these, Diana. The Bathory story is bigger than I thought."

Intrigued, she reached for them. One came from Philadelphia, the other from San Francisco, but both said the same thing—a woman had been stabbed to death in the city's theater district.

Foxe looked grimly pleased with himself. "On a hunch, I sent requests for information to a major newspaper in each city Damon Bathory visited on his current tour. Just gave the dates and asked if any newsworthy events had taken place about the same time. You see the result—replies from the *Philadelphia Inquirer* and the *San Francisco Chronicle.*"

"These women died while Bathory was in town?"

"At the end of his stint in each of those cities, late on a Saturday night or early on a Sunday morning, when he'd be on his way out of town and likely to avoid being questioned."

Foxe's logic was easy to follow. And alarming. Could Damon Bathory really have blood on his hands? She had been trying very hard to convince herself that he was nothing more than a talented writer and performer. Perhaps that had been a mistake. He did have an interest in some rather unpleasant subjects. And he claimed descent from an ancestor who had killed young women for their blood.

Diana shivered.

Mrs. Curran picked up each of the telegrams in turn. "Oh, my," she murmured, fixing a wide-eyed look on Foxe. "You think Damon Bathory killed these two women?"

"I think it will make a damned fine story if we can link him to the murders."

"That's not the same thing," Diana protested.

"He may have been responsible for their deaths." Foxe attempted to look hurt and missed by a mile. "Is this the thanks I get? I came here to warn you before you left to resume following your quarry. You must be on your guard, Diana."

Foxe's attitude made it difficult for Diana to take him seriously. Common sense suggested he was up to something. Besides, two deaths in two cities Bathory had visited seemed scant evidence of any connection. Bathory's involvement was highly conjectural. She'd seen the itinerary for the tour he'd just completed. The man had performed at twenty-eight stands in less than four months, crisscrossing the entire continent. She reminded Foxe of that.

"And who's to say there aren't twenty-eight dead girls, one in each city?" His eyes gleamed. The unlit cigar between his teeth bobbled as he worked himself up to a new level of enthusiasm. "Think of it, Diana! What a story!"

In her agitation, she gripped the edge of the table with both hands. "I do not write fiction."

Foxe snatched up the telegrams and waved them in her face. "What if it's all true? It could be. Philadelphia, last November. A young woman stabbed." He glanced at the top telegram for details. "Belinda MacKay, found in an alley behind the Muse Lecture Hall. Did she attend Bathory's reading the previous evening? Then here in San Francisco." He shuffled the yellow pages and flourished the second telegram. "January 9th. Lenora Cosgrove. Age twenty-eight. She was found in an alley, too. And likewise stabbed."

"Coincidence. By your logic, any member of any acting company might as easily have committed these crimes. There are dozens of theater troupes on tour at any given time. In each of those cities five or six plays, at the least, would have been presented on the same nights Bathory read from his works. And that does not count singers and circus acts and—"

"I take your point, Diana. But of all those performers, Bathory is the one who revels in blood and gore." He dropped his voice to a lower register. "And what if I were to tell you that both of these murders took place under a full moon?"

That suggestion elicited a gasp from Mrs. Curran but Diana's eyes narrowed with a sudden increase in her skepticism. "Did they?"

"Who knows?" Foxe chuckled and seemed to relax. He reached for another roll. "That's what I pay you to find out."

"This is the Saturday after he's completed a stand," Mrs. Curran murmured. "If he is the killer, does that mean he'll strike tonight?"

Foxe looked pleased at the thought.

"Where is your full moon?"

Foxe ignored Diana's sarcasm, making her reasonably certain that he had not made the special effort to come to Mrs. Curran's house because he thought one of his reporters was in danger. He'd wanted to catch her before she left. That much she believed. But his primary motivation had not been concern about her safety.

"What do you want me to do?" she asked.

"Keep following Bathory. Tonight, too. Do not let him out of your sight. No delegating this task to anyone else." He wagged an admonishing finger at her.

"You think Poke and the other street arabs missed something?"

"I think he's a clever lad accustomed to living by his wits. He's not above taking money from Bathory to edit what he tells you."

"You cannot ask this young lady to risk her life." Mrs. Curran glared at Foxe, warming Diana's heart. It was good to have caring, loving friends.

With an ingratiating smile for the older woman, Foxe rose from the table. "No risk. I have arranged for her to have a bodyguard." He shifted his gaze to Diana. "Today, when you follow Bathory, you are to let him see you. We'll draw him out. When he makes his move, we'll have our proof."

"When he tries to kill her? Are you daft?" Aghast, Mrs. Curran fanned herself, her gaze darting from Foxe's face to Diana's and back again.

Diana sighed. "This is likely to be a tempest in a teapot, Mrs. Curran. But if Mr. Foxe is right, I have an obligation to find out the truth. If Bathory was responsible for those deaths, he must be stopped."

Investigating Bathory as a potential criminal, she realized, would give her pursuit of him, her invasion of his privacy, a certain legitimacy. She shot Foxe a considering look. Was he providing her with what she'd said she wanted, the opportunity to go after real news? Or was this just another ploy to trick her into inventing scandal?

It was not until he'd left and she was preparing to set out for Bathory's hotel to relieve Poke, that Diana remembered a remark the elusive horror writer had made to her in his hotel room. He had encountered "a particularly annoying" female reporter near the start of his tour, he'd said.

Philadelphia had been one of his earliest stands.

In her head, in Bathory's deep, resonant voice, Diana heard again what else he'd said. "I dealt with her," he'd boasted, "in a most satisfactory manner."

But he'd only meant he'd taken her to bed . . . hadn't he?

CHAPTER FOUR

⊱⊰

Once again, the weather was bright and springlike. The temperature had quickly soared into the fifties and the only wind was a gentle southerly breeze.

Ben set out on foot at mid-morning to run a variety of errands, including a stop at a candy store. His mother had a weakness for a particular brand of imported chocolates difficult to obtain at home. In the mirrored wall behind the counter, he could see Mrs. Spaulding plainly. He had been right. She'd not given up. It was a good thing he'd made the arrangements he had for Aaron.

With the wisdom of hindsight, he knew he should never have agreed to this tour, but four months ago he'd had his own agenda—good reasons, or so he'd believed, for visiting the country's major cities.

What a waste! He'd learned that no one knew more about madness than he did himself. Most physicians understood far less and treated their patients with an appalling lack of humanity.

Ben studied Mrs. Spaulding's attractive reflection once more as he took his package from the sales clerk. It did no good to long for what might have been. He'd promised Damon Bathory's publisher to keep Bathory's identity a deep, dark secret. He could not reveal the truth without potentially dire consequences.

Eventually, though, someone would find out. Ben wondered if it would not be better to volunteer the information before that happened. For the moment, however, he had no choice but to honor his pledge.

When Ben left the candy shop, Mrs. Spaulding ducked into a doorway. A fragment of his conversation with Aaron came back to him as she trailed along after him.

"That woman following you is up to no good."

"You let me deal with her."

"You'll take care of her?"

"I'll take care of her."

ⅎℂℂ

While her quarry was in a barber shop, Diana waited outside, lulled by the very normality of his behavior this morning into discounting most of her earlier fears. She was inclined to dismiss Foxe's theory as wishful thinking on the part of a man desperate to unearth scandal. After all, if Bathory had meant to harm her, would he not have done so the first time they met, in that darkened lecture hall with no witnesses?

She continued to follow him throughout the morning and into the afternoon, all the while feeling safer and safer. And if, by chance, Foxe was right, then the bodyguard he'd promised her, a hulking brute named Bruno Webb, was not far behind. He'd been waiting on Diana's doorstep for her when she'd left Mrs. Curran's house.

When the afternoon began to wane, Bathory returned briefly to his hotel. He was dressed to the nines when he went out again. Looking neither left nor right, he proceeded to the Everett House. Diana did not dare follow him inside the brightly lit restaurant. Instead, she made do with watching him eat, staring at him through the window as her stomach growled.

Bruno disappeared briefly around the side of the establishment and returned, wiping his mouth with the back of his hand. Diana considered sending him back for something for her, but thought better of it. Bruno's job was to keep watch over her, not feed her.

When Bathory emerged, it was to stroll along the east side of Union Square. She hurried after him, confident he could not hear her footsteps in pursuit. High above their heads, perched on poles, noisy arc lights covered any sound she made. A troop of horsemen would have been hard put to make themselves heard over that incessant clicking and clacking.

Bathory appeared to be searching for an evening's entertainment. Someone would have taken his place at Heritage Hall, though Diana had no idea who. At Steinway Hall, there had been an afternoon concert but nothing was scheduled for tonight. The nearby Academy of Music was home to a pantomime called *Mazulm, the Night Owl* and he might also select from a variety of legitimate plays, all within a few blocks of his hotel. Henry Irving's well-respected company of British actors was performing *Louis XI* at the Star Theater. Diana noticed Bathory glance that way as he crossed 14th Street, but he proceeded on without turning, passing by the dark façade of the Union Square Theater.

Diana hurried by what remained of the structure, closed after the disastrous fire a few weeks earlier. Posters hopefully proclaimed that the theater would reopen in May, but that did not appear likely. Rebuilding had yet to begin.

A pity Irving's company was not presenting *Faust* tonight, Ben thought as he passed the ruins. He'd have been tempted to attend, if only to give Mrs. Spaulding pause for thought. The play would surely have struck her as appropriate fare for Damon Bathory. Even better would have been Richard Mansfield performing his virtuoso *Dr. Jekyll and Mr. Hyde,* but that talented thespian had left New York to tour.

Then he caught sight of the marquee of the 13th Street Theater.

It offered the perfect choice, the very production of *The Duchess of Calabria* he'd read about in Mrs. Spaulding's column on Monday. Blood and terror. Revenge and death. A fitting end to Damon Bathory's stay in the city. And it would have the added advantage of making Mrs. Spaulding squirm.

To force her to sit in the audience after printing such scandalous gossip about the performers seemed to Ben a fitting punishment for her sins. She had not enjoyed the production the first time. She would hate having to endure it again.

He affected not to notice when she was seated off to his right, an arrangement that enabled him to keep an eye on her during the performance. She spent a good deal of time scribbling in her notebook, as she had during his reading. He wondered why. It seemed a waste of print to attack the same play twice, but he supposed there was much she could still say about it if she chose.

The story had a number of difficulties, not the least of which was an adaptation that would have had the play's original 17th century author rolling over in his grave. The production was also severely marred by the fact that the leading lady kept losing her voice. It was obvious to Ben, if not to the others in the audience, that the Duchess suffered from a heavy cold. It would have been better—for those who heard her as well as for her own health—if she had allowed her understudy to go on.

Unfortunately for Ben, Mrs. Spaulding's earlier commentary had been unerringly accurate. Indeed, he now thought she'd gone easy on the actors. He suffered through to the end, but not without consequences. The sulfurous fumes from torches carried by characters on stage only increased a blazing headache brought on by the abysmal quality of the performance. That Mrs. Spaulding would once again take up her pursuit of him suddenly seemed intolerable to Ben. Where did the woman think he was going to lead her? Into some den of iniquity?

He'd tried scaring her with the Bathory ring at the lecture hall. He'd tried insulting her morals in his hotel room. He'd tried wearing her out by racing up one side of Manhattan and down the other. Nothing had worked. A new tactic was called for.

The crisp, bracing air outside the theater acted on him like a tonic. Anticipation simmered in his veins as he realized what it was he really wanted to do to about the tenacious Mrs. Spaulding. Should he?

If he acted on the desire uppermost in his mind, he'd hide himself. When she reappeared, looking for him, he'd turn the tables on her and become the one in pursuit. He was certain an opportunity to confront her in private would not take long to present itself.

Grinning at the sheer folly of the idea, he slipped into the shadows, furtive as any villain lurking in the pages of a horror story.

Diana was sick of following Damon Bathory. Not at all averse to losing sight of him "accidentally," she dawdled as long as she could on her way out of the auditorium, but this ploy created another problem. Several members of the cast, most of whom she knew well, had spotted her sitting in the audience. Nathan Todd, actor, director, and producer all in one, and an old friend, sent a note by way of the ticket seller to invite her to come backstage.

Under other circumstances, she'd have gone gladly, but ever since Foxe had made his additions to her review, she'd been avoiding an encounter with Lavinia Ross, the company's ingenue and the "Miss L. R." of the piece. Diana would want her wits about her when that confrontation came to pass. She owed the woman an explanation and an apology, and she intended that she would have one, but not tonight. After three hours of bad acting and smoking torches, her head pounded like surf during a storm.

Stopping at the box office, she scribbled a reply to Toddy's invitation, then took a deep breath and stepped outside. There was no sign of Damon Bathory, nor did she see Bruno Webb. She had the perfect excuse to give up and go home, but even as that thought crossed her mind, her sense of responsibility began to nag at her. Foxe had given her an assignment. More importantly, her readers had been promised a story.

Looking neither right nor left, Diana headed for "the Rialto," as 14th Street was called where it formed the south side of Union Square. There was still a chance she'd spot Damon Bathory before he got back to his hotel. Up ahead, the theater district was bustling. Hansom cabs and privately owned carriages vied with pedestrians for room to move. Hooves clattered on the cobbled streets. Wheels creaked. Adding to the din was a distant horse car bell, warning that a trolley was approaching on the tracks that ran down the middle of Broadway.

Without warning, someone seized Diana's arm, jerking her into the narrow passage between the Star Theater and the burned-out building next door. Before she could draw breath to scream, a hard hand covered in a rough wool glove clapped over her mouth.

Acting on instinct, she kicked out with both feet and aimed a blow at her assailant's face with her handbag. He knocked it aside. She heard it fall to the ground even as she was dragged deeper into the shadows.

Bathory, she thought. He was a murderer and she was his next victim!

A sense of disbelief swamped her. How could this be happening when there were so many people nearby? Did no one see? Did no one hear?

Diana increased her efforts to break free, but nothing she did succeeded in loosening the grip on her arm or the hand over her mouth. Slowly, inexorably, she was dragged towards the far end of the alley. Blocked by packing crates, debris from the theater fire, and a high fence, it offered no avenue of escape.

More by luck than design, Diana's boot connected with her captor's shin. He retaliated instantly, releasing her but striking her so hard across the face that her hat tumbled off and was trampled underfoot.

She had no chance to scream. In the second she was free, she could manage nothing louder than a strangled croak, too faint to be heard from the street. Then he got hold of her again.

Breathing hard, he once more clamped his hand over her mouth. Certain he meant to kill her, Diana did the only thing she could. She bit him.

With a bellow of pain and rage, her captor flung her away. She landed flat on her back in the alley, too winded by the impact of the fall to cry out.

Her ears still ringing from the earlier blow, Diana stared dazedly up at the fire escape high above. It nearly touched the high brick wall on the other side.

She was in an alley in the theater district on the Saturday night following Damon Bathory's last reading in this city.

Diana sat up with an abruptness that only increased her dizziness and the pounding in her head. Her attacker was no more than a dark shape in the encroaching blackness, advancing, about to seize her again. Terrified, she opened her mouth to call for help, but no sound came out.

Seconds elongated into an eternity as she tried to tell herself that this was just another nightmare. The pain radiating from her bruised face argued otherwise. The ominous figure loomed over her, silently threatening. Why didn't he get it over with? She was at his mercy.

Thoroughly terrified, Diana at last managed to scream.

Footsteps pounded into the alley.

At the sound, Diana's assailant whirled to look behind him. On Horatio Foxe's orders, Bruno Webb had been keeping an eye on her. Somehow, he'd missed her abduction, but at her scream he'd come running.

"Look out!" she shouted as a flash of light reflected off the lethal-looking blade in her assailant's hand.

Bruno's rush never faltered. He was taller and heavier than the man in the alley. One good close look at him and the attacker turned and fled. As Bruno stopped to assist Diana to her feet, the miscreant began to scale a board fence at the far end of the alley.

"Stop him!" she gasped, giving Bruno a shove. She sat back down again, hard, then watched in dismay as her rescuer lumbered towards the fence. By the time he reached it, he could do no more than catch hold of the back of the fellow's coat. With a wriggle and a kick, the villain broke free and hauled himself the rest of the way over the top.

Diana was on her feet, dusting off the back of her skirt, when a lantern appeared at the entrance to the alley. At last there was enough illumination to see, but it came too late for Diana to get a good look at her attacker.

The new arrival was a police officer—one Diana recognized.

The danger well and truly over now, she started to shake.

The 15th Precinct station house was the home of Manhattan's elite Broadway squad. Diana had been there before, visiting the precinct house in search of tidbits for her column. She knew several of the officers, including the one who'd escorted her from the alley, lending her his long, many-buttoned blue coat when she couldn't stop trembling and settling her in a chair in his captain's office with a cup of hot coffee to hold onto.

"Just tell Captain Brogan everything you remember," Officer Hanlon said kindly. "Then you can go home."

It was warm in Brogan's small, cluttered office, but she shivered as she recalled what had happened.

"Why did someone attack you?" Brogan sat behind a desk. Diana was in the wooden armchair opposite. Above them, an overhead lamp burned low, two jets under each of two shades flickering in unison. Brogan picked up a pen and held it poised over a blank sheet of paper.

"I don't know."

"Any idea who he was?"

She shook her head. It was the truth. She had not recognized him, but the man in the alley had not been in evening dress. "He was dressed in rough, wool garments. Very plain."

A frown creased her forehead as she tried to remember more, making her face throb. Her whole head pounded. Concentrating required more effort than she had energy to expend, but she was now absolutely certain of one thing. It had not been Damon Bathory who'd assaulted her. He would not have had time after leaving the theater to make a costume change.

She almost smiled at her inadvertent choice of words. Obviously, she'd spent too much time around theatrical people. It seemed more natural to think in terms of costumes than clothes.

"What did he look like?" Brogan asked.

"It was too dark to see his features."

Should she give them Bathory's name and share the information from the telegrams Foxe had shown her? If she did, they'd bring him in for questioning. She was not certain why, but she did not want that to happen. She needed to sort everything out in her own mind before she made any accusations.

To stall for time, she sipped at the coffee. It was thick, oily, bitter, and laced with whiskey so potent that it made her eyes water. Drinking it had the desired restorative effect, however, warming her, while at the same time giving her a few moments' respite in which to consider how much she wanted to tell the police.

Fishing for a handkerchief to wipe her streaming eyes, Diana was distracted by the realization that something was missing from her leather bag. Sadly worse for wear, both it and her mangled hat had been retrieved and returned to her.

"It's gone," she murmured.

"Money? His motive was theft?"

"There was no money in it." She'd tucked the five dollars Foxe had given her into her garter. That was for emergencies. But she'd used the last of her own money to buy a sandwich at the interval between the acts of the play. She'd been half starved by then.

"What is missing, Mrs. Spaulding?"

"My notebook."

"Perhaps it fell out when you dropped your bag."

"Yes. It must have. There was nothing important in it." Not even her notes on Damon Bathory. She'd filled the last notebook, similarly covered in green cloth, the previous day, and begun a new one tonight. The missing item contained only her scribblings during the performance. She'd not been writing a review, just jotting down random thoughts for future columns . . . and trying to avoid being spotted by the man she'd been following.

Brogan continued to ask questions, several of them delicately put, aimed at determining whether or not her assailant had taken liberties of a personal nature. At the time, she'd feared for her life and given not a single thought to her virtue.

"Thank goodness for Bruno," she said.

"Yes." Brogan consulted his notes. "Bruno Webb. He says he's an associate of yours. Just happened by, he says." There was a question in the sympathetic gray eyes.

"Yes. He works for the *Independent Intelligencer,* as do I." She was careful to volunteer nothing more.

After a few more questions, all routine, Brogan seemed satisfied with her account. "You may be sure we will be extra vigilant for the remainder of the night," he assured her. "We'll keep an eye out for the blackguard."

"I am relieved to hear it." Diana stood, shrugging out of Officer Hanlon's coat and returning it to him, but at the door she stopped and glanced over her shoulder at Brogan. "Are there many such attacks on an average Saturday night in the theater district?"

That the police captain seemed reluctant to answer did not surprise Diana. Now that she'd regained her composure, they'd all remembered she worked for a newspaper. No doubt he envisioned a list of unsolved crimes blazoned across the front page.

"Not many." He made a vague gesture with one hand. "Bright lights are a deterrent."

If the theater had not burned down, the alley would not have been so dark. Diana understood that. But what now struck her as peculiar was that the villain had selected her. Out on the street, the light had been excellent. A thief should have been able to see that there were more prosperous-looking folk out and about at that hour. It seemed a remarkable coincidence that she'd been warned that Damon Bathory might be in the habit of attacking and killing young women and then, that very evening, been attacked herself.

When Diana left Brogan's office, she found Bruno waiting for her in front of the chest-high sergeant's desk in the lobby. He rose from a hard wooden bench to cross the wide plank floor and offer her his arm.

"Mr. Foxe will pay for a hack," he said.

She did not argue, though Mrs. Curran's house was an easy walk from the precinct house.

During the short drive, her bodyguard sat silently beside her in the cab. His stoic mien did not encourage questions.

There were—Diana decided by the time she reached the sanctuary of her own room—three possible explanations for what had happened tonight.

Damon Bathory had not been the man in the alley, but he could have hired some thug to do his dirty work. Poke had seen him give money to that man in the park. As far as Diana could determine, however, Bathory wasn't aware she'd been following him, so why would he set someone on her?

A more logical suspect was Horatio Foxe. Had he staged this whole performance to convince her to go after Bathory with renewed dedication? Diana wouldn't put such a scheme past him. He was desperate to win his "war" with the other newspapers.

On the whole, however, she was inclined to favor a third option, the one the police had suggested. It made much more sense to believe that the incident had been entirely random. She had been in the wrong place at the wrong time.

SOCR

Ben did not intend to leave the darkened barroom of the Hotel Hungaria until he was certain Mrs. Spaulding had given up looking for him and gone home. He had no idea how long he'd been there. He'd ducked inside to avoid her pursuit, ordered a drink, and claimed a shadowy corner for himself. Once there, he'd become lost in his own dismal thoughts.

For one moment outside the theater, he'd been tempted to throw caution to the winds and voluntarily talk to his nemesis. Foolhardy. Imbecilic. Yet appealing. He was becoming obsessed with the woman. What was it about her? He tried to tell himself that she was ordinary, no one special, that he had simply been too long without a female companion. But there was something . . . he shook his head and polished off his drink. Time to go back to the hotel and get a good night's sleep.

Union Square was quieter, almost peaceful at this early morning hour. The fresh air came as a welcome relief and he inhaled deeply. In spite of his tiredness, he decided to take the long way around the three-acre park to get back to his hotel, to let the mild exercise relax him.

His perambulation brought him past the heroic equestrian statue of George Washington that stood at the southeast corner of the square and the pitiful remains of the Union Square Theater. The latter sight triggered a vague recollection of talk overheard in the bar. Something about a woman being accosted in an alley between the ruins and the adjacent Star Theater.

He made his way to its mouth and peered into the darkness but saw nothing of interest. He had already moved on when more of the comments he'd overheard while brooding over his solitary drink came back to him.

They'd run the gamut from sympathetic to outraged to foul obscenity. No one had mentioned the victim's name, but several of the Hungaria's patrons had speculated that she must be a prostitute. What other sort of female, someone had asked, went out unescorted at night?

Suddenly Ben knew the answer to that question.

A woman like Mrs. Spaulding.

As if compelled, he hurried back to the alley and ventured in. He did not expect to discover anything to tell him what had happened or to whom, but when his foot struck an object lying on the ground, he didn't hesitate to scoop it up and carry it back to the street to examine under better light.

The item was small and would easily have been overlooked. Perhaps the woman who'd been attacked had not even realized she'd dropped it during the struggle. Obviously the police had not found it afterward.

Ben stared at the green cloth cover. It was badly stained where it had fallen into a pile of refuse but he could not fail to recognize it. Standing under a lamppost, jaw clenched, he flipped it open to read the name and address neatly inscribed on the flyleaf.

ॐ

A telegram from Horatio Foxe awaited Diana when she awoke on Sunday morning. This fact did not surprise her. She'd expected Bruno Webb to go directly to their boss after escorting her home. The content of Foxe's wire, however, did take her aback.

"STAY ON BATHORY TRAIL," it read. "DO NOT WRITE ACCOUNT OF ATTACK."

Crumpling the cable in her hand, Diana bit back a curse. Of her three explanations, the one in which Foxe had been behind the entire business suddenly seemed by far the most plausible. It even provided a reason why Bruno had taken so long to show up when he was supposed to be right behind her.

She dragged a weary hand over her face, wincing when it came in contact with the bruise on her jaw. She'd have to use powder to cover it.

Diana sighed. She had not slept well. After the attack, she'd been calm on the surface, but as soon as her head had hit the pillow, all her doubts and fears had been set free. In troubled dreams, she'd revisited last night's events in the alley, and unhappy incidents from her past, as well.

Evan had struck her once in a fit of frustration over his failure to do justice to a role. That was one of the dangers inherent in loving a man with a creative temperament.

She'd felt powerless then. Now, she was angry, and too exhausted to do more than damn Horatio Foxe for getting her into such an impossible situation. She had to go on. If she did not, her editor was desperate enough to create a sensational story that bore no resemblance to the truth. That was why he wanted to delay printing a first-person account of an attack on one of his own reporters. He had a bigger story in mind. A completely untrue story.

The corollary to her logic was that Damon Bathory was entirely innocent of any crime. That being the case, how could she be a party to a plot to defame his character? She had no choice but to go to Bathory, not to demand an interview, but to warn him what Foxe had planned.

In the light of a new day, even one that was a bit overcast, Diana managed to convince herself that Foxe's threat to fire her for insubordination was all bluster. She could always appeal to his sister. Under threat of Rowena's nagging, he'd surely relent, forgive Diana, and take her back into the fold.

With luck that might even happen before she became destitute.

No effort of will could quite shut out the memory of near starvation after Evan had left Toddy's company to strike out on his own—and made a hash of it. They'd been down to their last two bits when he'd gotten into the poker game that had ended up costing him his life. Diana never had learned if he'd really been cheating. It had hardly mattered after he was shot by the disgruntled gambler who claimed he was.

Diana closed her eyes and took a deep breath. Evan had not survived, but she had. If worse came to worst, she supposed she could always go on the stage. The fact that she had not an ounce of theatrical talent shouldn't hold her back. The lack of acting ability certainly had not stopped Lavinia Ross from pursuing her career.

Diana's vision of a future in which she successfully played miscellaneous maids and waiting women, the female equivalent of spear carriers, amused her enough to allow her to consume her usual hearty breakfast with good appetite. After she'd eaten, she set out for the Palace Hotel at a brisk pace, determined to get this meeting over with. She did not realize that she'd just passed Bathory, on the other side of the street and heading in the opposite direction, until he was a good distance beyond her. Apparently lost in thought, he'd taken no note of her, either.

Doubling back, Diana had almost caught up with him when he joined the cluster of parishioners entering Grace Church for morning worship. Diana followed the crowd, momentarily bemused by the notion that the man who wrote such demonic stories should attend Sunday services. Once inside, she spotted him easily, but there was no room for her in his pew. She settled into one near the back of the church, prepared to wait for the end of services to speak with him.

More than an hour later, Diana stepped out of Grace Church into an afternoon that was still overcast but not yet stormy. She positioned herself near the wrought iron fence to wait for Bathory to emerge.

He was easy to spot—he was the only man not wearing a hat. Diana was about to call out to him when she saw him reach into the pocket of his coat and extract a small object. She had to bite back a gasp when she recognized her notebook, the one she'd lost in the alley.

Stunned, Diana ducked out of sight behind a large gentleman and his wife. Had she been wrong? Had Bathory been her attacker, after all? Had he stolen the notebook? Or gone back for it later?

Nonsense! She told herself she was imagining things. Hadn't she just reasoned everything out and decided she had nothing to fear from this man? He was not her attacker. He was the wrong shape. The man in the alley had been broader in the shoulders and much shorter than Bathory.

She hesitated too long. He left the churchyard heading away from his hotel. Her expression grim, Diana set out in his wake. She was no longer sure what she would do when she caught up with him, but following Damon Bathory seemed to have become a habit.

CHAPTER FIVE

෮෨

When Diana finally ran her quarry to ground, he was on the roof of the Equitable Building. He stood with his back to her, apparently contemplating the panoramic view of the Narrows, Staten Island, the North and East Rivers, and most of Manhattan and Brooklyn. This observation area at the weather station, run by the War Department's U.S. Army Signal Service to gain up-to-date information on storms and temperature, welcomed visitors at any time, but no one else seemed to be in evidence today.

Diana debated giving up and going home. Her jaw was throbbing, as were other assorted aches and pains she'd acquired by landing so hard on the ground in that alley. Moreover, the blister on her heel had opened again. She was having second thoughts about warning Damon Bathory of Foxe's suspicions, now that she knew he had possession of her notebook. But most of all, she'd begun to be afraid. When she'd followed him up here, she hadn't anticipated finding herself alone with him.

An instant before she could turn and flee, he swung around to face her, fixing her with his steady, compelling stare. His smile contained neither warmth nor humor, but his deep, resonant voice and hypnotic gaze held her still for his approach.

"You've been following me, Mrs. Spaulding."

Denial came automatically. "I haven't—"

"Shall I enumerate all the places you've turned up since you failed to get what you wanted from me in my hotel room? Later that day, you lurked outside an art gallery while I was inside. Yesterday, you dogged my footsteps to a candy store, the barber shop, and other places too numerous to mention. Last night you all but pressed your nose to the window while I supped at the Everett House. I could see you, only half-concealed by the shadows, peering in at me like a starving waif. I thought about asking you to join me," he added in dulcet tones, "but I decided you deserved to suffer for your impertinence. Then we both attended the same play."

"It is my job to review plays," she protested, but the game was up. At least he did not seem to know that she'd also followed him to Bellevue. For some reason that eased her mind. She did not think he'd be happy to hear she knew of his visit there.

"Your job," he repeated. "Yes. I see. And I am just another of your assignments."

Diana could rationalize that her need for an interview required her to stay, but she knew there was more to what she was feeling than that. More than she wanted to think about just now. Reminding herself she was not powerless, that she could run if she had to, she stood her ground.

Why did this man affect her so strongly? Whenever she encountered him, she felt she should beware of him; yet she did not seem to be able to heed the warnings flashing through her mind and simply walk away.

"Let's start again." The hard glitter in his eyes belied his reasonable tone of voice. "You followed me all day and evening yesterday, and the afternoon before that, and trailed downtown after me again this morning."

Reluctantly, she nodded.

He said nothing about Poke. She dared hope that meant he

had not noticed the watch she'd posted. That presented her with another problem, however. How could she get him to talk about the man he'd accosted in the park, the man he'd given money to?

"You meant to follow me after the play, but I slipped away from you."

Again she nodded. Remembering the notebook, she knew she should be frightened. She should run, but a strange lethargy had crept over her, sapping her of any desire to escape.

He came closer, his tantalizing mouth at eye level. She'd not noticed before how perfectly formed his lips were. They parted, revealing strong, white teeth, and a delicious warmth stole over her like a down coverlet. Without thinking, she took a step in his direction.

"I hid from you, Diana."

Her gaze flew upward to meet the consuming sensuality of his expression, but the use of her first name startled her enough to bring her to her senses.

She did not have to ask him how he knew it. She always wrote both her name and her address in her little cloth-covered notebooks.

"I thought about confronting you outside the theater," Bathory said. "I changed my mind."

In spite of all the unknowns, she believed him. The shivers running through her body did not come from fear. They had another origin entirely.

"Do you think I attacked you?" he asked. One gloved finger caught her chin and lifted her face until she was forced to meet his intense gaze once more. "Is that why you tremble?"

The unexpected touch, so close to being a caress, sent sensations rocketing along every nerve ending. Her mouth felt dry as dust, but she managed to choke out a question of her own. "How do you know about that? There's been nothing in the newspapers."

"There was talk in the neighborhood. I heard of the incident, though not who'd been involved, in the barroom of the Hotel Hungaria. That's where I went to hide, Diana. In a dark corner with a whiskey."

His free hand moved to touch the bruise on her cheek, his sharp eyes discerning it through her face powder. Diana flinched but did not retreat.

"Do you think I attacked you?" he repeated.

"I do not know what to think."

"Then you were either very brave or very foolish to have followed me here."

When he released her, she licked parched lips, then wished she hadn't. The innocent gesture provoked a new flare of heat in his eyes. It was gone again in an instant, but not before she'd recognized it for what it was. An answering awareness bubbled in her veins.

Damon Bathory reached into the inner pocket of his coat. When he withdrew his hand, it held her notebook. "Yours, I believe."

Although she'd known he had it, and had believed herself prepared to stay calm, the reality of the stained and dirty green cover brought back all the horror of what had happened to her in that alley. She felt her face blanch and when he extended the notebook towards her, expecting her to take it, a sudden panic made her retreat a few steps.

"I found your notebook well after midnight," he said in a gruff voice, pressing it into her hands but stepping away immediately. "On my way back to my hotel."

If he'd not retreated, Diana might have bolted. Somehow, putting even that little distance between them caused her nervousness to abate. She was able to think clearly again.

She drew in a deep breath and let it out slowly.

"Your story makes no sense," she said to his back. He stood by the railing that closed in the weather observatory, staring down at the city below. "The way from the Hotel Hungaria to the Palace Hotel does not pass anywhere near the ruins of the Union Square Theater."

"I took a walk around the park. Mild exercise before bed is an inducement to sound sleep."

Diana said nothing. He sounded sincere. He might even be telling the truth. An iron fence surrounded the three-acre park. She thought it was locked at night, but she supposed Bathory could have circled it on the outside. That did not explain, however, why he'd venture across the Rialto or why he'd decided to explore the pitiful remains of the Union Square Theater.

As if he heard her silent question, Bathory answered it. "There was talk in the bar of a woman accosted in the alley next to the ruins."

"And you thought of me?" Asperity tinged Diana's question. With his back to her she was no longer swamped by his powerful personality. She had regained her composure. He became just an ordinary man again. And her assignment.

"I was curious enough to take a look." He turned. "I found that in a pile of refuse."

"I want to believe you."

He leaned back against the railing. "Why?"

"I . . . I don't know."

But she did, and so, she sensed, did he.

For a moment, the look in his eyes made her think he meant to kiss her. She could all but see him closing the distance between them, taking her into his arms, and bending his head to touch his lips to hers. He would not let go, even if she struggled. And when he angled his mouth to give him better access, her resistance would slip away.

Lost in that imagined embrace, she was startled when a gust of wind buffeted her, lifting the hem of her dark blue coat and causing the wool to flutter at the top of her low boots. She blinked rapidly, coming to her senses.

"I . . . this . . . Mr. Bathory . . . "

His smile devastated her senses. Had he mesmerized her?

"Come," he suggested. "Share the view with me while we discuss how matters stand between us. From this height, the cable cars crossing the Great Bridge to Brooklyn look like ants."

She stepped away from him instead.

He laughed. "Do you think I mean to pick you up and throw you off the building?"

"Certainly not. It is simply too cold up here." She hoped he would accept that explanation for her shaking hands and uneven voice.

"Let us go indoors, then. To the Savarin? We can dine there, too."

That café, Diana knew, was on a lower level of the Equitable Building. "Yes. Fine."

Remember the interview, she lectured herself as he took her arm to lead her to one of the hydraulic elevators. She was not looking for a lover, only for copy for a newspaper column. She must ignore the frisson of awareness emanating from the point of contact between her arm and his hand.

Ten minutes later, Diana was seated across from him at a small table in a restaurant where white mahogany, onyx, and bronze dominated the decor, and expensive marble covered the floor. She had brought her wayward imagination under control and prevented her hands from trembling by keeping them tightly clasped in her lap.

"I had already reached the conclusion that you were not one to give up," Bathory said, after they'd ordered. "I tried to frighten you off with my ring at Heritage Hall. I attempted to use insults to drive you away when you came to my hotel room. Then I made a futile effort the next day, after I noticed you following me again, to bore you into abandoning the chase. Nothing has worked and I am left with only one course of action."

"And that is?" Her voice did not shake. Diana took that as a good sign.

"Why, to agree to your interview, of course. But only if you will tell me something about yourself first."

Cautious to begin with, Diana slowly relaxed. In the course of the next hour, she avoided revealing anything personal, but she did regale her dinner companion with a lively account of how the relatively new Savarin had lured its steward away from a more venerable restaurant, Delmonico's. By the time they'd finished the appetizers, she'd related a favorite anecdote about a runaway camel on Broadway. And, over the entree, she told him the story of Jim, the big trick cat who, until the fire, had made his home in the Union Square Theater.

"He was rescued unscathed, although he did get sopping wet in the process." The memory made her smile. "As soon as he was thoroughly dried out, the Union Square's manager hosted a reception in his honor at the Criterion."

"The cat was given a party?"

She started to confirm this but he waved her off.

"I don't know why I'm surprised. My mother has a cat she dotes upon."

Her smile broadened into a grin. "I'm sure she would approve of Jim's present whereabouts then. He has a suite at the Hotel Hungaria."

"Had I but known," he said with a surprisingly boyish laugh, "I could have bought him a drink."

Reminded that he'd been hiding from her there less than twenty-four hours earlier, Diana put down her fork. She'd been so caught up in conversation that she'd scarcely tasted the pheasant or the asparagus spears or the French bread. She had all but lost sight of her purpose in being with this man in the first place. And she had completely forgotten to be wary of him.

"Enough about me," she said. "You promised me an interview."

"There is a condition."

The lightheartedness vanished with startling speed. He was once again the dark, brooding man whose goal in life was to strike terror into the hearts of others. The transformation made Diana uneasy. Which was the real Damon Bathory? Or was he, like Dr. Jekyll, possessed of two separate and distinct personalities?

"Name it." The quiver in her voice was back and Diana despised herself for it, but it did not seem to be anything she could control.

"You must henceforth stop trailing after me like a bloodhound."

Offended as well as embarrassed, she forced herself to apologize. "I am not usually so bold."

"No. Just hell-bent on writing scandal. You'd do better to try humor. If those stories you just told me are anything to judge by, you have a flair for it."

Surprised by the comment, she took refuge in buttering a slice of bread she did not really want. She needed time to compose her response. By the time she looked up, he was staring at her with disconcerting intensity.

"I must earn a living, Mr. Bathory," she said in a quiet and blessedly level voice. "At the moment, in order to keep my job, it is necessary for the *Intelligencer* to entice readers away from rival newspapers. My editor, Horatio Foxe, believes you are the key. People will buy one paper over another if doing so enables them to learn things about you that they cannot find out any other way. In spite of what you may think, I have never invented an anecdote for my column. I may have speculated in the past about the inspiration for your writing and indulged in a bit of innuendo, but I do not make things up out of whole cloth."

"How reassuring."

Hearing skepticism in his voice, she sighed. "I cannot guarantee what my editor may insert into one of my columns. If I offer him some tidbits juicy enough, however, he will be inclined to print only my words. The content of the story will thus be my choice, not his. Your choice, in fact."

"Some might argue that is but a trifling distinction."

"I endeavor to write only what is true."

"As you see it."

"I am entitled to my opinions on plays and books."

"Is that why you were attacked, Diana? Did your column offend someone?"

Should she tell him or not? She did not pretend to understand this complex, compelling man, but after the last hour with him, she found it impossible to believe he could be a murderer.

"The entire incident may have been staged," she said bluntly.

In concise sentences, she gave him the gist of Horatio Foxe's theory and what few details she had about the two women murdered along the route of Damon Bathory's tour.

"Why are you so certain I'm not the one who attacked you?" he asked. There was no expression at all in his eyes.

Omitting any mention of the doubts she'd entertained because she knew he'd given money to a man in the park, she explained her reasoning.

"Your editor has composed a remarkable piece of fiction," he said, when she'd completed her tale.

Diana frowned. Somehow, she'd expected more reaction from him. After all, she'd just accused him of killing two women, maybe more.

"If Foxe speculates about this in print, the story could well cause people to stop buying your books. You might be taken in for questioning by the police."

"He's not likely to go ahead with the story once you tell him you know I wasn't the one who dragged you into that alley."

"He could say you hired someone. To stop me from following you."

One sardonic brow lifted, but he said nothing.

Flustered, she began to fumble in her leather bag for a fresh notebook. Only when she'd opened it to the first pristine page did she look at Bathory again.

"Ask your questions." He sounded amused. "Let us see what minor scandals you can unearth to replace the one your Mr. Foxe is so intent upon inventing."

Diana had to clear her throat before she could begin. "Where is your home?"

"Buffalo."

The answer came too pat, just as on that earlier occasion when he'd assured her that Bathory was a real name. Real, she thought again, but not necessarily his. As for Buffalo, she had her doubts about that, too. His speech pattern was all wrong. And earlier he'd accused her of following him "downtown." People from upstate New York tended to say "downstreet."

She declined to challenge him. After all, he might live in Buffalo now but not be a native.

"Where do you get your ideas?" she asked.

"Everywhere."

"From family stories?"

"You are thinking of the Blood Countess." He fingered his jade ring. "The Bathorys have an . . . interesting history."

"I knew you deliberately tried to frighten me that night. I realized it as soon as you disappeared behind the curtain."

The wickedness of his smile disconcerted her. "No nightmares?"

The sudden memory of her dreams and their content brought a flush to Diana's face. Ducking her head, she quickly changed the subject.

"Where were you going in such a rush on the day I came to your hotel room?"

"I went to Bellevue," he admitted after a moment's hesitation, surprising her with his candor. "A brief visit, but an illuminating one."

"Research for a new story?"

"I suppose you'd prefer to hear I was once confined there as a lunatic and visited the place for old time's sake?" He took a sip of post-prandial coffee.

"Were you?" Her heart had begun to pound so loudly, she was afraid he would hear it.

"No, but I do visit madhouses every chance I get."

The peach cobbler the waiter had brought for their dessert forgotten, Diana stared at him. "Why?"

"In the hope that doctors in one of them will someday develop a better way to deal with the insane." Strong emotion banished the earlier blankness from Bathory's face. "I saw one man at Bellevue who had been living on the street. He suffered from delusions of persecution. Heard voices. From the look of him, he'd once been a strapping brute. He probably had a family . . . a life he enjoyed . . . before he was reduced to an emaciated shell. Because one of the voices he heard told him to strike a man who'd only wanted to help him, the doctors considered him dangerous, a threat to himself and others."

"Why would he obey . . . a voice?" She did not know very much about madmen and wasn't sure she wished to.

"Some patients think the orders come from God. More likely from the Devil." Bitterness tinged his words.

"Is there no treatment?" She'd stopped taking notes, affected by his passionate intensity.

"Most such patients are simply given massive injections of morphine and chloral. This calms the hysteria but produces intolerable side effects. Thirst is the least of them."

"Horrible." Diana shuddered in sympathy.

Bathory did not seem to notice. "Every doctor I've talked to about the care of those who suffer blackouts, hear voices, or are subject to fits of rage insists the only safe place for such poor souls is an institution. To be locked in, kept away from all contact with sanity—there is the real path to madness. We must find better solutions, even for those individuals too deranged to be let loose on an unsuspecting community."

The problem of what to do with the insane clearly affected him deeply. Uneasiness stealing over her, Diana wondered why.

"What other choice is there?" she asked. "Surely you do not mean to suggest that the families of such people lock them in their attics?" That was in the best tradition of sensational fiction.

"Better that than the insane pavilion at Bellevue. And Bellevue is one of the better facilities." He picked up her discarded notebook and pencil and thrust them at her. "Write that Diana. Say that all madhouses are the same. Inhumane. Unenlightened. Often the doctors know less than the inmates."

"I sympathize with their plight, but it has already been written about."

"Old news?" The bitterness was back. "Yes. I've read Miss Bly's account. And some reforms were instituted afterwards. But once the public outcry died down, the patients and their illnesses were forgotten again."

"I would like to help," she told him, resisting the urge to reach for his hand, "but the only way I can put any of this in my story is if you provide some reason why it interests you particularly."

"I see. It would help, then, to say I have a mad wife locked up at home?"

His voice was so deadly serious, she did not know whether to believe him or not. "Do you have a wife?"

"Does it matter, so long as you have scandalous details for your column?" The disappointment in his tone made her wince. He had no reason to trust her, just as she had no reason to trust him, but she had thought there was a rapport developing between them.

They had finished their meal. Bathory called for the check and Diana took that as a signal that the interview was over. She put her notebook away.

They left the restaurant and walked back towards his hotel in silence. She'd leave him there and go home. Spending time with Damon Bathory was even more exhausting than chasing after him.

He noticed her limping and hailed a cab. When he'd climbed in beside her, he gave the driver her address.

"I can invite you in," she told him, "but only into the parlor and there will be a chaperone present. My landlady is most strict about gentlemen callers."

"You said earlier that you need this interview in order to keep your job." His most winning smile was firmly in place.

"Yes, but—"

"And if what you've already learned from me isn't enough, your editor will make something up out of whole cloth. Is that correct?"

"I fear so, yes."

"Then I've a proposition for you." He lowered his voice to a level that vibrated with sincerity. The effect of such charisma was difficult to escape and Diana was not inclined to fight it very hard. "If you promise not to follow me after I take you home, I swear I'll do nothing more exciting tonight than return to my hotel room and get a good night's sleep."

"All right, but—"

"Then, when we're both well rested," he continued, cutting her off, "we will meet again. Tomorrow, if you like, at whatever hour and place you say. Why, we can spend the entire day together, and in the evening go to a play. Shall we sit *together* in an audience for a change?"

"Most theaters are dark on Monday nights," Diana reminded him, beguiled by the wistful note in his voice.

He thought for a moment as their cab came to a stop in front of the house on 10th Street. "Will you allow me to take you to the circus instead? Eighty-six acts in three rings, or so the advertisements say."

A delicious sense of anticipation coursed through her at the prospect of spending more time with him. His lighthearted tone heightened the feeling. So did the appreciative look in his eyes. The admiration of a man for a woman he desired shone there. He made no attempt to hide it. Responding female to male, Diana forced the last of her doubts into a dark corner of her mind and smiled back at him.

"If we go in the afternoon," she said, daring to tease him a little "I can write a review of the opening performance."

"Done. How early shall I come for you? Interview first, I think. Business before pleasure."

Diana's smile abruptly dimmed.

"What is it?" He sounded genuinely concerned.

"I have an early appointment, but it shouldn't take long. Why don't I meet you in the lobby of your hotel at nine."

"A new story?" he asked.

"An old one. Unfinished business."

Diana was relieved when he did not press her for details.

Neither did he linger over farewells. When he'd gone, she drifted to the window and stood concealed by the lace curtains to watch him climb back into the waiting cab. She stayed there until it was out of sight, her fingers toying idly with the brooch at her throat. She listened until the last clip-clop of the horse's hooves faded away. Only then did she turn and, frowning, make her way upstairs to her tiny, solitary room.

She did not know what the morning would bring, but the last time she'd felt this edgy, this full of hope, she had been about to elope with Evan.

That had been the beginning of the most exciting time she'd ever known. It had also been the worst mistake of her life.

CHAPTER SIX

&)Q3

Diana had believed the weather forecast posted at the top of the Equitable Building and printed in every newspaper in the city, a prediction of springlike conditions on Monday. She had dressed accordingly in the pre-dawn hour, and by the time she realized her mistake, it was too late to go back inside to change clothes. Shivering, she climbed into the Hansom she'd hired, determined to arrive at Grand Central Station as planned, in order to keep the promise she'd made to herself before walking out of the 13th Street Theater two nights earlier.

She was not looking forward to the confrontation ahead, and the unsettled weather mirrored her feelings. During the night, a torrential rain had soaked Manhattan, causing the gutters to overflow. In the wee hours of the morning, the temperature had abruptly dropped, coating streets and sidewalks alike with a layer of ice and turning the downpour to sleet. The first hailstones struck the roof of Diana's cab soon after she set out. The precipitation had changed, yet again, to snow by the time she arrived at her destination. A gust of wind nearly strong enough to lift her off her feet struck her the moment she exited the hack. To add insult to injury, the driver demanded twice his usual fare.

"On account of the storm," he explained. "It's a corker."

Grudgingly, she gave up more money than she could afford and hurried into the many-turreted brick building. She'd hoped to stop and buy a cup of hot coffee to fortify herself, since she'd left Mrs. Curran's boarding house before her landlady prepared breakfast, but with the delay in getting here, it was nearly time for the early train to Hartford to depart. Squaring her shoulders, Diana made her way through the train shed at a fast clip.

Dealing honestly with Damon Bathory had been the right thing to do, she thought as she crossed the huge building. And so was begging the forgiveness of Lavinia Ross. Diana had braved the storm because she was determined to speak with the actress before Lavinia left on tour. Todd's Touring Thespians would be away from Manhattan for the next several months.

Embarrassment and guilt had plagued Diana in the week since Foxe made his unauthorized additions to her column. On Saturday night, forced to see again the very play she'd savaged, she'd realized she could not let Nathan Todd's company go off without trying to make amends. She could not undo what had appeared in print, but she could at least explain how it had happened.

She found Nathan Todd, a heavy-set, red-faced gentleman in his mid-forties, supervising the loading of props, costumes, and set pieces. In a booming voice that echoed in the open spaces above, he shouted orders to the baggage handlers. "Confound it! Be careful of that flat!"

He subsided into unintelligible grumbles, then fell silent when he caught sight of Diana.

She burst into speech, stumbling through her explanation.

"Any publicity is good publicity," Toddy declared, when she'd finished stammering out her apology.

"I am surprised you'll even speak civilly to me. I expected you to cut me dead."

Todd heaved a sigh so deep that the edges of his luxuriant mustache quivered. "What's done is done. I can hardly complain when the story's true. It wasn't any secret that Lavinia replaced Jerusha in my bed." He signed again, then managed a smile. "The gossip did nothing but help us at the box office. Your column brought them in droves."

"To gawk and speculate, Toddy."

He chuckled. "They think I'm a fine fellow, thanks to you. How can I be angry about that?" He puffed out his chest, which had the unfortunate effect of exaggerating a developing paunch.

"Dare I hope the others will be as understanding?"

Toddy's snort spoke volumes.

Jerusha Fildale, solid, reliable Jerusha, who'd taken Diana under her wing when Evan first married her, was not the sort to hold a grudge. Lavinia Ross was another story entirely.

As if conjured by Diana's thoughts, the young actress swept into Grand Central Station. She seemed to think the railroad platform, lit from above by both hanging lamps and skylights, was just another stage, a four-story-high set designed specifically to show off her dramatic entrance.

Diana could not help admiring the performance. And the costume Lavinia had chosen for it. She wore a fur-trimmed mauve traveling outfit in the latest style. A female passenger about to board the Chicago Limited caught sight of the fashionable attire and sighed with envy, no doubt imagining herself in Lavinia's place, traveling the country, seeing the world.

As she drew close to the other woman, Diana saw that the actress's face had been carefully painted and was artfully arranged into a smile. The effect was only slightly marred by the fact that wet snow had pocked her veil, adhering it in patches to her skin.

When she recognized Diana, Lavinia's mouth pursed with displeasure. "What are you doing here?" she demanded in her breathy, little-girl voice. The look in her eyes was one of intense dislike.

The hiss of steam and the loud clanging of bells momentarily drowned out Diana's answer. One train pulled out. Another was coming in. Conductors shouted, adding to the din.

In order to be heard, Diana stepped closer. With only inches between them, she could see that the dye in Lavinia's veil had begun to run. Mottled streaks of mauve decorated the actress's scowling face.

"I came to apologize," Diana said in a rush. "I know I cannot make up to you the harm that has been done to your reputation, but I want you to know that I never meant that story to appear in print."

"Who told you about me in the first place?"

That was the one question Diana did not want to answer. "Your relationship with Toddy was hardly a secret," she equivocated, thankful that the time for Lavinia to board the train was fast approaching.

Right on cue, Nathan Todd called for the members of his company to gather for departure. Diana watched as the first to respond, Charles Underly, did a classic double-take at the sight of her. Scowling, he gripped the top of his walking stick more tightly. No doubt he thought she had a nerve showing up here after all she'd said about his performance in print.

To Underly, at least, Diana did not feel she owed any explanation or apology. She'd given her honest evaluation of his acting ability—his portrayal of Ferdinand had been "bombastic and unbelievable." And to confirm her assessment, Underly had gotten even worse reviews from other New York newspapers.

"Cow," Lavinia muttered, drawing Diana's attention back to her.

The epithet had been directed at Jerusha Fildale, whose entrance caused a stir sufficient to put Lavinia's in the shade. The long-time star of Toddy's company, Jerusha knew how to command attention. This morning she did so by sporting a hat which seemed to be a recreation of an eagle's nest, complete with bird. Diana wondered how she had kept it from being drenched or blown away in the gale outside.

Intent upon upstaging her rival, Lavinia turned her back on
Diana and sashayed across the platform. Every male eye in the
vicinity followed her bouncing bustle. Her tight-waisted corset
tipped her forward at a highly suggestive angle.

That, Diana thought, was something she would not mention
in her column, although she would put in a notice about Toddy's
tour. Careless comments about the morals of one actress slandered
them all and most, as Diana well knew, were as upright as any
women obliged to work for a living.

Better than some.

As Diana scanned the crowd, she had to smile. People's reactions
were so predictable. Only three females unconnected to the
theatrical company waited to board the train to Hartford. One
looked fascinated, the second repulsed, and the third envious. The
faces of the men revealed an equal diversity of expression—here
salacious speculation, there desire, and there—

There, Diana realized with a sense of shock, was Damon
Bathory with a pile of baggage beside him. She felt as if she'd been
drenched by the icy water pooled on the glass ceiling above.

He was leaving, sneaking out of town when he had promised—

Too infuriated to think straight, she seethed in silent rage until
a whistle sounded to warn everyone on the platform that the train
was about to depart. Propelled into action by the sound, and by
the call of the conductor, Diana hurried forward.

The engine pulled only five cars and a caboose on this run,
four for passengers and one for baggage. Bathory entered a first-
class car.

It did not matter to Diana that she was unprepared for a journey.
Grimly determined that, this time, she would discover the whole
truth about Damon Bathory, she boarded the train.

At this early hour, there were not a great many travelers. The
members of Todd's Touring Thespians—seven men and three
women—had a coach-class car to themselves. Diana had known
most of them for years, and they knew her, both as Evan Spaulding's

widow and as the woman who wrote "Today's Tidbits." Hamilton Fields, Ralph Leighton, Jeremy Fargo, and Amos Singleterry had been with Nathan Todd's company back when Evan was alive, as had Jerusha Fildale and Patsy Jenkins, a plump and cheerful older woman who played character parts. The new additions were Underly, Lavinia, and a young man named Billy Sims. Patsy sent a cheerful smile Diana's way. Underly and Lavinia greeted her appearance with hostile stares.

Diana hastily slid in next to Jerusha Fildale on one of the bench-style seats and turned beseeching eyes towards the woman who had once been so much more than a mere friend.

In the past, Jerusha had always taken Diana's part, even once against Evan. If, in their days at school, Horatio Foxe's sister had assumed the role of the sibling Diana had longed for when she was growing up, then after her marriage it had been Jerusha who had fallen into the role of slightly older but much more worldly-wise relation.

"I'm sorry," Diana whispered. "Forgive me?"

Jerusha glowered. She frowned. Then she sneezed. She still had the heavy cold that had marred her performance in the title role of *The Duchess of Calabria.*

"You should take better care of yourself," Diana chided her. "Why did you go on if you were sick?"

Jerusha beetled her brows. "The alternative was to let Lavinia butcher the part." She fished a delicate, lace-trimmed handkerchief out of her bosom, blew her nose with a resounding honk, and glared at Diana through bloodshot eyes.

"Oh."

"Yes—oh. But there's no need for you to apologize. I knew what you did for a living when I told you about Toddy and Lavinia."

Impulsively, she hugged Diana, engulfing her in a wave of lavender scent tinged with the less pleasant smell of horehound drops. She was sucking on one to ease her cough and sore throat.

Her generosity only made Diana feel worse. Jerusha had

confided in her as a friend, sharing the painful details of Nathan Todd's betrayal of her affections. He'd abandoned a long-time relationship with Jerusha for a fling with the younger woman, a no-talent hussy whose only previous experience on the stage had been as a magician's assistant.

"I know Toddy says any publicity is good publicity, but I never meant so much to be printed."

Jerusha shrugged. "I am resigned to my situation now, and your column did do some good. After it appeared, every one of our performances sold out."

"Yes, so Toddy said."

Suddenly, Jerusha grinned. "And Lavinia was fit to be tied. Did my poor old heart good to see her so angry."

"Does she know you're the one who talked to me?" Diana asked.

"If she didn't before, she does now." Jerusha swiveled around, a self-satisfied smirk on her face.

Diana glanced back. The subject of their discussion sat two rows behind them, next to Toddy, who looked a trifle puzzled by Diana's presence.

"Ticket, miss?" The conductor stood beside her, his hand out.

Diana burrowed in her bag for money and came up short. To get enough to pay for a ticket all the way to Hartford, she had to dip into the emergency billfold secured by her garter. As she paid the conductor, she tried not to think of how very little money she had left. If Damon Bathory changed trains in Stamford or New Haven, she would not be able to afford to pursue him.

"You hadn't planned to make this trip," Jerusha observed.

"No," Diana agreed as the red-faced conductor moved on.

A few rapid calculations sent her spirits plummeting. She'd need to send a telegram to Horatio Foxe at the first stop to ask for more funds and for authorization to send news dispatches over the wires leased from Western Union by the Associated Press.

"Cash in the ticket before we leave the station," Jerusha urged her. "There's no point in coming with us. Even if you pursue

Lavinia all the way to the next stand, she won't accept your apology."

"That's not why I'm here."

Diana pictured Damon Bathory in her mind, trying to convince herself she was doing the right thing. Confusion threatened to overwhelm her. What was it about the man? The previous day, completely under his spell, she'd lost all perspective. That was the answer, she supposed. He was a sorcerer. And what else? This time, she meant to find out. She'd not allow herself to be charmed by him again!

Jerusha tugged at her sleeve. "What are you up to, Diana Spaulding?"

A low whistle sounded as the train shuddered into motion.

"There is someone I followed onto the train," Diana confided as they left the station, "but not Lavinia."

It was too late to change her mind. The train plunged into a tunnel that would keep them underground until they emerged, far to the north, at 125th Street.

"Who?" Jerusha's hoarse voice broke on the question. She was about to lose it again.

"Someone I don't want to see me. By blending in with all of you, I can pass unnoticed." Why would anyone look at a plain brown wren when the eye was drawn to brightly colored parrots?

"Who?" Jerusha repeated, this time in a whisper.

"A man. I was to meet him later today for an interview. Instead, I discovered him here, boarding this train. I mean to find out where he's bound." He was not going to Buffalo. That much was certain. This train was headed in the wrong direction.

She'd been a gullible fool last evening, letting herself believe everything he said. Take her to the circus? Hah! No doubt he'd only pretended to enjoy her company, letting her think he was beginning to care for her as a woman in order to lull her into forgetting to be cautious. She'd been as completely taken in as one of those addlepated young ladies who'd flocked to his readings.

If she hadn't seen him today, by accident, she'd have had a long wait in that hotel lobby. Had he even left her a note? Somehow, she doubted it. He'd lied to her, cast out seductive lures, all so he could sneak out of town like a thief in the night.

Jerusha reached out to touch the colorful bruise on Diana's jaw. The light coating of face powder she'd used to cover it had been washed away by the storm. "Did he do this to you?"

"No."

She started to say he was not that kind of man, then fell silent. Any man was capable of physical violence when angry and she'd seen flashes of temper from Damon Bathory. He'd frightened her more than once.

He'd also touched her with a tenderness that had made her ache.

Once he'd admitted to knowing she was following him, she should have realized that the rest of his story would not survive close scrutiny. Why, he'd had plenty of time to come up with all sorts of nefarious schemes to get rid of her! He might even have hired that thug who attacked her.

"He's hurt you in other ways," Jerusha said. "You care for him and he doesn't return your feelings."

When Diana tried to deny it, Jerusha just looked smug.

"I can tell by the look on your face. You never were any good at hiding your emotions."

The realization that her friend might be right jolted Diana. Was more than her pride involved? Had her heart fallen victim, as well?

In a very short time, her feelings had become impossibly tangled. Not since Evan's whirlwind courtship had she experienced so many changes of emotion.

"What am I doing here?" she whispered in sudden panic.

"Well," Jerusha said with a smile, "you claim you're after a story for that newspaper of yours."

"Yes. Yes, of course I am." Squaring her shoulders, Diana tried desperately to reorder her priorities.

The very fact that Bathory had run away from her meant that he had something to hide. She might have a personal reason for wanting to find out the truth about him, but she was also sure that she could turn what she learned into the scandalous story Foxe had demanded.

Thinking more clearly now than she had at any time since she'd impulsively boarded the train, Diana considered how much it would be prudent to reveal to her traveling companion. If Bathory's ultimate destination was not Hartford, or if he did get off the train sooner, then she might need to rely upon Jerusha's generosity for the wherewithal to continue her quest.

Diana turned to study the woman beside her. Jerusha had removed the outlandish hat to reveal brassy blonde hair and, as if to contradict that effect, tiny mother-of-pearl earbobs. She dressed, as all the company did, to attract attention and draw in the paying public, but in spite of the bright clothing and heavy cosmetics she wore, she looked tired and ill. There was no opportunity to stop and rest on tour. She must go on, sick or not, until she either recovered or collapsed on stage in the middle of a performance.

"You should sleep," Diana told her.

"I'd rather hear about your man."

"He's not my man."

"It would take my mind off my misery," she wheedled.

After only a token protest, Diana gave in. By the time she'd finished her account, an edited version of events of the last few days that left out both Horatio Foxe's theory about the murdered women and any mention of the attack on herself, the train had crossed the Harlem Bridge and left Manhattan behind.

"Damon Bathory." Jerusha sounded impressed.

Diana rested her head against the back of the mohair-covered seat. "If I don't get this story, I could lose my job."

"He made quite an impression in San Francisco," Jerusha said. "We were there at the same time he was, you know."

San Francisco? A queasy feeling came over Diana. The second

murder had taken place in San Francisco.

If Bathory had lied, if he had been behind the attack on her, could that mean he might have murdered those women, too?

Did she dare trust her sense that he was not the sort of man to hurt a woman? Her instincts had not been all that reliable when she'd married Evan.

She remembered what she'd told Horatio Foxe, that by the logic he'd used, a member of any theatrical company on tour at the same time as Bathory might have committed those murders. Slowly, she turned to survey the other occupants of the railroad car.

"Was this the same company Toddy took to San Francisco?" she asked Jerusha.

Her friend looked surprised by the question. "Why, yes. Billy Sims and Charles Underly joined up shortly before we began that tour."

Diana regarded each man in turn. Sims played opposite Lavinia in the comedies. He doubled as a stagehand when Toddy needed him to. In her review, Diana had described his acting as wooden. For all his good looks—carrot-colored hair, vivid green eyes, and a winning smile—he did not convey much personality from the stage.

He caught her looking at him and gave her a cocky grin. Diana answered with a weak smile, noticing two things that suddenly made her uneasy. Those green eyes of his were oddly flecked with gold, giving them an unsettling brightness. And he had a scratch on the side of his face, as if someone had clawed at him in an attempt to escape his clutches.

Sims could have nicked himself shaving, her more rational side said. After all, she could not remember marking her attacker in that alley. Surely, her imagination was running away with her. And yet, for size and shape, it could have been Billy Sims who'd accosted her. And he wore a plain wool coat, just as her assailant had.

Disconcerted, she broke eye contact with him, shifting her attention to Charles Underly. With his head bent, she could not see his features, but she remembered that he relied upon contortions and exaggeration rather than more subtle expressions when he trod the boards.

His hands were folded over the top of a silver-headed walking stick. She'd never seen him off stage without it, although he did not appear to need it to get around. Diana assumed that carrying it was an affectation, but it did seem to rule him out as the man in the alley.

As if Underly felt her gaze, he raised his head and looked directly at her. Diana braced herself, expecting to see dislike, derision, or disdain in his bloodshot eyes. She had, after all, panned his performance in *The Duchess of Calabria*. Instead, she got a blast of simmering hatred that seemed to go far deeper than simple pique over a bad review. If looks could kill, she thought, she'd be in her death throes by now.

When Jerusha started to cough, Diana was glad for the distraction. She patted her friend's back while Jerusha fumbled in her bag for a small bottle of Hale's Honey of Horehound and Tar, a patent medicine that claimed to stop any cough, even one caused by consumption.

"Where was the company last November?" Diana asked when Jerusha had put the bottle away and cleared her throat. There was one easy way to put her foolish fears to rest.

"In New York. Don't you remember? We'd disbanded for a bit to reorganize. The last ingenue, Louisa Carver, had just left to get married. That's why Toddy had to hold . . . auditions. He went all the way to Philadelphia in search of actors who'd suit."

"Philadelphia!" Diana's voice rose higher than she'd intended. She did not dare look around to see if anyone had heard, but she was careful to whisper her next question. "When?"

Jerusha gave her an odd look. "Early in the month. I don't remember the exact date. Came back with all three of them. Underly. Sims. And Lavinia."

"Could it have been the 9th?"

"It could have been. Whatever is the matter with you, Diana? You've gone pale as a cheesecloth scrim."

"Nothing." And it was true, she told herself. Nothing but an excess of imagination.

She'd been overexposed to tales of terror of late. No wonder she was jumping at shadows. To think that the same man had killed both those women was preposterous, let alone that anyone she knew had tried to harm her. Besides, if Bathory hadn't had time to change "costume," neither had Underly or Sims. Or Toddy.

Of the four men on this train who had been in both cities where young women had been murdered, and in New York when she was attacked, only one posed any threat to her. But not because he could turn out to be a cold-blooded killer. Damon Bathory might have other dark secrets, but she could not convince herself he was capable of murder.

Would he be very angry, she wondered, when he found out she was still after her story? After him?

It didn't matter. As long as she was careful not to be alone with him, she would be perfectly safe from his wrath . . . and from all other strong emotions, as well.

As Diana listened to Jerusha chatter about plans for the current tour, she was glad that, for the moment, Damon Bathory had no notion she was on this train. She must have herself firmly under control before she met him again. These foolish, contradictory feelings she was enduring now would never do.

If she had any sense, she thought, she'd hope he did elude her. Then she could go back to New York and tell Horatio Foxe the truth—she'd gone after the scandal but had failed to find any.

CHAPTER SEVEN

❧❧❧

The gent's washroom was already occupied by two men when Ben Northcote entered. He did not recall seeing either of them in the parlor car, but then he'd not been paying much attention to the other first-class passengers.

He maneuvered around a heavy-set, red-faced fellow of forty or so in order to pump water into the ceramic basin and sluice it over his hands. The other man stood with his back to them, changing his collar in front of one of the two mirrors. When the train lurched suddenly, causing his hand to jerk, one end of the new collar flew up and slapped him in the face.

Ben hid a smile as he dried his hands on the roller towel. He was about to return to his seat, when the man whose laundry added starch with such a heavy hand turned to his rotund companion and spoke a familiar name. "What's Diana doing here, Toddy?"

Ben stilled. It wasn't such an unusual name, yet . . . Interested to hear the answer, he pretended to find a spot of dirt on the back of his right hand. He scrubbed industriously at it while he eavesdropped.

"She's hoping to get Lavinia to accept her apology. That's what Lavinia thinks, anyway."

"Makes no sense." The man at the mirror sounded peeved, but Ben could not tell if it was the topic of conversation or his losing battle with the collar which annoyed him. "She spoke to her on the platform. Why tag along after us onto the train?"

This time his question received only a grunt in reply. The one called Toddy had gone into the smaller, adjoining compartment that held the commode. In reality, it was no more than a box with a mahogany seat that opened to the tracks below. For all the luxury of the appointments in first class, a primitive dry hopper was the best they could provide in toilet facilities.

"Is she going all the way to our next stand? I didn't see any luggage?"

Toddy's reply was muffled but understandable. "I doubt she intended to come along, Charles, but Lavinia snubbed her and our Diana has always been persistent. Probably followed her on impulse."

"Why is she sitting with Jerusha, then?"

"Because I am occupying the seat next to Lavinia."

There was no longer any doubt in Ben's mind that "their" Diana was the one he knew. Indeed, now that he put the names Jerusha, Lavinia, Toddy and Charles together, he recognized the two men as actors in *The Duchess of Calabria*. This portly fellow was Nathan Todd, who managed the company and took most of the leading male roles. Charles was Charles Underly, easily the least talented person in the troupe. Jerusha would be Jerusha Fildale, the leading lady of Todd's Touring Thespians. Lavinia was undoubtedly the notorious "Miss L. R.," who'd used her body to ease her path to a featured role in the play. She'd had to, Ben thought, remembering her portrayal of Julia, the Cardinal's mistress. She had little ability as an actress.

Underly, having at last subdued his collar, reached for the public brush and comb tethered by cords to the white marble top of the paneled washstand. He winced as he restored order to the thick mane of his hair. Either he'd encountered a snarl or he was hung over. The bloodshot eyes reflected in the mirror made Ben suspect the latter.

"You know what happened the last time Jerusha and Diana had a little heart-to-heart chat," Underly muttered as Todd emerged from the cubicle.

The older man heaved a sigh so deep that the edges of his mustache quivered. "What's done is done. The gossip didn't hurt us at the box office. Still, I could have done without the backbiting backstage."

"You spoke civilly enough to Diana at the station. In your place, I'd have turned my back on her." He reached for the silver-headed walking stick he'd left propped against the wall. "Or wrung her pretty little neck," he added in a mutter.

"We can hardly complain when the story's true."

To avoid making the two men suspicious of him, Ben left the washroom, but he lingered just outside. Their voices reached him well enough through the door.

"Next you'll be telling me she didn't mean what she said about my interpretation of the role of Ferdinand."

"For God's sake, Charles. You've had worse reviews."

"She's Evan Spaulding's widow, Toddy. She might have been kinder. To hear Jerusha tell it, your troupe was like family to her once. It's betrayal, that's what, to go to work for that newspaper and dissect the talents of Spaulding's colleagues."

"That's what reviewers do, Charles." Todd sounded resigned.

"Then she should have found other work."

"As what? A seamstress? Maybe you'd rather she walked the streets?"

Ben heard the sound of the latch being lifted and beat a hasty retreat. He might not know what had motivated Diana Spaulding to choose the profession she had, but he was certain he knew the answer to Underly's earlier question. Once again, she was following Damon Bathory.

And once again he would have to find a way to put an end to

her pursuit.

∞⟩⟨∞

Fools," Jerusha muttered.

Diana came out of her reverie with a jerk. "Who?"

"Them." She indicated Nathan Todd and Charles Underly, who were just returning to the coach.

In the few seconds it had taken the two men to cross from one railroad car to the next, they'd been coated in white. Even Toddy's mustache was caked with wet snow. Underly shook himself like a dog, then glared at Diana as he passed her seat.

"Where did they go?" She'd been so lost in her own bleak thoughts that she hadn't noticed them leave.

"First-class parlor car. To use the gents' washroom."

Diana suppressed a laugh.

"Sheer insanity to have braved the elements in such a blow," Jerusha declared.

"You'd do the same if it weren't storming."

Diana would herself, especially when encumbered by a bustle of any size. The first-class ladies' washrooms were small—three-feet-by-six at most, with a smaller, adjoining compartment to hold a commode—but less luxurious cars did not contain any washing facilities and the cramped, airless closets provided for the basic necessity were barely large enough to back into with one's skirts already raised.

"Insanity," Jerusha said again. She was staring fixedly at the scene beyond the square window.

Diana leaned past her for a closer look and had to admit the weather had turned into a formidable blow. A silent, swirling white fury obscured every detail of the passing landscape. "Perhaps this is just a local squall."

"Oh, la, I hope so, but it seems to be getting worse by the minute."

As much as Diana wanted to maintain a more positive outlook for the rest of the journey, she feared Jerusha was right. The train did not seem likely to carry them out of the storm. It appeared to be moving into it instead. She was trying to think of a remark that would cheer them both when her stomach growled loudly.

Embarrassed, Diana felt color climb into her cheeks. This was getting to be an annoying habit, as was missing meals in order to follow Damon Bathory.

Jerusha chuckled. "No breakfast?"

"No time. I'll get something at Stamford." According to the schedule, that was the first stop, followed by New Haven and Hartford.

She wouldn't, of course. She didn't dare waste what little money she had on food. Nor could she buy sandwiches or coffee from the water boy, if she was to afford a hotel room of the cheaper sort wherever she ended up. "I have a few things with me." Jerusha pulled a small satchel from beneath the seat.

Diana stared at fruit and dried beef and cold chicken in amazement. There was even a glass of jelly. "You've enough for several days there. I thought the stand in Hartford lasted almost a week."

"It does. And we've only short trips after—Springfield, Boston, Portland, and, at the end of the month, Bangor. Then on to Burlington, Saratoga Springs, and Albany. But it never hurts to be prepared. You know how it is with trains. Most of the stops last less than ten minutes and never more than twenty. Barely time to get out and stretch your legs, let alone buy a meal."

Shifting a fraction closer, Diana peered into the satchel. "I don't suppose you stashed an extra coat in there?"

Jerusha's sharp glance surveyed the outfit Diana had chosen to wear for her confrontation with Lavinia. The stylish Modjeska jacket was decorated with beaver fur in the collar and cuffs, but the lining was only fancy quilting, warmer than the satin used in some walking outfits but little protection against the icy blasts of air that eddied into the railroad coach through the loosely-fitted sashes. The pale gray color had been another impractical choice. It would soon be stained with soot and grime.

"Pitifully inadequate," Jerusha declared. "You'd be an icicle already if we weren't sitting right next to the heat."

The coach boasted two stoves, one permanently fixed at each end. Periodically, someone added another stick of wood to keep them going.

"I would have worn my warm blue Ulster with its cape," Diana assured her, "but I expected the day to be clear and warm. That was the forecast." As if to underscore her foolishness, the wind howled and rocked the railroad car, increasing the interior's pervasive chill.

"I have a steamer trunk and Gladstone bag in the baggage car. I can spare a blouse. Perhaps the broadcloth dress. I hardly ever wear it."

Diana gave Jerusha's hourglass figure an amused look before shifting her gaze to her own, far less impressive bosom.

"Needles and thread," Jerusha added, winking at her. "Pins and hair pins. You'll need flannel underwear. A handkerchief. A dressing gown. Slippers. Toilet articles. A flask and drinking cup. A jar of cold cream."

"I might be better off borrowing a pair of trousers and a jacket."

"Oh, la! That you could think you'd be closer to a lad's build than to mine!" Shaking her head at the notion, Jerusha rose and went back among the company to scrounge for clothing.

Diana swiveled her head to monitor her friend's progress. The request produced only further venom from Lavinia Ross. Patsy began at once to burrow into a satchel that was the twin to Jerusha's. With another wink at Diana, Jerusha extended her search to the men.

"Two of you would fit in my britches!" Toddy bellowed, laughing heartily.

The joviality seemed overdone, even for him, and when Lavinia tugged on his arm, he hastened to bend close and listen. Whatever she whispered erased his smile. He did not look Diana's way again.

Charles Underly did not deign to comment when Jerusha approached him, but he did sneer at her request. Pursing his lips, he glanced in Diana's direction, giving definition to the act of looking down one's nose.

"Here," Jerusha said when she returned from her expedition. "This should help. Patsy had a spare." She thrust a heavy, knitted shawl at Diana.

Barely had she got the borrowed garment around her shoulders when she felt the train begin to slow. Up ahead the whistle sounded.

"We can't have reached Stamford yet."

As one, Diana and Jerusha turned to stare out the window, but there was nothing to see except a blinding curtain of snow driven sideways by the wind.

With a lurch, the train halted entirely, belching steam with a sound like a dying elephant. Diana bounced forward. If she'd not caught hold of the ashwood armrest, she'd have ended up in a heap in the aisle.

Bundles tumbled from the nickel-plated luggage racks overhead and Toddy, who had just stood up, lost his balance and landed hard on the plank flooring. His curses filled the air, louder than the assorted moans and cries of alarm from the rest of the troupe.

Rubbing her elbow, the same one she'd bumped in the cab, Diana righted herself. This time it had connected with the window frame.

There had been no collision, no crash. No grinding noises or explosions. She supposed she should be grateful for small favors, but what she suspected had happened was bad enough.

An hour later, they'd not moved so much as an inch. Far from leaving the bad weather behind, they appeared to have traveled straight into the heart of it. They were snowbound in the middle of a blizzard.

Diana stared out at the storm and sighed.

"What are you thinking?" Jerusha asked.

"That no one knows where I am, or that Damon Bathory has left Manhattan. I wish I had some way to send a telegram to Horatio Foxe."

"If a train can get stuck in this snow, then the telegraph lines are most likely down."

Diana suspected her friend was right. Conditions had grown steadily worse since they'd stopped. She could see nothing more than an inch away from the window, and only that much through one of the few small patches of glass that were not coated with ice.

Turning away from the view, such as it was, Diana toyed with the idea of taking out her notebook and jotting down her thoughts. Foxe would expect her to write an account of what was happening to her. "Stranded on a Train" the headline would read.

Or, "Dead on Stranded Train."

She shuddered at the thought. "We'll all be icicles before the day's over," she predicted in gloomy tones.

"Not if we move about to keep warm," said Jerusha. "I suggest dancing."

"Dancing?" Astonished by the thought, Diana stared at her. She heard the door to the coach open and felt a blast of cold air, but was too fascinated by her companion's suggestion and the anticipation in Jerusha's voice and manner to look away. "Dancing?"

"The tarantella, perhaps. Something lively to keep the blood flowing and take our minds off being cold. The only thing that would be more useful would be a nice bottle of brandy to warm the insides." Her gaze shifted over Diana's shoulder as footsteps paused in the aisle beside them. With a bright smile, she added, "Or a big strong man to cuddle up to."

Without looking, Diana knew who stood behind her. So much for keeping her presence secret from him! With a sense of impending doom, she turned to face Damon Bathory.

Face ruddy and hair and beard frosted from having crossed the stormswept platform between cars, he stared back at her with an expression cold as ice sculpture. "What a charming ensemble you are wearing, Mrs. Spaulding," he said in that deep, resonant voice of his. "Did you select it just to meet me?"

Blast the man! Her temper flared, banishing embarrassment and guilt and common sense, as well. "You knew I was here! You lured me aboard this train!"

That annoyingly sardonic brow lifted. "Do you think I also arranged for the blizzard?"

She flushed but did not look away. "I would not put it past you! Sorcerers can conjure up all sorts of evil things."

"Trust me, Diana. I did my best to escape New York without being followed."

"You lied to me."

"Yes."

"About everything?"

His eyes darkened. "No. Not about everything."

Her breath caught. In confusion, Diana dropped her gaze to hands she held tightly clasped in her lap.

Jerusha coughed, then extended a hand past Diana. "Mister Bathory, I presume?" She all but purred the question.

"Miss Fildale. A pleasure." He bowed over her hand and kissed it, bringing his chiseled profile into Diana's line of vision.

"Oh, la! You give me all sorts of new thoughts on how to stay warm."

"Better than alcohol, I trust. Imbibing heavily tends to make people careless and that invites frostbite. It is not a pretty sight, nor is the resulting loss of fingers or toes."

"Charming," Diana muttered. She could guess the sort of tale Damon Bathory might create from this experience. Frozen corpses reanimated in the manner of Mrs. Shelley's Frankenstein monster. Horribly disfigured creatures who—

"Don't scowl so," Jerusha hissed, giving Diana a thump on the upper arm. "Your face will get stuck that way."

Bathory had turned his attention to the other occupants of the coach. Diana glanced over her shoulder at them, then wished she had not. Avid curiosity came back at her in palpable waves. They'd overheard her exchange with Bathory and drawn their own conclusions.

Seeing the salacious speculation in Lavinia's eyes, Diana wished she could crawl under the seat and hide. She settled for visualizing Horatio Foxe's face when she presented him with the sensational story he'd demanded.

Behind her, Bathory's mellifluous voice outlined their situation. "The most practical course is for everyone to gather in one place," he concluded, "and since the parlor car is the most comfortable, I suggest you all move there."

"How astonishing," Jerusha murmured. "We're being invited to join the posh set."

"Kind of you, m'boy." Nathan Todd spoke for all the members of his troupe, and not one of them needed to be asked twice. Gathering their possessions, they exited the coach en masse.

They were greeted on the other side by a formidable matron. Diana recognized her as the passenger who'd looked so repulsed by the sight of Jerusha and Lavinia promenading on the platform at Grand Central Station.

"I am Mrs. Wainflete," she informed them.

"Pleased to meet you, ma'am!" Toddy grabbed her hand and shook it, causing her considerable consternation. "We're grateful indeed for your hospitality. And to prove it, we'll pay our passage by entertaining you. You have at your disposal, madam, one of the finest theatrical companies in the world. We'll perform a play from our repertoire. Any one you select. What would cost you three dollars for an orchestra seat, you shall have today for free."

Mrs. Wainflete seemed somewhat mollified, although it soon became clear she'd not favored inviting them in. Like the others who'd bought first-class tickets, she'd paid twenty-five dollars to ensure that she wouldn't be obliged to mingle with the riff-raff.

Jerusha pushed Diana in the direction of a buffet outfitted to serve coffee, tea, and light refreshments and pressed a sandwich into her hand. "Eat."

Mrs. Wainflete returned to her pedestal armchair, a recliner covered in red plush and furnished with white cloth arm- and headrest-covers, a foot cushion, and an individual heating coil connected to the small stove that sat in one corner.

The man who identified himself as Mrs. Wainflete's husband, reed thin with wispy hair and a mustache to match, stayed as far away from his formidable wife as he could get, staring out of one of the parlor car's large windows.

"Can't see a blasted thing," he complained, peering into the storm, "and I vow this handrail's turned to ice." Wincing, he lifted his bare fingers from the silver-plated surface.

"You'd best close the curtains," Bathory advised. "We should keep in whatever heat we can."

It did not surprise Diana when Wainflete obeyed. Damon Bathory had that effect on people.

"Surely the stove will keep us warm." Mrs. Wainflete's voice was sour as vinegar.

"We have no way of knowing how long we'll be stuck here."

"A few hours—"

"More likely a few days."

"Surely you exaggerate, sir." Mrs. Wainflete appeared to take the possibility of being stranded for any length of time as a personal affront.

"I hope I do," Bathory said. "The trainmen, be they porters or brakemen or conductors, are trying to dig us out. If they are unsuccessful in their attempts, they will need every able-bodied man to take a turn at the shovels, and even that may not be enough."

Diana concentrated on sipping a cup of tea, but she was instantly aware when Bathory left the parlor car to collect more passengers from another coach.

Jerusha snickered.

"Why do you laugh?"

"Because you relax as soon as he's gone. You bristle like two cats in each other's presence," she observed, still audibly amused. "And he is as fascinated with you as you are with him."

"That's hardly likely," Diana muttered. Besides, Bathory had a dark, secretive, dangerous side. Diana would not be fooled into forgetting that again, or tricked into trusting him.

"He is a very pretty fellow, Diana Spaulding." Jerusha leaned closer. "If you want my advice, you should keep right on following him until he lets you catch him."

෧෨෬

The snowdrifts blocking the tracks appear to be a good twenty feet high," the conductor announced. "We will not be moving again for some time." The blue of his uniform was almost obscured by rime.

Fifty-two heads swiveled his way. Over Mrs. Wainflete's protests that there were not enough chairs in the parlor car for everyone, Bathory had insisted on assembling all the train's passengers in one place. There were only nineteen recliners, but the rest of the passengers did not seem to mind the thought of sitting, or even sleeping, on the floor. The parlor-car floor was covered by a thick carpet.

"Are there any plows on this side of the drifts?" Bathory asked the conductor.

"Keeps on snowing, we'll need a mighty big plow. One weighted with twenty-five tons of pig iron and as many as a dozen engines to push it. Not something we get much call for in southern Connecticut."

"What about bucking snow with the cowcatcher?"

Plainly, Bathory had traveled by train in the winter before. So had Todd's Touring Thespians, and Diana with them.

"We'd have to do more shoveling first. Need to back up the track about a mile to do it right, then pull the throttle wide open, and kerchug! Right into the wall of snow." The conductor's smile was grim. "I'll grant you that the impact can drive an engine two or three car lengths into a drift, but then the crew has to go out and clear the snow before we can do it again."

It sounded a long, dangerous process to Diana.

"How many men in your crew?" Bathory asked.

Mrs. Wainflete looked outraged. "Surely you don't mean to invite the help into first class?"

"It makes sense to pool all our resources, especially food and heat. Bodies pressed together keep each other warm."

"I will not stand for it," she shrieked. "The railroad—"

"The engineer and fireman will want to stay with the engine, and the brakemen and baggage men will be more comfortable in the caboose." The conductor was accustomed to soothing irate passengers. "Doesn't take much to heat it, being small, and that's where they sleep on long hauls anyway."

Mrs. Wainflete settled down and nodded her approval. "I am glad to see some people know their place." She sent pointed looks at several of the coach-class passengers, hoping to encourage them to go back to the other cars.

No one obliged.

"We'll need cuddling to keep warm, even in here," Jerusha whispered.

"At least we're not out in the elements." The wooden sides and bullnose-shaped roof of the railroad car protected them from the snow and wind. But Jerusha was right. The longer the train sat motionless on the tracks, the colder it would get. The mahogany panels on the interior walls and the oak veneer of the ceiling added little in the way of insulation to a car constructed of pine. The ventilators, installed on the level of the overhead racks, let warm air escape right along with the fumes from the oil-burning center lamps.

They would indeed be forced to share each other's warmth if they remained here long. The thought of bundling with Damon Bathory made Diana feel a trifle giddy.

"The baggage car," she blurted.

"What's that, Diana?" Toddy asked.

"There must be more provisions and warm clothes in the baggage car. Someone should investigate."

She made the mistake of glancing at Damon Bathory when she spoke. He stared back, a speculative expression on his face.

From the relative protection of the platform between cars, Diana watched the snow fall. It showed no sign of abating. Vicious gusts threatened to topple her from her perch and made her borrowed shawl feel thin as gauze. Aside from the wind's howl, the only other sounds in this eerie white world were the loud pinging of the cooling engine and Damon Bathory's irritated voice.

"What are you doing out here? Do you want to freeze to death?"

Ignoring him, Diana continued to run her gaze over the countryside, searching for some sign of habitation. Not a single building broke the expanse of field and forest as far as she could see, and yet she knew that Connecticut was one of the better populated states. With visibility limited by blowing snow, she supposed there could be a whole town just beyond the next rise and she'd never know it. The most obvious sign of habitation— smoke from chimneys and smokestacks—would not be seen at any distance under these conditions. Fenceposts, even small buildings, had already been covered over by drifts of snow.

A heavy weight landed on her shoulders. She yelped and tried to push it off as images from the dream she'd had the night she'd first met Bathory came back to haunt her.

His hands clamped down over the long black cloak of his costume, holding it in place. "Don't be a fool, Diana."

She went still.

"Come back inside the baggage car," he said in a gruff voice. "It's safer there."

Whether there was a double meaning in his words or not, she saw the sense in them. She went in ahead of him.

Crowded with the props and set pieces belonging to Todd's Touring Thespians, the baggage car had so far yielded a few warm clothes to the search party, but little in the way of edibles. Just as Bathory and Diana entered at the front end, shaking show from their clothing, a young trainman came in from the caboose side.

"Mr. Brown, sir. Sam's been hurt. He's in the crummy."

The conductor, Elias Brown by name, followed him out. To Diana's surprise, Bathory went after them. Hatless as always, she noticed. If the cold affected him, he did not show it.

The others were ready to head back to the parlor car, carrying various bits of clothing and other potentially useful supplies. Diana hesitated. She rationalized her impulse by telling herself she was a journalist, that it was her job to find out what was happening and report on it. Going after Bathory this time would have nothing to do with Jerusha's advice. Diana was simply trying to earn a living.

When Diana pulled the cloak close about her over the shawl, she caught a whiff of wet wool and another, more elusive scent that clung to the fabric. His essence, she thought. Was that alone enough to ensorcell her?

She was almost glad of the cold blast of air that greeted her when she stepped out onto the platform between cars. It banished all thoughts save reaching shelter once again.

Just inside the doorway of the caboose, what trainmen called the "crummy," Diana stopped and stared. Sam, the injured man, his face gray with pain, sat upright in a straight-back chair. Bathory knelt at his side, concentrating so hard on peeling away the uniform coat and shirt beneath that he did not notice Diana's arrival.

"At best you've dislocated this shoulder," he said in a soothing voice. "At worst, you've broken your collarbone. What were you doing on top of the railroad car?"

"My job," Sam said. "Brakies ride on top. That's where the iron wheels are, the ones that work the brakes. When the engineer whistles for a stop, one brakie starts from the front and one from the rear."

"How do you keep your balance?"

"Running boards along the top of the cars. But we have to jump from one to the next. Thirty inches between." The injured man hissed in a breath when Bathory probed gently from neck to shoulder. "Always figured it'd be the coupling'd get me."

"You were lucky, then. You didn't lose a finger or a hand, you weren't crushed between cars, and when you fell, the snow softened your landing. But I am going to have to set this collarbone."

"You a doctor?"

The moment of hesitation before he answered alerted Diana to the evasion that followed. This was a pattern she'd encountered with him before. He never answered the question. He said only, "I've set fractures like this before. Will you trust me to do right by you?"

After a moment, the brakie nodded.

A short time later, using the padded lid of a tobacco tin to add pressure directly over the break, Bathory had set Sam's collarbone with a skill that spoke of a suspicious degree of practice. He wound a long bandage, crossed and recrossed at the point of the fracture, over and around the brakeman's shoulders in a figure eight to hold everything tight.

"Can you still breathe?" he asked.

Sam managed a grin. "Well enough. You do good work, mister. Better than some sawbones I've met."

Bathory helped him to one of the caboose's built-in bunks. Together with the personal possessions of the trainmen, and supplies for cooking and heating, the beds took up most of the room in the small, snug crummy.

"Rest," he ordered, and turned to go back to the parlor car. For the first time, he saw that Diana had been watching him.

"Will he be all right?" she asked.

"He'll do."

Before his advance, she retreated. Mr. Brown remained behind in the crummy. She walked faster, but Bathory caught up with her in the now-deserted baggage car.

"We need to talk."

"Not here."

"Where better? Fewer interruptions."

This close to him, her heart rate speeded up and she had to remind herself to breathe. She itched to move nearer even as what was left of her common sense warned her that she must get away, that it wasn't wise to be alone with him.

He smiled, but there was something menacing in his expression.

In sudden panic, Diana turned and ran.

Bathory was too quick for her. He circled her waist with one arm and a moment later they were face to face, her bosom pressed tightly against his chest, her arms pinned to her sides. His grip tightened until she could feel each of his fingers through the fabric of cloak, shawl, and Modjeska jacket.

"What am I going to do about you?"

"Let me go." It sounded as if she were begging. Diana closed her eyes, mortified.

"I don't think so."

First she felt his rough palms, warm against her cold face as he held her still. Then his beard tickled her cheek, just before his lips brushed hers.

The kiss she'd imagined in New York had aroused her. The real thing was devastating. He seduced her with firm lips, the soft rub of his beard, the gentle caress of his hands on her upper arms.

His touch shifted to her back, eliciting an immediate response she felt powerless to control. Craving. Hunger. A clenching deep inside. Her body longed to welcome him even as her mind struggled against the attraction.

"No," she protested, shocked at how close she was to yielding and by her sudden suspicion that, with this man, she might learn to appreciate all the earthy pleasures her late husband had only begun to teach her.

Her objection came out so softly that, at first, Diana did not think he'd heard. Then, slowly and with obvious reluctance, he lifted his head to stare down at her.

The primitive hunger in his dark brown eyes made her stomach jitter and her bones melt. Her skin tingled. She could feel her cheeks burn.

"This . . . we . . . we cannot . . ." A shudder ran through her, fear and longing mixed together so that one blended into the other and neither could be separated out.

"No," he agreed.

Just that fast, the fires she'd seen in his eyes were carefully banked, if not completely doused. He set her away from him.

"Go back to the parlor car," he said, "before I change my mind. Keep the cloak. I have no further need of it."

Bereft, she could not contain a tiny cry of dismay. At that, more horrified than before, she managed one wobbly step, then two. Turning, using all her willpower to hold back a sob, she bolted for the door.

CHAPTER EIGHT

✄

Eat up," said Mrs. Grosgrain, a sea-captain's widow from Rhode Island. She was a round, red-faced, cheerful little person. Diana remembered her as the woman who'd been fascinated by Lavinia and Jerusha when she'd watched their entrance into the train shed. She and Mrs. Wainflete had set out a modest repast for luncheon.

"Go easy," Mrs. Wainflete warned. "Remember that we must ration what we eat." Having accepted Bathory's dire predictions, she was now prepared to enforce rationing with a heavy hand.

The inventory of food supplies had been disheartening. In addition to the fruit, dried beef, cold chicken, and jelly in Jerusha's satchel, and similar supplies one of the other women carried, they had only a dozen eggs, two cans of Borden's condensed milk, and the cakes and sinkers from the buffet in the Pullman.

"Once the snow stops falling, we'll be able to reach nearby farms. They'll have food we can buy." This reasonable assumption was voiced by Mrs. Preble, the third woman from Grand Central Station. The look in her eyes, as she'd watched Jerusha and Lavinia with avid interest, had been envy.

"We don't know where we are or how far from civilization," Diana pointed out. They might be just on the outskirts of some town or miles from any habitation. There was no way to tell.

After they ate, Todd's Touring Thespians helped them pass what was left of the afternoon by performing a light comedy called *The Cheerful Wives of Chatham*. In this farce, Lavinia Ross and Jerusha Fildale played rivals for the affections of the character played by Nathan Todd. It was not much of a stretch for any of them and as a result the production was far more enjoyable than *The Duchess of Calabria*.

A light supper that much resembled luncheon followed, and after that Mrs. Wainflete made her next attempt to take command. "The womenfolk," she announced, "will sleep in the drawing-room car, while you gentlemen remain here in the parlor car." The other Pullman contained small, private drawing rooms whose sofas and armchairs converted into beds.

"Better than being jammed in like canned sardines," Jerusha whispered in Diana's ear.

Lavinia looked rebellious and clung to Toddy, but Mrs. Wainflete wasn't having any of that. With a quelling look, she began a lecture on morals and propriety.

Once they got on their high horse, people like Mrs. Wainflete could not be swayed. In the end, it was easier to give in.

ഗ‍ാര

Diana awoke on Tuesday morning to a lull in the storm, but it did not last long. They'd only just sent out scouting parties, in the hope of finding a farm or village not too far from the tracks, before the snow began to fall again.

Several hours later, it was the team of Bathory and Todd that rode back in triumph on the seat of a farm wagon on runners. They brought with them a good supply of ham sandwiches, boiled eggs, and coffee. Hot, fresh coffee. Just a sip of the dark brew made Diana's spirits soar, but she could not help noticing that Nathan Todd did not share in the general jubilation.

"What's wrong, Toddy?" she asked, drawing him apart from the others to stand by the handrail in front of the parlor car windows. He'd flicked the curtains aside to stare bleakly out at the continuing snow.

"That Bathory fellow's most unreasonable."

"In what way?"

"While we were out hunting for a farmhouse, I took the opportunity to tell him I'd heard that those stories he writes are deuced popular."

Diana said nothing, but she had an inkling of what was coming.

"Told him that fellow Mansfield's making a fortune touring in *Dr. Jekyll and Mr. Hyde.* I offered Bathory the chance to see one of his tales adapted for the stage. Do you know what he said?"

Diana could imagine. Mansfield had more talent in his little finger than the entire company of Todd's Touring Thespians put together.

"He turned me down flat." Clearly hurt by the rejection, Toddy huffed and fumed, then gestured impatiently at the scene beyond the window. "And look at that! Thunderation, Diana! Every flake that falls is costing me money."

She murmured sympathetic words. This time they were sincere. Todd's Touring Thespians had been scheduled to play five nights in Hartford. If they were stuck here much longer, Toddy stood to lose not only the box office receipts from that stand, but also his profits for the entire tour.

"Talk to him for me?" he suggested. "I've a feeling he'd listen to you."

"I have no influence over Mr. Bathory, Toddy."

"Could if you wanted."

The taunting words haunted her the rest of the day. She'd been avoiding Bathory since their kiss. The coward's way. How was she to continue their interview if she didn't talk to him?

Jerusha's sniffles gave her the excuse she was looking for. "Do you have any remedies for a catarrh?" she asked, sidling up to

Bathory as he stood by the window. The curtains were pulled back a scant inch to allow him to look out at the night sky.

"Why do you think I'd know?"

"You knew how to help Sam."

"Common sense."

"Well, then, what does common sense recommend for Jerusha?"

"Rest. Liquids. The patent medicine she's taking won't do her any harm." His penetrating gaze made her uneasy. "She's on the mend. I can hear it in her cough and so can you. What do you really want from me, Diana?"

"The same thing I've always wanted. To interview you."

"That's all?"

"That's enough."

An awkward silence descended. Before either of them could break it, Lavinia Ross minced up to them, seizing Bathory's arm and simpering. "Oh, Mr. Bathory," she said, batting her eyelashes and running one fingertip along his sleeve. "You mustn't disappoint me. Toddy says you've written the role that will make my career."

Diana stared at her, trying to imagine her as "the Blood Countess." In some respects, it would be type casting. In others, more important to the success of a play, she'd be a disaster in the part.

He was more patient with Lavinia than the ingenue deserved, but his answer was still no. Thwarted, she flounced off to be consoled by Toddy.

Bathory took Diana's arm and escorted her to the table where the coffee had been dispensed. Only the dregs were left, but for once Diana did not feel hungry. "Did you act, too, when you were married to a player?" It was a bit more private where they stood. Although people pressed in on every side, they were separated from the other actors by the length of the parlor car.

"I have no talent on the stage, but I traveled with the troupe and made myself useful sewing costumes and cooking."

And while she'd been thus occupied, Evan had frequently gone off on his own. She had not realized for months that he'd kept secrets from her before they wed. He'd been a compulsive gambler. Worse, he'd gambled on her family being willing to buy him off. They'd disowned her instead.

Bathory caught her chin in his hand and lifted her face, forcing her to meet his eyes. "What makes you so sad?"

But she shook her head. "Your turn. Tell me something you like to do."

"Climb mountains," came the prompt reply. "I've been up Katahdin in the east and Pike's Peak in the west."

She shivered.

"What?"

"I had a bad experience on a mountain once."

He waited.

"My husband wanted to branch out on his own. He and Toddy didn't always see eye to eye on who got what role. So we left the troupe in Denver one year and set off towards Leadville. Leadville has a fine opera house and Evan had made arrangements to meet several other actors there and form a new company."

She fell silent, seeing that long ago day in her mind's eye. It had been a lovely autumn morning when they'd set out, but by the time they'd reached the mountains in their open buggy, winter had descended. Not a blizzard like this one, but bad enough.

"The horses knew how to keep to the road, so we plodded on even after the weather got so bad we couldn't see where we were going. Evan was determined to get through." They'd been near the Continental Divide, about as high as a person could get. "Just before we were to begin the steep descent from Mosquito Pass, the brake on the buggy broke."

His hand closed over hers in a gesture of comfort. Affected by her memories, she did not immediately pull free. She saw again the moment when the open vehicle plunged downward, out of control.

"It careened on two wheels, then crashed into a boulder. I don't remember many details after that, except for the instant when I peered over the splinters that were all that remained of the seat and saw that we were precariously perched at the edge of an abyss. What appeared to be a bottomless crevasse threatened to swallow us, buggy, horses, and all. After we overturned, Evan was able to pull me free of the wreckage, but we lost all our possessions. And the horses." The memory of the animals' dying screams had kept her awake for weeks afterward.

"And when you reached Leadville?"

"More disasters. Some of the actors never arrived. Evan quarreled with the others."

They'd lived in a tiny room above a tobacco shop and had been close to starving to death before Evan got a job as a Faro dealer in one of the gambling houses. At five dollars a day for a six day week, they might have saved enough to rejoin Todd's troupe, if Evan hadn't been convinced he could win even more. He'd lost instead. Repeatedly.

Once he'd even tried to bet her.

She pulled free of Bathory's grip and hugged herself, suddenly cold.

"Evan died. I managed to scrape together enough money to take the train to San Francisco, where a friend of mine took me in."

Rowena would have been happy to keep Diana with her as a companion, but her husband had frowned on the idea. A wife who'd associate with someone who traveled with a troupe of actors risked society's censure.

"Your turn again," she said with a too-bright smile.

"I've nothing of that caliber. I've never been married."

"Cheat!" Her voice sounded gay but she wanted to curl up and have a good cry. She was not certain which man was the cause of her tears, Evan or Damon Bathory. She only knew she was close to an emotional edge.

"We're not private enough here for my secrets," Bathory said.

"Your friends already know your life's story, but when I tell you mine for the first time, I'd just as soon you were the only one to hear it."

His words had the ring of sincerity, but she found them difficult to swallow. He'd lied to her before. Why should she trust him now?

When Toddy interrupted them to make another bid to buy Bathory's stories, Diana used the excuse to put some distance between them. She stayed away from him the rest of the evening, and went early to bed, the first to brave the trek to the drawing-room car.

A few of her fellow passengers, wrapped up in extra clothing, were already asleep on the floor as she made her way towards the door. Others passed the time playing cards. All three actresses, accustomed to late nights, were still wide awake and talking among themselves.

The storm showed no sign of abating. Not only was it intensely cold, but the stinging, wind-driven snow lowered visibility to the point that it was impossible to see her hand in front of her face. Anyone foolish enough to step down from the platform and take a few steps away from the train risked being lost till spring thaw.

With relief, Diana entered the drawing-room car and hurried down the narrow aisle past the other drawing rooms, each set off by a combination of partitions and heavy drapes, until she reached the cubicle she'd been assigned. The curtain that hung across the entry to form a door fell back into place as she passed through.

The interior was dark. The silence around her seemed as penetrating as the cold. Shivering, she crawled under the covers, still fully clothed, but it was a long time before she slept. When she did, she dreamed of Damon Bathory.

∾∾

The storm passed for good around ten o'clock that night. On

Wednesday morning, the farmer returned, this time bringing pork sandwiches, cake, and milk.

Refueled by the food, the passengers organized work parties. Every able-bodied male pitched in to help with the digging out. They had no idea how long it would be before help came, but each foot of snow they could clear on their own put them that much closer to breaking free.

By evening, everyone was exhausted. Nathan Todd looked more harried than he had the night before. He even snapped at Lavinia Ross. When he later changed tactics and exerted himself to appear cheerful, that false jocularity grated as badly as Underly's constant whining.

Mrs. Wainflete continued to complain and was outraged when Billy Sims amused himself by flirting outrageously with her. Lavinia sulked. Jerusha Fildale brooded. And sneezed. And coughed. Damon Bathory, looking physically done in, appropriated one of the reclining chairs for himself.

Diana steeled herself to approach him again. It might be some time yet before the train could be freed from its icy prison, or the end of their ordeal might already be in sight. Either way, she had an obligation to talk to him.

He appeared to be half asleep, but when he caught sight of her through his lowered lashes, his eyes snapped open. "What in God's name are you wearing?"

"Whatever I could beg, borrow, or steal. I wasn't prepared to set off on a journey when I followed you onto this train."

"Why did you?"

"I was angry. You lied to me."

"Diana—"

"I suppose I understand why."

"You had enough for your story." Before she could agree, he apparently decided it was safer to return to the subject of her attire than to pursue a discussion of the plans they'd made to go to the circus together. "That outfit is unusual, but it suits you."

Wary of flattery, she glanced down at herself. The blouse was forest green. Jerusha's. Deep purple fabric swathed her lower half. From Mrs. Preble. Gold slippers peeped out from beneath the hem. Mrs. Grosgrain's contribution.

"Is that what they call rational dress?"

She nodded. The skirt was split, turning it into wide-legged trousers.

"My mother would approve of such a sensible garment."

Encouraged by the personal nature of his comment, she perched on the arm of his chair, ignoring the interested looks from members of Todd's company and Mrs. Wainflete's censorious glare. "Is she an active woman?"

"More than you'll ever know."

"Which of your careers is she more proud of, writer or doctor?"

The flash of anger in his eyes was frightening to behold. "You never stop, do you?" The words were harsh, guttural.

"It's obvious you're a physician." She'd suspected when she'd watched him set Sam's collarbone and had become convinced when he'd given his opinion of Jerusha's condition.

"You're an expert, are you?" He looked like a grumpy bear, disturbed in mid-winter, but she thought she detected the hint of a smile in his voice.

"Have I stumbled upon one of your deep, dark secrets?" she teased, hoping to lighten the mood. "Are you really Dr. Bathory, mad scientist?"

He closed his eyes and ignored her.

No amount of coaxing would get him to resume their conversation.

In the end, frustrated, Diana gave up. She'd try again in the morning, she decided. Wrapping Bathory's cloak around her, she left the parlor car.

A blast of cold air buffeted her as she stepped outside. The surface was icy beneath the slippery soles of her shoes. She should never have worn the frivolous things. Fumbling for handholds, she inched across the open space towards the door to the drawing-room car.

She heard a faint snick behind her, but did not look back. It required all her concentration to manage each tiny step forward.

A sharp tug at the back of the black cloak caught her off guard. It felt as if the hem had snagged on something, but Diana had no time to discover what or how. Jerked off balance, she felt her left foot slip sideways. Her other ankle twisted with an audible pop, and she lost what remained of her balance. Flailing wildly, she tried to catch hold of something, anything, that would help her stay on the narrow, slippery walkway.

The futile effort came to an abrupt, calamitous end when the back of her head made sharp contact with something blunt. A shower of stars and a burst of pain sent her reeling. Dazed, she saw the world go black around her even as she felt herself pitch headlong into a drift of cold, unforgiving snow.

CHAPTER NINE

෪)ঞ

Diana bolted upright with a cry and opened her eyes.

Damon Bathory sat beside her on her bed in the drawing-room car.

When he put his hands on her shoulders and tried to force her to lie down again she instinctively fought him.

"Be still," he ordered.

"Diana, do as he says. You're hurt."

It was the second voice, Jerusha's, that she obeyed. Her head hurt too much to go on struggling.

"What happened?" Her voice sounded weak and raspy.

"You fell crossing to the drawing-room car," Jerusha said.

"There's a lump on your head." Bathory looked puzzled. "The snow you landed in was deep and relatively soft. I don't understand how you managed to knock yourself out."

"My cousin Chloë was caught out in bad weather once."

Diana turned towards Mrs. Wainflete's strident voice, then wished she hadn't. Even the smallest movement sent shards of pain through her skull.

"She was unconscious and cold as a corpse when they found her," Mrs. Wainflete continued. She crowded into the cubicle with

Diana, Jerusha, and Damon Bathory. "My great-aunt Fanny saved her life by wrapping her in a sheet smeared with molasses."

"A bath in tepid water would have been as effective," Bathory murmured distractedly, "and Mrs. Spaulding was not out there long enough to need such radical treatment."

"She's not badly chilled?" That was Jerusha.

"The cloak kept her relatively warm."

His cloak, Diana thought, and shivered.

"We need to get her out of these wet garments and into something dry." He started to unbutton her blouse.

"Mr. Bathory!" Mrs. Wainflete sounded scandalized and Diana felt her bat his hands away.

She wanted to tell the old battle-ax to mind her own business, but the pounding in her head confused her. Had she fallen? Or had she been pushed? And if she'd been pushed, had it been Bathory who'd pushed her? Was he savior or enemy? Friend or fiend? She had no way of telling.

"Who found me?" she asked.

"I did," Jerusha said. "We all decided to retire shortly after you left the parlor car, but neither Patsy nor Lavinia noticed you there in the snow. I did."

Bathory's voice was all gentleness now. "Do you hurt anywhere else? Ribs? Back? Neck?"

Diana closed her eyes to the concerned faces hovering above her and forced herself to concentrate. Only then did she realize that the throbbing in her ankle was more intense than that in her head.

"When I *slipped*," she said slowly, emphasizing the word as she opened her eyes to watch Bathory's face, "I twisted my ankle."

She saw concern in his expression, and something more. It was as if he felt her pain. That impression was so strong that it temporarily banished her doubts.

"I slipped on the ice," she murmured.

This time she almost believed her own story. After all, wouldn't someone have noticed if Bathory had followed her out of the parlor car? Mrs. Wainflete certainly noticed, and bleated in protest, when he reached beneath the divided skirt of Diana's rationals, shoving aside one leg of the red flannel union suit she'd borrowed from Jerusha to run deft fingers over her injury. Holding her foot in one hand, he kneaded her calf with the other, his fingers warm on her cold skin and strong enough to rub away the cramps that had come from tensing her muscles against the pain.

As soon as she relaxed, he stripped off a bright pink stocking to get a better look at her injured ankle. Diana wondered what had happened to the little gold slippers but she didn't ask. She was too preoccupied with what he was doing to her. In stoic silence, she bore his poking and prodding.

Mrs. Wainflete was not so obliging. "Mr. Bathory! You cannot handle a young woman's limbs that way! It isn't decent."

"I am a doctor, Mrs. Wainflete. It is quite all right for me to examine her."

"He is a physician," Diana said through gritted teeth, but by the look on the woman's face, she did not believe either of them.

"It isn't broken," Bathory said. "Just a slight swelling. But it wants wrapping and you should stay off your feet for a day or two."

"I will wrap it," Mrs. Wainflete informed him. "Your medical knowledge, Mr. Bathory, is appreciated, but you are no longer necessary."

"Mrs. Wain—"

"I have bandages. And laudanum."

"No laudanum," Diana whispered. She knew how it affected her.

Bathory did not allow Mrs. Wainflete to bully him, but neither did he pay attention to Diana's protests. Laudanum, he agreed, was an excellent idea.

Diana fell silent, all her darkest suspicions reawakened. Laudanum dulled memory. Was that what Bathory wanted? Was he afraid she'd recall that someone had caused her to tumble into the snow?

"No laudanum," she said again, but in spite of her objections, she found herself bandaged, bundled up, and dosed with a potent mixture of alcohol and opium.

"Swallow," Mrs. Wainflete threatened, "or I'll slip it in your food. You need rest."

Diana obeyed, hoping she'd be left alone so she could throw up the potent mixture, but Mrs. Wainflete did not oblige. She was still sitting beside the bed when Diana drifted into drugged sleep.

The first nightmare engulfed her soon after.

She was in a theater, apparently one of the company performing there since she was in a dressing room containing the crocodile skin gripsack and tweed bag and steamer trunk she'd been accustomed to use when she traveled with Evan.

It was the Union Square, she thought, confused. Before the fire. Or was it during? Panic assailed her at the first whiff of smoke.

The scene changed. She saw herself huddled in a corner of the dressing room, clutching a large, angry cat close to her bosom. Jim, the big trick cat that lived at the Union Square.

The door burst open, its flimsy wood splintered by a kick, and Damon Bathory rushed in. Two long strides brought him to her side. He wasted no time on questions or explanations, simply hauled her to her feet and then off them, swinging her high against his chest.

The cat, hissing and spitting, escaped her hold and fled, bounding through the now open door.

It had been locked, she thought. Someone had locked her in. Someone had wanted her to perish in the Union Square fire.

"Put your arms around my neck, Diana," Damon Bathory ordered. "Damnation, do it!"

The fabric of her dress was slick beneath his gloved hands and he had difficulty keeping hold of her. With every step he took, she came closer to slipping out of his grasp. As they neared the stairs she made a concerted effort to escape. He meant her harm. She was sure of it. Squirming, she cried out in a raspy, smoke-roughened voice, but his arms were clamped like steel bands around her knees and shoulders. She could not escape.

The scene changed again. Bathory had reached the wings.

A tremendous crash echoed through the building, causing Diana to scream and bury her head against his shoulder. She clutched at him willingly, as a source of protection.

When she opened her eyes again, the dust had cleared and she could see that a large mass of burned beams and planks of wood that had once formed part of the balcony had fallen directly onto a small group of firemen. Their fellows attacked the debris, attempting to pull them out before they could suffocate or catch fire. *That really happened,* she thought in the part of her mind that knew this was a dream.

"Can you walk?" Bathory asked, setting Diana down on the stage floor.

"Yes." But her voice was hoarse and she felt his loss as he moved towards the fallen firefighters. Then panic returned.

Someone had tried to kill her.

She turned and ran in the direction of the stairs that led to the stage door.

"Look out!" he called, but the warning came too late.

She could not avoid the thick length of hose snaking its way back and forth across the stairwell. Her foot struck the unexpected obstacle to send her pitching forward.

With a scream, Diana tumbled head over heels. She heard the unmistakable crack of bone against wood as one of her limbs struck the open door at the bottom of the stairs, but there was no accompanying burst of pain.

The only thing she felt was the brush of Bathory's hands, running over her limp body with practiced skill.

She woke unsatisfied and itchy.

She was not alone. Bathory stood nearby, watching her.

She started to reach for him, then realized that Mrs. Wainflete was also in the cubicle, snoring in a chair just a few inches away.

"Go back to sleep," Bathory said.

When she awoke again, she was alone. Remembering her laudanum-induced dream, Diana brooded. Someone had attacked her in an alley in Manhattan. Now she'd received a knock on the head that could have resulted in her death from exposure to the cold. If Jerusha hadn't noticed her in that snowbank and called on Bathory to help pull her out, she'd be dead now.

That any one person should face two such life-threatening events in less than a week was extraordinary. The most logical explanation was that someone had deliberately tried to harm her. Someone who had been in New York and was now on this train. Toddy? Sims? Underly? Or Damon Bathory?

Too much imagination, she told herself. Any one of them would have had to be insane to try such an uncertain way of getting rid of someone. And wouldn't the killer have stabbed her?

Coincidences happen all the time. Why on this train alone there had been two falls, her own and Sam's. As a journalist, Diana knew better than anyone that truth was often stranger than fiction.

She considered Damon Bathory and realized she simply did not want to believe the worst of him. She'd seen too much of a gentler side of the man, a side that made her wonder how he could be capable of writing those terrible stories, let alone committing a real act of violence.

As if she'd conjured him with her thoughts, he reappeared in the doorway of her cubicle. "Mrs. Wainflete has been outvoted," he said. "We cannot spare the fuel to heat this car as well as the parlor car."

With no more explanation than that, he swept her into his

arms and carried her off to join the other passengers, pausing only long enough to gather up her borrowed shawl and cloak.

He also insisted upon staying close to her. Very close.

The passengers crowded into the parlor-car passed the time telling stories, several of which Diana had heard before, since members of Toddy's company told them. After a while, however, as another evening drew on, there was only the murmur of quiet conversation, and some of the men, who'd worked hard shoveling all day, fell asleep without even attempting card games or other pastimes. Bathory made a bed out of the cloak and shared it with her, keeping one arm around her shoulder to protect her from being bumped and to warm her. Diana gave up protesting after the first few minutes. He wasn't listening to her anyway, and it was very comfortable.

"Tell me something," she whispered. "When you first came back to our railroad car to invite us here, why weren't you surprised to find me?"

"I'd overheard a conversation in the gents' washroom an hour or so earlier, between Charles Underly and Nathan Todd. Underly wanted to know why you were aboard." Bathory smiled. "I am well aware there is more than one woman in the world named Diana, but I had a premonition that Underly might be referring to you. Todd said you came aboard in the hope of getting Lavinia to accept an apology."

"That is why I went to Grand Central at such an early hour." Diana explained how the story of the love triangle of Jerusha, Toddy, and Lavinia had gotten into her column. She could not tell if Bathory believed her or not. "I did not expect to find you there."

"You left me no choice. You were too persistent."

"Was it necessary to . . . to . . ."

"Try to charm you? Rest assured, Diana, that was not all playacting. If I had not felt it crucial to avoid having my private life made public, I'd have done much more than take you to supper."

"Oh."

Bathory cleared his throat. "Yes. Oh."

There did not seem to be anything else to say.

Diana drifted into sleep soon after, and woke to the first pale light of day. She was still wrapped tightly with Bathory in the warm folds of his cloak. Her first thought was that she ought to be scandalized. Her second was that she was safe in his arms.

She felt more alive when she was with him. She'd not been this filled with energy since those giddy days right before she'd eloped with Evan.

The comparison gave her pause, but she chose to believe she was older and wiser now. She'd not repeat the same mistakes she'd made in the past. What harm, then, could there be in enjoying the heady pleasure of this man's unique company?

When others began to stir, Diana realized that there was an unusual amount of activity outside the parlor car, too. A party of rescuers had arrived to finish the task of freeing the train from its prison of snow. In the end, it took a snowplow pulled by twenty-eight horses and hundreds of men shoveling in front of it, to get them unstuck, but by midday they were at last able to press on to Stamford.

At 1:30 that afternoon, the train pulled into New Haven. Diana was one of the last to step, gingerly, onto the platform. Her ankle was tender, but she managed with the help of a cane, the fancy one Charles Underly always carried. Jerusha had appropriated it for her.

The other passengers milled about, most trying to make arrangements to go on to their original destinations. Bathory disappeared, but only long enough to hail one of the hotel wagons lined up at the depot.

"I'm taking you to the Columbia House," he informed her.

She knew the name. It was one of New Haven's finest hotels. "I cannot afford to stay there."

"You'll be a guest in my suite. With two separate bedrooms,

you can be as respectable as you want to be."

"Oh, but I—"

"I feel . . . responsible for you." There was a warmth in his tone that did nothing to dispel her uneasiness.

She fought it with banter. "Does that mean you're willing to admit to all and sundry, and my readers, that you are a physician?"

"I am willing to do all sorts of things, if you agree to come with me."

When he looked at her that way, it was impossible to resist.

"All right, but I must send a telegram to my editor first."

"A precaution?"

"A courtesy."

But telegraph lines were down in that direction. A hand-lettered paper, posted next to the distinctive black and yellow metal sign of the Western Union office, gave no indication of when they'd be up and running again. Diana was not really surprised. After a storm so severe, it only made sense that communications were still disrupted.

Diana!" Jerusha hurried towards her along the platform.

Toddy and Charles Underly followed after her, trailed more slowly by Lavinia Ross.

"Wonderful news!" Jerusha called. "The train can go on to Hartford. We leave in ten minutes, which means we can still make the last night of our stand." She engulfed Diana in a lavender-scented hug. "Will you be all right on your own?"

They both looked around for Damon Bathory. He had gone into the Western Union office. Diana could see him through its bay window, conversing with the man on the other side of the brass grill.

"I will manage, Jerusha." Diana forced a smile. Her friend's cough was much improved, but both eyes and nose still looked red and sore. "You must take care of yourself and stop worrying about me."

When Charles Underly reached them, she solemnly handed over his cane.

"Can you do without?" Toddy asked. "Underly, give that back to her. You can always buy another."

Underly sulked. "I need my cane. You know it's specially made."

Bathory interrupted, emerging from the telegraph office to take Diana's arm. "She has me to lean on," he said. "She has no need of a cane."

Jerusha sent him a piercing look. "Can we trust you to take good care of her, sir?" They all turned to stare at him.

"It was her desire for a story about me that landed Mrs. Spaulding on this train in the first place. I am honor bound to make certain she gets back to New York."

"Good man," Toddy declared, slapping him on the back. "But, another word with you before you go?"

They stepped aside. Diana assumed Toddy meant to make one last attempt to persuade Bathory to give him dramatization rights to his stories. "Good luck to him," she muttered.

"Good luck to you," Jerusha said, and slipped a small silk purse into Diana's hands.

She peeped inside and was astonished at the sum it contained. "I cannot take your money!"

"Consider it a loan, just in case you do not wish to let someone else pay your way. You have no means yet to return to Manhattan, and even if the tracks were completely clear, it is never wise to be entirely dependent upon a man's charity."

Murmuring her thanks, and further admonitions for Jerusha to mind her health, Diana slid the purse into her leather bag. It was with mixed emotions that she watched her theatrical friends depart, leaving her alone in a strange city under the protection of the most compelling and dangerous man she'd ever met.

CHAPTER TEN

❧❧

Ben signed the register at the Columbia House with a flourish: Mr. and Mrs. Damon Bathory. It gave him an odd feeling to do so, but he forced his qualms aside. She had agreed to let him take care of her. What did one more small deception matter?

"I need to purchase a few things," Diana murmured as the bellboy collected their luggage, almost all of it Ben's.

Reminded of the state of her wardrobe, he sent the bags on to their suite. The desk clerk provided the name of the best dress shop in the city.

"You need proper clothing if you don't want to be gossiped about," he insisted over Diana's protests as he hustled her into a cab.

"Far be it from me to create scandal," she agreed, "but a dressmaker needs time to sew clothing. I need a department store with ready-made fashions."

Reluctantly, he changed their driver's orders, surprised to find that he had been looking forward to ordering a new wardrobe for her.

At first she would not look at anything other than bare essentials. "Too expensive," she complained when he pointed out a gown that would go well with her complexion, "and unnecessarily dressy."

"Let me buy it for you. It's the least I can do."

"You are already doing too much. In fact, I insist on paying half the cost of the hotel."

"It is my fault you were on that train. My fault you're stranded here now."

She started to say something, then changed her mind. She fingered the fabric of the dress. "A loan, then. To be repaid as soon as I return to New York."

"Yes. Fine." He'd have agreed to a good deal more just to see her in that dark green silk.

"I will need an address, to send you the money."

"Try on the gown."

The look she sent him over her shoulder as she carried it and another off to a changing room sent what remained of his good sense out the window. He scribbled on a piece of paper and had it ready to hand to her when she returned. A fictitious street and number. In Buffalo.

To his disappointment, she did not model the silk, but did promise to wear it to supper in the hotel dining room that evening. She plucked the slip of paper from his hand, glanced at it, and tucked it into her bag, then was engaged by the sales clerk in a discussion of undergarments.

Diana's pleasure at having free rein in the ladies' department made Ben realize how much he was enjoying himself. He liked buying pretty things for her. While she tried on a serviceable wool dress, he picked out a cameo brooch. And when she would have selected a plain brown coat, he talked her into a fur-trimmed, dark green garment.

"It is your color, my dear. It makes the best of your hair."

"You will turn my head with such flattery, sir," she warned him.

"I hope so, madam." He had, after all, every intention of taking her to bed that night and seeing that glorious hair spread out on a white pillowcase. A pity he could not arrange for green silk on their bed as well.

By the time they reached their suite and Diana closed herself in one bedroom with a hotel maid to dress for supper, Ben could think of little else but making love to her. Unfortunately that urge was accompanied by an inconvenient desire to tell her everything about himself. He even wished he had not been so quick to give her that false address.

As he changed into his own evening attire he wondered when his feelings towards Diana had gone beyond simple lust. Dangerous waters lay ahead. No question about that.

He grinned at his reflection in the mirror. He'd always enjoyed taking a canoe through the rapids on the Kenduskeag in the spring. Giving his cravat a last pat, he went out to meet his fate.

She looked magnificent in the dark green silk, as he'd known she would. Her mahogany-colored hair had been twisted up in an elaborate knot. He looked forward to taking it down.

Ben removed the box with the cameo from his pocket, took out the brooch, and pinned it just at the center of Diana's modest neckline. She shivered as his fingers brushed her neck.

Then her stomach growled, and shared laughter took them out of the suite and down to the lobby.

"One stop on the way to the dining room," Diana begged. "I want to try to send a telegram again."

₭℞

The hotel housed its own branch office off the lobby, staffed by a Western Union telegrapher, a harried-looking young woman whose green eye shade was crooked.

"Still no direct contact with New York City," she informed Diana, pushing at the drooping elastic armbands that held her sleeves away from her wrists. The telegraph key at her elbow was silent, the only sound in the office the ticking of the clock on the far wall.

"Not surprising," Bathory said. "Shall we go in to supper?" He offered her his arm.

The waiter seated her, but when Bathory should have taken his chair, he sent her an apologetic look instead. "I meant to ask the telegrapher about incoming messages. Will you excuse me while I go back and check with her? I won't be long."

He returned within five minutes, giving Diana just time enough to decide what she wanted to eat. He smiled at her, but a line of worry creased his brow.

"Is something wrong?" she asked.

"Nothing that can't be fixed. But I should be asking you the same question. Is there some reason why you are so anxious to reach that editor of yours? Is there something . . . personal between you and this Horatio Foxe?"

"He's my employer. And I have been wondering, naturally, what he's done about my daily columns since I've been gone. With this storm, he may not have been able to publish the newspaper at all."

"Is that all there is to your relationship?"

It took her a moment to understand what he was hinting at and when she did she couldn't resist an enigmatic answer. "It is now."

"And before? Was he your lover?"

She couldn't hold back a smile. He sounded as if he were jealous. "When I first knew him, I looked on him as an older brother."

Bathory eased back in his chair, his manner more relaxed than it had been. "You seem to have a plentiful supply of those. Or do you regard Nathan Todd as a surrogate father?"

"More like a jolly old uncle."

That forced a wry laugh out of him. "No doubt that's why he took me aside this afternoon and warned me to behave like a gentleman towards you. Just because you have friends who are actresses, he said, doesn't mean you can be treated like a woman with loose morals."

Diana gaped at him. "Toddy said that?"

"That and more. He explained that, as Evan Spaulding's widow, you were family to his troupe, and that they looked out for their own."

At Bathory's urging, Diana shared some of her favorite anecdotes about Toddy and Jerusha during the meal. And one or two that involved Horatio Foxe and his sister Rowena. He talked about his recent travels.

Diana sent him a shy smile as she toyed with the last bite of the chocolate trifle she'd ordered for dessert. She found it easy to imagine sharing a lifetime of meals with him and never being bored.

Abruptly, Bathory pushed his chair away from the table and stood. "Shall we return to our suite?"

She readily agreed, although she did feel a bit nervous about being alone with him.

"You're favoring that ankle," he remarked as they left the dining room."

"It's a little tender."

"Let me take a look at it," he insisted when they reached the small sitting room between their bedrooms. Diana obediently sank into one of the chairs.

He went down on one knee on the floor in front of her and lifted her foot until it rested atop the other knee. With a tender touch, he began to remove her boot—she'd refused the offer of dainty evening slippers to go with the gown. He took his time over the buttons.

She could always go back to asking questions, Diana thought a bit desperately. Conduct that interview. Had he not promised to cater to her every wish while they were in New Haven?

Then he swept away her stocking and touched her bare ankle and she felt the shock of that contact all the way to her womb.

All afternoon, all through their meal, he'd made her feel things she'd not experienced for a very long time.

Sorcerer, she thought. Demon.

She'd be a fool to let herself fall under his spell again . . . but she could not seem to stop herself.

She'd followed him onto the train, not as a reporter but as a woman. She could admit that to herself now. She'd been so angry at him because he'd disappointed her.

She'd already been half in love with him.

She very much feared her fall was now complete.

She awoke the next morning to find him gone, along with his luggage. Frantic, she dressed in as much haste as she could manage and hurried down to the lobby. He was just turning away from the Western Union window when she caught up with him.

"My train leaves in an hour." His face was the enigmatic mask she was coming to hate. Even that sardonic eyebrow would have been an improvement.

"Did you intend to say good-bye this time?" She tried to sound curious rather than hurt but wasn't sure she succeeded.

"Yes. I'd have come back upstairs to tell you the suite is paid for through the next two nights, if you need it."

She gaped at him. "Liar!"

"No. No more lies. I mean to tell you everything . . . but not just yet."

"When?"

"When I return."

"Where from?"

"I can't tell you that." When she started to protest, he pressed one finger to her lips. "I swear, Diana, I will come back to you. Go home to Manhattan and wait for me."

She gazed at him, shaken by the terrifying knowledge that she'd fallen in love with a man who was going to break her heart.

"Take care of that ankle," he added. "You should avoid walking far for at least another day." With that, he left her standing by the hotel's Western Union office, fists clenched at her sides and tears pricking her eyelids.

The same telegrapher who had been on duty the previous evening was there again this morning. "Doesn't look like messages for Manhattan will get through anytime soon," she offered when she recognized Diana. "The whole city's at a standstill. Mountains of snow."

Just then a loud rattling demanded the young woman's attention. While she dealt with the steady clatter of incoming messages in Morse Code, Diana stared at the contents of her tiny office, welcoming any distraction. A line wire entered through the wall, connecting a telegraph pole outside to the telegrapher's key, which sat on a table next to a cut-off switch, a steel-pen-and-ink-bottle ensemble, and a supply of message blanks. On the wall between the operator and the half door that kept customers at a distance, were a series of hooks upon which message papers were filed after they'd been sent. The top one was close enough to read.

As the words leapt into focus, Diana's heart began to beat faster. This had to be the telegram Damon Bathory had just sent. She leaned closer, squinting to see the address. Belatedly, reading the destination, she was able to identify the trace of regional accent she'd heard, time and again, in his voice, confirming her conviction that he'd sent it. *Not* Buffalo. She hadn't expected it would be.

The message, which said only that he was on his way home, was unsigned. That didn't trouble her. What did was the fact that it was addressed to a woman. Mrs. Abraham Northcote.

If Bathory was a pseudonym, as Diana had suspected all along, then his real name could well be Northcote. Abraham Northcote?

If he'd lied about his name and his address, he might also have lied about having a wife. In fact, he probably had. Evan had found it easy enough to deny her existence any time some nubile and star-struck farm girl had wanted to throw herself at him.

What a fool she was! Return to New York and wait? Oh, yes, and he'd take her to the circus, too! She'd had the right idea in the first place—forget all about this strange, charismatic man who wrote horror stories. She should go back to that plan.

But in her heart, she knew it was already too late. If what she now suspected—that he was married—was true, then he deserved to have his real identity exposed just for deceiving her.

She drew in a deep breath, then another.

No matter what the truth was, she could not hope to put him out of her mind or her heart until she knew the whole story. Not for the newspaper, but for herself, she had to continue her pursuit of Damon Bathory.

"Good news, miss," the telegrapher said, interrupting Diana's thoughts. "My prediction was wrong. I can send to New York City now. Three dollars for ten words."

Diana seized a message blank, then paused, chewing thoughtfully on her lower lip. She needed authorization to relay telegrams through a press operator. Foxe would also have to send her a voucher for a cash disbursement. She intended to repay every cent "Damon Bathory" had spent on her.

It took more than ten words, and Diana was very glad of Jerusha's generosity when she paid for them. She used a little more of her friend's money to buy a carpetbag in which to pack her few possessions. She was tempted to throw away the things Bathory had bought for her, but she could not spare any of her clothes. The cameo brooch she buried deep. It hurt too much to remember how hopeful she'd felt when he'd pinned it to her gown.

When she consulted a train schedule, Diana learned that the earliest connection she could get would bring her to her destination at 5:45 in the morning. Better to wait a bit, she decided. Go later and arrive at a reasonable hour. But when she went back to the suite, intending to nap until it was time to depart, she found that memories of the previous night would not let her rest.

She paced.

And fretted.

And did not sleep.

When it was finally late enough to leave the hotel, she felt as if she'd been through a wringer. Jaw set, temper simmering, she limped up to the station master's window at the railroad depot.

"Where to, ma'am?" the agent asked.

"Bangor," she told him, reciting the city named in the telegram to Mrs. Abraham Northcote. "Bangor, Maine."

CHAPTER ELEVEN

≈⊃⊂≈

Another telegram awaited Ben in Boston. He swore when he read it. The crisis was over. Aaron was no longer missing. There had been no need to rush home, no need to leave Diana so soon.

Better this way, he tried to tell himself. He would go back to New York for her when everything had been resolved. He needed to settle a few things before he could be completely honest with her.

First among his problems was Aaron, who had taken a very long time to get home. According to this latest telegram, he'd told their mother he hadn't been caught in the storm. But neither had he been able to recall much of what had happened to him since he'd left Manhattan a week ago. He'd remembered arriving in Stamford and then, much later, in Boston.

Could he have returned to New York in the interim?

Ben did not like the direction of his thoughts. Surely it was a coincidence that Aaron had been in Philadelphia when that woman had been killed. And even if he hadn't left New York after all, or had gotten off the train, or had returned from the first stop, he'd have had no reason to hurt Diana.

But Ben remembered his brother's concern in the park that

they do something about being followed. By the time they'd met in the coffee shop and Ben had put Aaron on the train for home, Aaron had been acting as if he'd forgotten all about Diana. But with Aaron, one never knew.

This is crazy, Ben thought, not without irony. Aaron was no killer. And he certainly could not carry out a series of pre-meditated crimes. Besides, Aaron had never been to San Francisco, where that other woman had been murdered.

Bone-weary, he scraped a hand across his face and took a seat on a straight-backed wooden bench to wait for his train. Briefly, he considered finding a hotel and getting some sleep before he continued on to Bangor. There was no rush now, but neither was there any reason to delay going home.

The moment he rested his elbow on the iron arm rest, new doubts assailed him. His brother had seemed in perfect command of himself when they'd parted company. Ben had let his guard down. Aaron was smart enough to get himself home on his own, but he was also clever enough—devious enough—to have made new plans, especially if he'd believed he had a good reason to.

He'd had a strong reaction to Diana Spaulding. Ben wondered if she affected everyone that way. In spite of his concern about his brother's whereabouts he had himself been unable to get her out of his mind on the train journey from New Haven to Boston. If Aaron had been similarly obsessed, and beset by an irrational dislike of the woman, could he have felt driven to slip back into New York and attack her?

Ben rubbed his pounding temples. Aaron could have been the man in the alley last Saturday night, but he could not have been on the train with them. He could not have been responsible for Diana's fall.

Had there been something sinister about Diana's near-fatal accident? He'd almost broached the subject with her before he left New Haven, almost asked if she thought someone might have struck her from behind. Or given her a push. But he hadn't wanted to spoil their time together.

On the surface, such an attack seemed unlikely, but he wished he hadn't been half asleep at the time. He hadn't even seen Diana leave the parlor car, let alone anyone following her. He hadn't known she was in danger until Jerusha screamed for help. If there *had* been two attacks on her, Ben could only take consolation from the fact that Diana would soon be safely back in New York. Everyone else on the train—including him—was headed somewhere else.

When his thoughts circled back to Aaron again, Ben stood and began to pace. The sooner he got home, the better. He had a few pointed questions to ask his brother. What happened next would depend upon Aaron's answers.

80CR

Diana arrived in Bangor, a city of some 17,000 souls, in late morning on the special Sunday "paper train." She was stiff and sore after sitting up all the way from New Haven. All the minor injuries she'd sustained over the last week throbbed in unison.

At the depot, a conveyance waited to pick up passengers for the Windsor Hotel. Since it sounded a respectable sort of place and the driver looked clean, she hobbled over and allowed him to assist her into a seat. Her meager baggage was hoisted into the back, landing with an audible thud. Diana scarcely noticed. She was too tired, and her ankle felt as if it had swollen to the size of a ripe melon.

After a few minutes, when it appeared that she was to be his only passenger, the driver mounted the box and clicked his tongue at the pair of bays in the traces. They set off through a goodly city that Diana was in no shape to appreciate, although she did notice a few of the same signs of spring she'd seen in Manhattan before the blizzard. There was still some snow on the streets, but wheels had all but replaced runners on most of the horse-drawn vehicles, and she caught sight of a robin on one brown and muddy lawn.

The driver noticed the direction of her gaze. "Bangor Tigers'll be back soon," he said enigmatically.

"I beg your pardon?"

"That's the true sign of the season. The first woodsmen come back to the city after the winter in the wilds. Best not to go out unescorted at night for the next few weeks, and stay away from Exchange Street and Peppermint Row. Those fellas are no great respecters of womankind, if you know what I mean."

Bemused, Diana thanked him for the warning.

The Windsor was a presentable place, bigger than she'd anticipated but relatively inexpensive at $1.50 a night. Grateful for small favors, Diana checked in, spending Jerusha's last fifteen cents to tip the porter. This ensured that he'd bring up kindling and a hodful of coal and light a fire for her. A few hours later, warm at last, Diana fell into an exhausted sleep that lasted well into the next day.

Much restored——although she was still limping a bit——she made her way to the Bangor office of the Western Union Telegraph Company. A scene of chaos and disarray met her. The clicking out of dots and dashes sounded like the buzz of angry bees.

"Moving," a harried-looking fellow told her. "We'll be in our new digs downstairs a week from today."

In the meantime, confusion reigned. Diana was obliged to wait while the young man consulted his supervisor, who in turn sought the guidance of the manager. Diana had plenty of time to fret.

If Foxe had not responded to the telegram she'd sent from New Haven, she would be in dire straits. She couldn't even afford to eat unless he wired money, having exhausted the funds Jerusha had lent her with this impetuous journey to Maine.

Diana knew of only one person who lived in Bangor, and she could scarcely seek out the mysterious Mrs. Northcote and throw herself on her mercy, especially if it turned out that Damon Bathory was Mr. Northcote. She needed time to discover more about the situation here before she approached anyone.

To her immense relief, several communications from Horatio Foxe had arrived. He'd sent a voucher for a sizeable sum, which she collected on the spot. Further, he'd authorized her to send future dispatches through the press operator.

She waited to read the personal message he'd sent until she'd fortified herself with a substantial meal. The telegram was congratulatory. He approved of her decision to follow Damon Bathory and applauded her continued quest to discover his secrets, but he added an unexpected bit of information to the end of the communication.

Diana reread the brief words. Their meaning did not change. Foxe had learned more about Belinda MacKay and Lenora Cosgrove. He'd established another link between the two women, besides the fact that each had been stabbed to death in an alley in the theatrical district of her respective city.

The luncheon Diana had just consumed threatened to rebel. Her hands turned to ice, to match the chill running down her spine.

Belinda MacKay had written a theatrical gossip column under the name Dolly Dare. Lenora Cosgrove, anonymously, had been a theater critic. Both women had attended one of Damon Bathory's lectures and then complained in print of the excessive violence and gore in his *Tales of Terror.*

"Is something wrong, miss?" the waiter asked.

"No. No, of course not." She hastily tucked the telegrams away and paid her bill.

Once outside in the cool, crisp air, her mind cleared. This news did not change anything. Not yet. It did, however, make the next task on her agenda all the more urgent to accomplish.

Horatio Foxe thought she'd come here in pursuit of a story. Now he expected her to find evidence that Bathory was guilty of murder. Diana's real purpose had been to find out if he'd lied to her. That was still her goal. She'd decide what to do about determining guilt or innocence once she found proof of his real identity.

After asking the way, she went to the offices of Bangor's morning paper, the *Daily Whig and Courier*. She had meant all along to discover as much as she could about the Northcote family before she approached any one of them. It had even occurred to her that she might have made a terrible mistake and jumped to an entirely erroneous conclusion. It was possible Mrs. Abraham Northcote had no connection to Damon Bathory at all, or was a housekeeper or a neighbor.

Looking for any mention of the name Northcote in back issues of the *Whig and Courier,* Diana soon found a reference to Mrs. Abraham. The woman to whom the telegram had been sent appeared to be a pillar of local society. She'd been an honored participant in festivities the previous Labor Day.

Working backwards, Diana found Mrs. Northcote's name on guest lists for various teas and charity events. Not until she'd encountered a half dozen references, however, did one mention that Mrs. Abraham Northcote was a widow.

My mother has a cat she dotes upon.

Damon Bathory's casual remark took on new importance as Diana continued searching the newspaper archives. Determined to proceed in a logical, professional manner, she worked her way through several years' worth of old newspapers. Not once did she find the surname Bathory, but there were other mentions of Northcotes. One Aaron Northcote appeared to be an artist. Benjamin Northcote was a physician.

"Finding what you want, miss?" A newspaper employee peered anxiously at her over the tops of his wire-rimmed spectacles.

Diana hesitated, reluctant to reveal too much to a stranger. On the other hand, direct questions generally produced answers. "Do you know the Northcote family?"

A cautious nod answered her. He poked the glasses teetering near the tip of his long narrow nose back into place a half second before they could tumble to the hard plank floor.

"I only ask because I want to be sure I have the right family. Mrs. Abraham Northcote is, I gather, the matriarch?"

The clerk's suspicions seemed to ease a little. "That's right. She and her two unmarried sons live up in that big house on the west side of the city. The one with the gargoyles on the fence."

That seemed to fit!

"One of the sons just got back from a trip, I believe."

"Both of them were gone a spell, one longer than the other."

A hail from the front of the building, where a customer waited to place an ad, prevented Diana from asking anything else, but what he'd already said appeared to confirm the conclusion she'd come to as she'd skimmed through an account of a showing at a gallery maintained by the Bangor Art Association.

"Damon Bathory" had visited an art gallery in Manhattan, a gallery that displayed a landscape by one "A. N."

Aaron Northcote?

She had found the artwork disturbing—in the same way Bathory's stories were unsettling.

Was it possible she'd been wrong about "Damon Bathory" being a physician? Perhaps he had simply observed one at close hand. Dislocated shoulders and turned ankles were both common injuries. An artist and writer with a doctor for a brother might know enough to feel confident treating either. The more Diana thought about it, the more logical it seemed to her that a painter might also be a writer and that he'd choose to publish his stories under a pseudonym in order to keep the two careers separate.

Satisfied she'd done enough background research, Diana collected copies of the Thursday, Friday, Saturday, and Monday editions of Bangor newspapers to take back to her hotel room. After supper, she read every word of the *Whig and Courier* and the evening *Daily Commercial.* She no longer searched for mentions of the Northcotes. Now she was after accounts of the storm in New York City.

She'd left home just before the entire island of Manhattan had been brought to a standstill by the blizzard. Hundreds of people were dead, and the chaos was unimaginable. Seeking news of friends, reassurance that no one she knew had died, Diana read every item she could find on the storm.

It was hard to believe that only a week earlier there had been the promise of an early spring in the air, especially when she read an account of a man lost in the snow in Union Square during the height of the blizzard. Diana tried to envision it. No lights. Drifts so deep he was stuck in one for twenty minutes. She could only shake her head in amazement.

Another story, reprinted from Friday's *New York World,* reported that some cab drivers were charging as much as fifty dollars to drive passengers through streets clogged with drifting snow. The *World* had apparently organized snowshoe brigades to go out and gather news. That paper also reported that an ice bridge had formed across the East River, making it possible for people to walk from Manhattan to the opposite shore.

Diana wondered if the presence in the Bangor papers of excerpts from the *World* meant that other Manhattan dailies had been able to continue publishing. If so, what had Horatio Foxe done about her column? The exposé of Damon Bathory he'd promised readers should have run last Wednesday. He'd have been ecstatic had he known that she and Bathory were even then stranded together on a train in Connecticut. Diana supposed Foxe had made up a story, as he'd threatened to do. For all she knew, he might have penned a whole week's worth of columns using her name. Or perhaps he'd announced her disappearance to the world and made something scandalous out of that. She winced at the thought before a more likely possibility occurred to her—given the storm, he'd no doubt suspended publication of "Today's Tidbits" in order to fill the paper with news of the blizzard.

In the Bangor papers, most of the copy was devoted to New England news. Only a few columns contained "Incidents of the Storm," but from those she gathered that hundreds of people all across Connecticut and Massachusetts had been stranded in isolated farmhouses, in train stations, and on the trains themselves, many without heat or food. For the first time, Diana realized just how extensive the blizzard had been and how much damage had been done by it. It gave her a queer feeling to read that the greatest number of trains had been stranded for the longest period of time in the area around New Haven.

In Bangor, although trains had stopped arriving from New York and Boston, local rail service had continued unabated. Indeed, Bangor had experienced only a light snowfall, the usual sort of winter precipitation. By early afternoon on that same Wednesday Diana had been snowbound in Connecticut, the sun had reappeared here, melting snow with such rapidity that people complained about sloppy walking conditions.

When she'd read all the newspapers she'd collected from beginning to end, Diana sat staring at them. What now? Damon Bathory was probably Aaron Northcote. He'd lied about his name and where he lived. Had he also lied when he swore he'd come back to her?

She buried her head in her hands.

Bathory—she could not call him Aaron, not yet, and she'd always had difficulty thinking of him as Damon—would not be pleased to discover she'd followed him again, but she could not leave Bangor without warning him. Foxe was more determined than ever to implicate him in the murders of those two women. Worse, Diana's editor now knew she was in Bangor. Even if she refused to reveal what she'd discovered here, he had enough to go on to uncover Bathory's real identity for himself. She had no choice. She had to arrange a meeting with Aaron Northcote. Whatever else the man was, she did not believe him to be a cold-blooded killer.

At noon the next day, Diana waited, growing ever more anxious, at a table for two in the dining hall of the Bangor House, the city's largest hotel. She had sent a note to the Northcote home to suggest that Aaron meet her for luncheon.

Initially, she paid no mind to a man approaching her table. He was not Damon Bathory. Only when he stopped next to her did she realize he seemed familiar.

Diana frowned. The stranger had eyes of an odd copper color and brown hair. Although he had a build similar to Damon Bathory's, he was less muscular, showing evidence of a sedentary life style. Beneath a fine mustache, even his beardless jowls were fleshy.

"I don't recognize your name," he said, "but your note intrigued me."

Diana blinked at him in surprise. "You're Aaron Northcote?"

He frowned, staring intently at her face. "I've seen you before."

"I don't think so. I've only just arrived here from New York."

This announcement seemed to alarm him. "You didn't warn me," he said.

"I beg your pardon."

"I'm not talking to you."

His strident tone made Diana nervous, and very aware that everyone else in the dining room was staring at them. "Mr. Northcote, I think there's been some mistake."

"I thought we'd seen the last of her." He muttered the comment to a point beyond her left ear, as if there were someone standing there. Then, without warning, he bolted, moving so suddenly and violently that he toppled the table and knocked Diana right off her chair on his way to the exit.

Unhurt—but so astonished that for several moments she couldn't find words—Diana sat on the floor of the restaurant and stared after the departing artist.

The *maître d'* rushed over to her, solicitous and concerned. "Are you all right, madam? Shall I send for a doctor?"

"No, of course not. I'm perfectly fine." She started to get to her feet, hampered by her bustle and heavy skirts.

A hand wearing a ring with a familiar family crest appeared in front of her, offering assistance.

"What luck," the *maître d'* exclaimed. "Here's Dr. Northcote. I had not realized you were back in town, doctor. Welcome home."

Diana's heart began to race as she rose to her feet, lifting her head to meet the brooding gaze of the man she'd last seen in New Haven. "I had the wrong brother," she whispered.

She looked, Ben thought, as confused and shocked as he'd felt when he'd found the note she'd sent Aaron. *Diana here.* He could hardly credit it.

"We need to talk," he said, careful to conceal any hint of the tumultuous emotions coursing through him.

He held her chair, then seated himself opposite her and signaled to the waiter. They were still the center of attention. Behaving as if their meeting was an everyday occurrence seemed the wisest course. And until he knew why Diana had turned up here, he dared not let her know how his heart had leapt at the sight of her.

Even beset by doubts, he felt a sense of relief wash over him. Her arrival made one decision easy. He had no other choice now. He must tell her the whole truth about Damon Bathory.

"Your name is Benjamin," she said. It was not quite an accusation, but close enough.

"Ben."

"Ben," she repeated, sounding a bit breathless. She offered him a tentative smile.

"I meant what I said. I'd have come to you."

"I thought you'd be angry that I followed you again."

"Should I be?" Alerted by the odd note in her voice, he narrowed his eyes. His hand froze in the act of lifting a water glass to his lips.

She was prevented from answering by the appearance of the waiter. After they'd ordered, he reached across the table and took her hand in both of his.

"Why didn't you return to New York, Diana? And how did you know I would be here?"

"I saw the telegram you sent to your mother," she blurted. "I thought she was your wife."

She'd been jealous? Uncertain whether to be encouraged or wary, Ben said nothing. He didn't want to risk betraying how deeply his own feelings ran.

Uncertainty made conversation stilted. So did the proximity of other diners. With painful awkwardness, they made small talk until the arrival of their meal. For a few minutes after that, they ate in silence. Ben had no idea what he put in his mouth. It all tasted like sawdust.

"How's the ankle?" he asked.

"Better," she said, without looking up.

He felt his eyebrow shoot up. "I doubt that."

"Still sore," she amended.

"When did you arrive in Bangor?"

"Late Sunday morning."

"I should have known I couldn't get rid of you so easily." It took a concerted effort to sound more amused than irritated but she seemed to take his tone of voice as an encouraging sign. Watching her as closely as he was, he saw her shoulders relax and some of the tension go out of her neck.

"I thought I'd solved the mystery," she told him, and recounted the steps that had led her to fix on Aaron as Damon Bathory.

Her explanation answered more questions than she realized. "So you did go back to that gallery in New York. I thought you might have."

"Yes. Your brother is a talented artist."

"He comes by it honestly."

"What do you mean?"

"You'll find out soon enough. And you'll have a story for your Mr. Foxe, as well, if you still want it."

Her face blanched.

"What's wrong?" He put down his fork and took her hand once more. It trembled in his grasp.

"I might have considered going quietly back to New York to wait for you, once I knew you weren't Abraham Northcote," she confessed in a voice so soft he had to strain to make out her words, "but something else came to light in Horatio Foxe's pursuit of scandal."

Taking a deep breath, she related her editor's latest discoveries about the two murdered women. Ben's consternation grew with each word she uttered. If Foxe combined these speculations with the Northcote name in print, the story had the potential to tear Ben's family apart.

"You're certain he isn't making this up? You did say he wasn't averse to inventing scandal, and it seems odd this information didn't come out when he first sent his queries to those two newspapers."

"I imagine only a few people knew those women were journalists. My byline doesn't appear on 'Today's Tidbits,' and female reporters often use pseudonyms. You don't think Nellie Bly is her real name, do you? She borrowed it from the Stephen Foster song."

"But surely their own newspapers—"

"Perhaps they didn't write for the papers Foxe queried, but for their rivals. In any case, I need your help if I'm to convince my editor to abandon this story."

Ben did not reply. A flicker of memory came to him. Frowning, he murmured. "I met Dolly Dare."

At the startled sound she made, he smiled reassuringly. "No, I did not kill her. But you already know she came to one of my lectures, and that reporters were always trying to interview me."

"Did you seduce her?"

His ill-advised attempt to frighten Diana in his hotel room in New York came back to him. "Was she the woman near the start of the tour who seemed . . . affected by my reading? No. That was someone else."

Diana frowned at him, obviously wondering if he'd admit it to her if he had taken Dolly Dare to bed. "How is it you remember her, then?"

"I remember the name. I clipped reviews out of newspapers in every city I visited and sent them home for my mother to paste in her scrapbooks. For that matter, I recall the unsigned review from San Francisco, too." He grimaced. "Vicious criticism does tend to stick in one's mind. As I recall, that anonymous critic accused Damon Bathory of being responsible for the corruption of a whole generation of young people. Said they couldn't help but turn violent if they were brought up on a diet of Bathory's tales."

"I am sure you were not the only one of whom these women did not approve. And it is still entirely possible that there is no connection but coincidence between the two murders, even if the victims were both journalists. As a motive, killing someone over a difference of opinion seems very weak."

"Strong enough when it's your creation that's been torn apart in a public forum."

Diana sighed. "I do not believe I will go back to writing scathing reviews of plays or books. They cause too much harm."

"It would not be sufficient motive for me," he assured her.

"But your stories were savaged by the press. He can argue that—"

"No," Ben said.

"You won't help me convince Foxe of your innocence?"

"You misunderstand me, Diana. Finished?" He gestured at her plate.

She looked surprised to see she'd eaten most of the meal. "Apparently I am."

The smile she provoked quickly vanished. What he meant to propose was deadly serious. He plunged ahead. "I had already decided to tell you the truth, Diana, but there are reasons why the details must not be published just yet. There are people who need to be warned before any revelations are made."

"I am not the one you must convince," she said. "It's Horatio Foxe who threatens you."

"Do you trust me, Diana?"

"Yes." The reply came without hesitation, gladdening his heart.

"Enough to collect your things from the hotel and come home with me?" The invitation was a risk, but not as great a one as leaving her to her own devices. "I want you to meet Mother."

She hesitated, then gave a tentative nod.

ଧଞ୍ଚ

Diana had already realized that the Northcotes were well-to-do, but she was unprepared for her first glimpse of the estate. Wrought-iron gates decorated with fearsome-looking gargoyles were opened by an aged servant to reveal a steep, curving drive leading to a mansion with a Mansard roof and a square tower at the front, the latter topped by a widow's walk. Beyond the main house were several outbuildings, including a stable and a carriage house.

The old manservant closed the gate behind them . . . and locked it.

"Do you see patients at home?" Diana asked. There was certainly room enough for an office with waiting and examining rooms in this huge house.

"No, but I do have a laboratory in the basement where I compound medicines and . . . well, it has several uses." He seemed to withdraw a little as he brought the horse to a stop in the ivy-covered porte-cochere.

Laboratory? Diana did not like the sound of that. She associated the word with a place where experiments were conducted. Suddenly all the thoughts she'd been trying to suppress surged to the fore. Despite his charm, Ben Northcote was still Damon Bathory, the man whose mind had conceived horrifying images and chilling scenarios. And he was also Dr. Northcote, a scientist with an intense interest in madmen and their treatment. As he handed her down from the buggy, Diana wondered if she had made a terrible mistake in coming here.

Inside the Northcote house, Diana barely had time to note the overall luxury of the decor before a sturdily-built woman of medium height swooped down on her. Her dress was an expanse of black velvet broken only by jet beads at the wrists and hem, and by a heavy gold brooch at her throat.

"Who is this, Ben? Who have you brought me?" She made it sound as if Diana might be the evening's entertainment.

"This is Diana Spaulding, Mother, the columnist I told you about. Diana, this is my mother, Maggie Northcote."

Graying hair framed a surprisingly youthful face. Mrs. Northcote's eyes, alight with curiosity, were the same curious copper color as her other son's.

"Today's Tidbits?" Abruptly, the eyes narrowed.

"That's right." Diana's wariness increased.

"You have a way with words, my dear," Mrs. Northcote said.

Ben helped Diana remove her coat and shrugged out of his own, then escorted both women into the parlor. "The time has come to tell Mrs. Spaulding the truth," he said when he'd installed Diana on a loveseat.

With exaggerated nonchalance, Mrs. Northcote arranged herself on a rococo sofa. She took care that the light from the chandelier fell on her in the most flattering way possible. The elaborate scroll work on the back of the piece of furniture created the illusion that she sat upon a throne.

The woman's eyes, Diana realized, reminded her of a cat's.

Ben remained standing, one shoulder negligently resting against the window frame. "With your permission, Mother?"

Mrs. Northcote gave a regal nod.

"I am not the Northcote who wrote those horror stories," Ben said.

"Aaron?" she guessed.

"No." Nodding his head towards his mother, he said, "Allow me to present the real Damon Bathory."

CHAPTER TWELVE

❧❧❧

A *woman* had written those tales?

Caught off guard by Ben's announcement, Diana murmured, "Oh, my," in a faint voice while her thoughts whirled. It had never crossed her mind that the imagination of one of her own sex could wax so vivid, so violent.

At the same time, she felt a rush of relief. Ben Northcote was not Damon Bathory. He was a physician. A care giver. He was . . . normal.

Benjamin Northcote. A doctor. A blessedly ordinary man. Well, not ordinary, exactly. In some ways he was quite extraordinary, but he was not some Dr. Jekyll/Mr. Hyde as she'd once feared. Nor was he a self-centered, vanity-driven performer.

He was not another Evan.

The comparison struck her forcibly. Was that what she'd thought? What she'd feared as much as anything when she'd believed Ben was the author of those stories? Had she been afraid she was about to repeat the greatest mistake of her past by falling in love with another creative, tormented soul?

Mrs. Northcote cleared her throat. "Of course, now that you know the truth about Damon Bathory, we'll have to kill you."

Diana gasped, unsure what to make of such a preposterous statement.

"Behave yourself, Mother." Ben's voice contained only mild reproof. "She's harmless," he added, directing the remark to Diana.

"You never let me have any fun," Mrs. Northcote complained, and Diana was not entirely sure she was joking. There was something . . . odd about her.

"She's teasing you, Diana," Ben reassured her.

When he crossed to the loveseat and sat beside her, she slowly began to relax. With him there to look after her, surely she had nothing to fear.

"Mother had already agreed to reveal Damon Bathory's true identity to the world. Now that you're here, you may as well be the one to break the story."

This was what she'd been after, Diana told herself. Horatio Foxe would have his exposé. She would keep her job without being obliged to invent a thing. Best of all, the fact that Mrs. Northcote had written the stories shattered Foxe's theory that "he" had murdered reviewers who'd panned them.

"Why delay?" she asked. "The sooner this is made public, the better."

"I need to inform my publisher of the decision," Mrs. Northcote said, "and break the news to a few close friends. Most of my acquaintances already consider me an eccentric, but they have no notion just how unconventional my behavior has been."

"How long?" Diana felt uneasy again, in spite of Ben's comforting touch.

"Time enough to discuss that later," he said before his mother could reply. Taking Diana's elbow, he propelled her to her feet. "I'm sure you want to rest a bit and settle in before supper."

A few minutes later, Ben showed Diana into a large, richly furnished bedroom. A glance was enough to show her that her belongings were already there and had been unpacked by a servant.

"I know we need to talk," Ben said, already leaving, "but right now I should get back to Mother."

"Ben! Wait. I do understand. I think. Why you didn't tell me sooner."

He turned back to her, his shoulders filling the doorway. "Please believe that I didn't care for all the secrecy, not even in the beginning." He sent a rueful look in her direction. "With the wisdom of hindsight, I know I should never have agreed to go on tour. But four months ago I had my own agenda. I decided to indulge myself. The decision bore bitter fruit. Even before I met you, I longed to return to my own life, but I'd made a promise. I was committed to fulfill Damon Bathory's obligations."

He took his promises seriously. She did know that much about him.

"I wanted to tell you the truth in New Haven, Diana." He dragged his fingers through his hair as he looked away from her to stare out the window at the lowering sky. "I wanted to tell you even before that night. But I'd sworn to Mother and to Damon Bathory's publisher that I'd keep her identity secret. I must have been mad to agree to that."

"Eventually someone would have found out."

"So I reasoned for myself. Far better to volunteer the information. But in New York, and in New Haven, I was still bound to honor my pledge. I was not the one who'd have to face dire consequences if the truth came out too soon."

"You had your own reasons for going on tour," Diana reminded him.

"Yes. I told you about my visits to the hospitals. I have a . . . patient who concerns me. Someone who displays many of the symptoms of a hysteric."

The idea of madmen loose in society made Diana uneasy, but she remembered how passionate he had been on the subject when they'd supped together in New York. She was not sure what question would have come out next, but before she could open her mouth to ask Ben anything, he bent towards her.

"I need a few minutes with Mother before we dine," he said, and kissed her lightly on the end of the nose. With that, he went out, closing the door behind him.

Diana did not move until Ben's footsteps had faded away down the hall. Then she went straight to the wash basin to slosh cold water onto her face in a desperate bid to bring order to the jumbled thoughts whirling in her brain.

Dripping, she gripped the sides of the oak commode and stared at her reflection in the mirror affixed to the high back. Her eyes looked haunted. What had she done? She fumbled at the built-in towel rack, then buried her face in the soft cloth.

She'd trusted Damon Bath— No. She'd decided to trust Ben Northcote. She loved Ben Northcote.

But she did not know anything about him, except that, whatever his name, he'd cast a spell over her.

She knew still less about his family and his life here. She fingered the fabric clutched in her hands. A life of luxury. She folded the towel and returned it to the rack, then slowly turned to assess her surroundings.

All the furniture was oak, all of it heavy and most ornately carved. But instead of roses or some other flower, the usual decoration on such pieces, these furnishings sported scarab beetles, intricately detailed. And spiders and scorpions and serpents. Diana moved from piece to piece, pausing to run her fingertips over the glossy surface of a bureau. It had been polished with lemon-scented wax.

Perfectly normal, she thought. Unfortunately, she didn't believe it.

Last of all, she studied the bed, a massive affair with four posters and a canopy. Diana stepped closer, braced for more carved insects, then stopped abruptly and bit back a cry of alarm.

Curled up, dead center on the counterpane, was a huge, long-haired black cat. It regarded her with unblinking eyes—copper-colored eyes that bore an eerie resemblance to Mrs. Northcote's.

"I suppose you're her pet," Diana said to the feline. Appropriate, she thought, that Damon Bathory should have a black cat as a familiar. "I wish you could talk," she added after a moment. "You probably have all the answers I need."

The enormous beast blinked at her but made no other response.

Sinking onto the end of the bed, Diana cautiously extended a hand. The cat sniffed, then licked her fingers. Encouraged, Diana stroked the soft fur. When it didn't protest that either, she lifted it—him—onto her lap. What was one more risk?

She sat there, petting the Northcotes' cat, until she felt calm enough to face a disquieting truth: there were still secrets in this house. Something more than Mrs. Northcote's *nom de plume* had her exchanging guarded glances with her son. Diana's feeling of wrongness was strong, almost strong enough to make her flee back to the safety of the hotel.

She realized she had taken an extraordinary risk, made an impulsive, perhaps foolish decision, because of how she felt about Ben Northcote. When first they'd met, she'd tried to protect herself by remembering the emotional turmoil that was inevitable when one came to care for a creative, artistic person, but it had done no good. Even before she'd found out that Ben was not Damon Bathory, she'd known she could not control her feelings where he was concerned. It was as if, at last, she'd found the other half of herself.

A gentle rapping sound broke in on Diana's thoughts. The door opened a moment later to reveal a slender young woman in a black dress and white apron. She carried Diana's green silk gown, freshly pressed.

The cat hissed and kicked Diana with his back feet until she released him. The maid stepped prudently to one side as the animal streaked past her, then bobbed a curtsey.

"Beggin' your pardon, mum, but Mrs. Northcote wonders will

you be needin' any help with your dressin'?"

Diana started to refuse, then realized that Ben and his mother weren't the only ones in this house who could satisfy her curiosity. It would be wasteful to overlook a source of information when it was dropped into her lap. She told the young woman to come in.

"What is your name?" Diana asked.

"Annie, mum."

"Well, Annie, I am Mrs. Spaulding and I am delighted to make your acquaintance. Tell me, does the cat have a name?"

"Cedric, mum. At least that's what Mrs. Northcote calls him."

Diana smiled at her. "And is there some other name that you use for Cedric?"

"Not me, mum, but the cook, she calls him the devil's spawn."

When she'd hung the gown in the armoire, Annie spoke again. "I'm very good at fixing hair, mum."

"Excellent."

Diana had wondered how she was going to keep the girl with her long enough for an interrogation. Diana did not really need help to change her clothing. Even if she'd brought her entire wardrobe with her, she'd have been hard put to offer Annie much employment. Unaccustomed to having a servant, Diana always took care to select garments she could get into and out of on her own.

Diana encouraged Annie to chat about herself as she worked and soon learned the girl was one of eight children. "The first to get a job when we all come to America from Ireland," she told Diana proudly.

"Do any of the others work here?" Diana asked.

"Oh, no, mum. There was just the one post open."

"I've not met the rest of the staff, except for the gatekeeper. A taciturn fellow." Her mind's eye provided a picture of an elderly man with a big key.

"That's Old Ernest. He calls himself the *grounds*keeper. And sometimes he drives Mrs. Northcote in her carriage. Then there's

Cora Belle, the cook. And Eudora, the housekeeper, and I'm the maid of all work."

"That's four. Are there others?"

Diana watched with interest as color blossomed in Annie's cheeks. "There's Joseph, mum."

Although Annie was vague about his precise duties, Diana gathered that Joseph was young and strong and spent most of his time in the carriage house.

"Why the carriage house?" she asked. A stable would have made more sense if his job was to care for the horses. The only things most people kept in carriage houses were their buggies and wagons.

"He has his room there. And Mr. Aaron's studio is on the upper floor."

"He works for Mr. Aaron Northcote, then?" Diana studied the girl's reflection in the mirror.

Momentary confusion made Annie's brow wrinkle as she tucked a wayward curl into the stylish coiffure she was constructing for Diana. "He works for Mr. Ben," Annie said after a moment. "We all do, except Ernest. Mrs. Northcote pays him."

When she didn't volunteer anything further, Diana tried a new ploy. "I saw one of Aaron Northcote's paintings in New York. He is a very talented artist."

"I wouldn't know, mum. He doesn't let me clean in his studio." There was a new primness in her voice and her lips pursed in disapproval.

"Surely Joseph has taken a peek," Diana teased her. "Didn't he tell you what he saw?"

Annie hesitated, then lowered her voice and leaned close to Diana's ear. "He saw scandalous things," she confided. "And heard them, too. Mr. Aaron, he has women up there at all hours of the day and night, and more than one of them has come away sobbing after he's done with her."

☙❧

At the appointed hour for supper, Diana descended the elaborate cherrywood staircase. She paused at the foot, disconcerted by the way the oval mirror above a Louis Quinze *bombé* bureau reflected the ornately carved griffin on the newel post.

Such things were fashionable, she told herself. But she wished now that she had not devoured so many of the novels of Mrs. Radcliffe and her imitators when she was a girl at school. Squaring her shoulders, Diana marched down a long, dimly-lit main hallway, its highly polished cherrywood floor partially covered by thick Oriental carpets. The dining room was at the far end, its entrance guarded by two huge gargoyles positioned on either side of a cherrywood arch.

Ben came to meet her and showed her to one of the three places set at an enormous oval dining table. "My brother will not be joining us," he said before she could ask. "He's something of a recluse. Shy. Especially when women are around."

"He was willing to meet me at the restaurant when I thought he was you."

Ben shrugged. "He was curious."

Diana might have pursued the subject of Aaron, but to prevent it Ben turned to his mother, who was seated on his other side. "I believe Mrs. Palermo is going to have twins," he told her.

Annie served the soup.

Mrs. Northcote and her son discussed the Palermo family in excruciating detail, then went on to speak of other local matters. Diana ate in silence, feeling more ill at ease by the moment. A vivid imagination, she decided, could be a distinct disadvantage. Her sense of a wrongness about this place, a wrongness about Mrs. Northcote and, perhaps, about her other son, the one who was shy . . . and appeared to talk to people who weren't there . . . grew stronger.

"You're looking much too somber, Diana," Ben said abruptly.

She stammered an apology. "My thoughts wandered."

"There's a penalty for that," he said in a teasing tone of voice. "I insist you tell Mother that story you related to me in New York—the one about the camel."

She had shared the tale with him, Diana remembered, because she'd been trying to avoid talking about anything more personal. Was that his motivation now?

"Yes, do tell." Mrs. Northcote's insistence left her houseguest no choice but to oblige.

"It happened in January," Diana began. "A camel, an elephant, and a donkey were all featured in the Kirafly Brothers' spectacular at the Academy of Music. Bolossy and Imré Kirafly," she added for Mrs. Northcote's benefit, "are Hungarian-born performers turned theatrical producers. They have been Manhattan's principal purveyors of spectacle for the last dozen years. Nightly after the show, the animals are taken in charge by keepers and driven to a stable on Prince Street."

She paused for breath, taking a sip from her water goblet. Ben smiled encouragingly. Mrs. Northcote's face wore a bland expression.

"On this particular evening, the camel led the procession, which went by way of 14th Street to Broadway, then turned south. Just as they reached 12th Street, the camel broke free."

She leaned forward, determined to engage her hostess's interest.

"A camel running wild is a frightful novelty, Mrs. Northcote, even to jaded New Yorkers. Horses and humans alike dove for cover to give the marauding beast room. Portly gentlemen and stout ladies strolling along the sidewalk suddenly displayed the agility of acrobats in order to escape danger. The rabble soon scented fun and joined in the chase with an ear-splitting chorus of yells. The noise further maddened the poor camel."

"Where was the animal's keeper?" she asked.

"In pursuit, but the beast ran in a zigzag pattern. The poor fellow was hard put to keep up. And distracted by the elephant. For quite some time, friend camel ran down Broadway unmolested."

"You mustn't leave loose ends. The keeper's role is important."

"Er, yes. Well, to continue, the noise and lights confused the runaway beast and he vented his fury in roars and kicks, and that in turn caused horses pulling carriages to rear and plunge. The driver of an express wagon had just left his conveyance in front of the St. Denis Hotel, in order to deliver a trunk, when he heard the racket up the street. He dropped the trunk to dive for the reins and was barely in time to keep his team from making a rapid-transit trip through the hotel café."

Diana expected a chuckle at this point, if not an outright laugh, but she got no response at all from her audience. Determined to inject a little more verve into her storytelling, although she was already gesturing with both hands while she spoke, she cleared her throat and continued.

"Grace Church is opposite the St. Denis." She glanced at Ben, remembering that she'd followed him to services there. "It boasts an iron fence. When the camel left the express wagon, it bolted across the street. A woman passing by on the sidewalk saw it coming, screamed, and tried to run, but one foot slipped on an icy cake and down she fell, plump in the camel's path. It was a critical moment, but just as those watching braced themselves to witness a terrible collision, the camel sprang over her prostrate form like a hurdle racer and fetched up against the iron fence of the church. He struck it with such violence that the concussion knocked him flat."

Mrs. Northcote made a tsking noise.

Ben chuckled. "A knock-down blow."

"But not sufficient to lay Mr. Camel low for long. Even as the woman scrambled to her feet and fled, the, er, hunchback terror started off for another stretch down Broadway."

She thought that a rather good turn of phrase, but neither of her listeners seemed impressed.

"The camel seemed to sense that his stable was somewhere in

that direction and he was bent on getting there at a pneumatic clip, but as he approached the Sinclair House, another hotel, a private carriage containing a gentleman, his wife, and their baby, wheeled into view going up Broadway. The driver's eyes went wide and his horses had an attack of St. Vitus dance as they realized that the camel was making a bee-line for the carriage. His bowed head was in close proximity to one of the glass doors when, at the last possible minute, two men sprang to the rescue. They seized the camel by the nostrils, one on each side, kicked him in the forelegs, and threw the beast, holding him firmly until help arrived."

"The approved technique for subduing a camel," Ben told his mother, *sotto voce*.

"In a little while," Diana finished, "the keeper appeared on the scene and that was the end of Mr. Camel's adventure."

"How did those two men know what to do?" Mrs. Northcote asked.

Ben grinned. Since he'd heard the story before, he answered before Diana could. "They told reporters on the scene that they'd both had previous experience wrangling camels."

"Coincidence," Mrs. Northcote scoffed. "It never works well in fiction."

"But this is all true," Diana protested.

"Do you think people will believe preposterous things just because they really happened?" Mrs. Northcote asked. "On the other hand, with a little work, this might make a good story."

"I thought it *was* a good story." Diana felt more confused than ever.

"I mean if it were written down. As fiction. Not just as you told it, of course. It wants tinkering. You must turn the basic chase into something more. Explain away the two men who just happened to know what to do. Perhaps the entire incident was a sinister plot to ruin the Kirafly Brothers. Arranged by a theatrical rival."

"More likely a publicity stunt," Diana muttered, disconcerted by Mrs. Northcote's comments. In New York, Ben had told her the tale was humorous, and suggested that she might write that sort of thing instead of gossip columns.

"That could work," Mrs. Northcote said in a thoughtful voice. "Keep asking yourself 'what if?' until you've found exactly the right combination of details. Then slap a snappy title on the whole and you've got yourself a nice little package to sell to a magazine."

"Is that how you do it?" Diana—her pique forgotten—asked because she was genuinely curious to know.

"Most of the time." Mrs. Northcote waited, plainly expecting more questions.

Diana did not want to disappoint her. "Why did you choose a male pseudonym?"

Damon Bathory's alter ego blinked solemnly at her. "Because some people have an irrational prejudice against women in any occupation men dominate. Aside from Mary Shelley, I know of no other woman who has ever written stories like mine. Oh, a few females pen novels containing dark secrets, mysterious villains, ghosts and ghouls and things that go bump in the night, with virginal heroines, of course, but those tales do not come close to exposing the evil underbelly of human depravity, or the torments of the misaligned mind."

"Do you risk censure, then, by revealing all at this juncture?" Diana could well believe it. She'd not considered that aspect of the situation before and the thought sobered her.

"I always wanted to be honest with my readers." Mrs. Northcote's expression was deadly serious. "My editor dissuaded me. First he insisted no one would believe that a respectable matron could write so convincingly about murder and mayhem. Then he said they'd be horrified if they did believe it."

Diana thought of Horatio Foxe and was forced to agree. Men could be very small-minded.

"A company in Boston publishes my books," Mrs. Northcote

continued. "They were the ones who insisted I pretend to be a man. Six months ago, they suggested that I find someone to impersonate me and embark on a lecture tour. I persuaded Ben to do it. Knowing he had his own reasons for wanting to visit several of the cities on the proposed route, I seized upon what seemed an admirable compromise."

He'd wanted to visit insane asylums. Remembering that, Diana sent a questioning glance his way. His expression enigmatic, he ignored it.

"Since his return, he has persuaded me that subterfuge is unnecessary, that my sales figures are high enough to overcome any qualms on the part of my publisher. Since he will not stand in for me again, I am inclined to do as he wishes. I do not know what the result will be." She heaved a theatrical sigh. "They may decline to accept any more stories from me. My writing will come to an ignominious end."

"Not likely," Ben muttered. "The publicity will undoubtedly cause sales to soar. Your publisher will profit and so will you."

Diana had more questions, but Ben deftly deflected them. The rest of the evening passed without further discussion of his mother's unorthodox career or the news story Diana was to write about it.

Not until she was in her room once more, trying to ignore the storm raging outside her windows as she prepared to go to bed, did Diana realize how easily Ben had distracted her. All he'd had to do was smile.

She resolved to be more sensible in the future. She'd focus on getting answers to her questions. And she would not let her imagination run away with her. If the wind had not howled just then, producing an involuntary shiver, she might have had more faith in her ability to keep that second vow.

Hurriedly, without help, she undressed and put on her nightgown. In the morning, she'd insist on interviewing Mrs. Northcote. Then she'd write her article. After that . . . .

At this point, Diana's optimism failed her once more. She still felt Ben was keeping something from her. Worse, he had given her no real indication of what he had planned for them. Did they have a future together?

You are not some impressionable young virgin, she lectured herself. She'd married Evan without enough forethought. She hoped she had sense enough not to repeat that particular mistake.

Not that Ben had asked her to marry him.

All he'd said was that he had intended to keep his promise to return to New York. He'd intended to tell her the truth about Damon Bathory.

She climbed into the huge bed, snuffed the candle, and tried not to think about the bugs carved into the headboard. She'd be fit for one of Ben's madhouses if she didn't get a good night's sleep.

Resolutely, she closed her eyes. Everything, she told herself firmly, would sort itself out in the morning.

CHAPTER THIRTEEN

⁂

He's already left for the day," Ben's mother told Diana when she came downstairs the next morning. The older woman was dressed in a frothy concoction of laces and bows that Diana took to be some sort of night wear. It was eccentric, but in a charming way.

"He has a separate house in town for his office," she continued as Diana helped herself to a selection of foodstuffs from a well-stocked sideboard in the breakfast room. "When he bought out another doctor's practice, he took over both the patients and the building."

"I understand he has a laboratory here."

"Oh, yes. In the cellar. Would you like to see it? I'm fairly certain there are no cadavers there, though."

Diana choked on a bite of toast. "Cadavers?"

"Oh, yes. Ben did a lovely dissection just before he left on tour."

Forcing herself to chew and swallow, Diana digested this information. "Is Ben, by chance, the local coroner?"

"How clever you are!" Mrs. Northcote calmly buttered a roll. "A hunter found the body in the woods near here. Ben did an autopsy in the hope of discovering what killed him. And when. There wasn't much to work with by then."

Apparently relishing every word, Mrs. Northcote provided far more detail than Diana ever wanted to hear again. When she could stand no more, she abruptly stood. "I believe I will go into town."

"In this downpour?" Mrs. Northcote gestured towards the windows. As it had all through the night, rain fell in sheets, obscuring the view. "As your hostess, I must insist you stay close to the house today."

Had the gates been locked behind Ben after he left? To keep her in? Or to confine someone else?

Diana told herself she was being fanciful. Mrs. Northcote was . . . unusual, but certainly not that fictional stereotype, the madwoman in the attic.

"Do I make you nervous?" Ben's mother asked.

"No, of course not," Diana lied.

"Then you will not mind meeting me in the parlor in an hour. I've a yen for your . . . company."

When Mrs. Northcote had gone back to her room to dress, Diana finished her breakfast, then amused herself by wandering through the other rooms on the first floor of the house. She found stairs leading to the basement but did not go down. Neither did she venture into the kitchen.

"He's a queer duck and no mistake," said a woman's voice just as Diana was about to open that door.

It belonged to one of the other female servants Annie had mentioned, or so Diana assumed. Eudora or Cora Belle. Diana had not yet decided to make her presence known when the unseen woman spoke again.

"Half the time he seems to be lost in his own little world, not noticing anyone around him. Then, so sudden it makes a body gasp, he's paying more attention than is proper, staring at places on a woman that a well-brought-up gentleman ain't supposed to let on he notices. You stay away from him, Annie. And if he asks to paint you, you say no."

"I'm a good girl," the maid protested. "And I know the sort of woman he has pose for him."

"Scandalous, that's what I say!"

Diana turned away, reluctant to thrust herself into the middle of what was obviously a private conversation. Remembering the painting she'd seen in New York, she could understand why Annie was being warned off. The women in the seascape had not been wearing much. Diana thought they were intended to be mermaids.

At the appointed time, Diana ventured into the parlor. Ben's mother was already there, once again all in black. She posed by the piano, waiting.

"Virgins are so difficult to come by these days," she said as she ran idle fingers over the keys. The sound was jarring, since the instrument was badly out of tune.

"Why do you need one?" Diana asked.

She beckoned Diana closer. "Look at my face. How old do you think I am? I have the skin of a woman fifteen years my junior. Do you know why? I keep my youthful appearance by bathing in the blood of virgins. It is an old family tradition."

"I see. Then you must be related to the Bathorys." Diana hoped she sounded nonchalant. The excessive glee in the other woman's voice seemed more than just eccentricity.

Mrs. Northcote fingered her brooch, looking disappointed that she'd failed to shock Diana. The same crest that had been on the ring Ben had worn in New York graced this piece of jewelry, confirming Diana's guess.

"I was born Magda Bathory," Mrs. Northcote admitted.

Diana swallowed hard. When Ben had said Bathory was a real name, he'd meant it. And if it wasn't his precisely, it did belong to his ancestors. Bathory blood ran in his mother's veins . . . and in his.

"Elizabeth Bathory was a sixteenth-century Hungarian countess." Mrs. Northcote's expression softened into a fond smile.

"She literally drained the blood of her victims, keeping it in great vats until she required it for her baths. Dear Elizabeth killed hundreds of young girls before she was finally caught and tried and sentenced to be sealed up forever in a room in her own castle."

An involuntary shudder wracked Diana's slender frame. It took all her fortitude not to turn and flee. The horrible thought that Ben had been visiting insane asylums because his own mother was going mad had already occurred to her. Had all those troubling stories come, as she'd first suspected, from a disturbed mind?

"You should see the expression on your face, my dear. It is really quite gratifying."

"Mrs. Northcote—"

"Maggie, dear. Call me Maggie."

And with that, "Maggie" began to chatter about everyday things, including her work schedule. When she'd explained that mornings were her most creative time, she excused herself to go off and write, but she paused in the frame of the pocket doors.

"Ben won't be home until late. Today's the quarterly meeting of the trustees of the Maine Insane Hospital." Before Diana could respond to that, Maggie surprised her yet again. "I don't want you to be bored. I know. I'll give you my new manuscript to read. You can tell me what you think of it over dinner."

She sent Old Ernest to deliver the pages to Diana's room. He had a face like a prune and a surly demeanor, seeming to resent the presence of someone in the house who was not a family member. When Diana tried to talk to him, he replied only in grunts. She soon abandoned the effort.

Maggie's work in progress, a novel, was the tale of a woman trapped in a castle complete with dungeon. The story quickly captured Diana's interest. If nothing else, she could relate to the heroine.

She was still reading when, late in the afternoon, a note arrived from Ben. "Mrs. Palermo is in labor," he wrote. "There are problems. I may not be home at all tonight." He added no personal message, but Diana consoled herself with the thought that he'd been pressed for time.

To Diana's relief, Maggie did not make any further attempts to frighten her. She did not want to discuss her manuscript either. Instead she chatted about Bangor, and the weather, and persuaded Diana to tell her about life in New York City. Ben's name was not mentioned—nor was Aaron's.

The next morning, Ben had still not returned, although he had sent word that Mrs. Palermo had been safely delivered of healthy twin boys. Once again, Diana and Maggie had the breakfast room to themselves, but this time Maggie was already fully dressed in the black that seemed to be her uniform. She said little, but as Diana ate she could feel the other woman staring at her. Being watched that way was a singularly unnerving experience.

Diana glanced towards the window. No rain or snow. Only overcast.

"I believe I will go out for a breath of fresh air," she announced, abruptly abandoning the breakfast she'd barely touched.

"Watch your step," Maggie warned.

Pausing only long enough to don the coat Ben had bought for her in New Haven, Diana fled. Cautiously, she descended a set of broad stone steps that led to the dooryard. The way was treacherous underfoot. The previous day's rain had frozen in icy patches, but someone had sprinkled sand along the driveway and Diana was able to walk as far as the ornate gate at its foot without undue difficulty.

The gate was locked.

The gargoyles cleverly worked into the wrought iron leered at her, as if mocking her attempt at escape, and Diana's sense of being imprisoned increased when she peered through decorative but sturdy bars at the bleak and empty road beyond. She hadn't realized the terrain was so rugged and hilly or how far away the nearest neighbor was. There was no other house in sight, although she could make out the smoke from a chimney in the distance.

Trees obscured what must surely be a panoramic view of Bangor from the top of the next hill. She knew she could walk into the center of the city . . . if she could only get past this locked gate.

She rattled the padlock, but it was secure. She could not open it without a key. If Ben Northcote's intention in bringing her home with him had been to keep her from contacting Horatio Foxe, or anyone else, he'd succeeded admirably.

It was an uncharitable thought, most likely untrue, but as long as she was locked in, she could not entirely dismiss it. With an ever deepening sense of foreboding, Diana turned to look back at the Northcote house. There was one way to find out. She could march right up to Old Ernest and demand to be taken into town.

Just as Diana reached the front door, Maggie emerged wearing a voluminous black cloak that reminded Diana of the one Ben had worn on stage. "Ah, there you are, Diana. Come along."

"I was just on my way into Bangor," Diana protested.

"You can visit Ben's office some other time. Right now I want you to meet the rest of the family."

With decidedly mixed feelings, Diana allowed Maggie to pull her towards the back of the mansion. She *was* curious about Aaron.

Maggie sailed right past the entrance to the studio above the carriage house. She had a tight grip on Diana's arm and almost dragged her along. Diana wondered what other relatives lived on the estate. This was the first time anyone had mentioned them to her.

They passed a garden. Although it was difficult to tell much at this time of year, the area appeared to be used to grow shrubs, flowers, and herbs as well as vegetables. In spite of recent rains, snow still covered the beds.

Beyond, the path became uneven underfoot. Patches of mud were interspersed with puddles, making it difficult to navigate, and in shady spots there was ice. Diana had to concentrate just to stay upright, but Maggie was sure-footed as she wove her way through a profusion of immense trees, mostly beech, elm, and maple. At the center of a stand of ash stood a small stone building. Until the last moment, even without their foliage, the trees had concealed its presence.

"Come along," Maggie insisted, giving Diana's arm a tug when she hesitated. "They won't hurt you," she added, grinning. "They're quite dead."

She let go to draw an oversized bolt and open a heavy wooden door. It swung back with a loud creak to reveal a short flight of stone steps leading downward.

Reluctantly, not at all reassured by Maggie's cheerful disclaimer, Diana followed her through the arched opening and into the crypt.

Like the house, the Northcote family vault was of fairly recent construction and sturdily built. With solemn ceremony, Maggie produced a tinderbox and lit several of the lanterns stored in niches along the walls.

Although the crypt was below ground level, the flagged floor was dry. No rainwater or melting snow had seeped in. The air was close but did not smell stale or unpleasant. More reassuring still, the current residents of the Northcote family crypt had chosen to be sealed in stone. There were no coffins stacked like cordwood in sight.

"You'll want to read the inscriptions," Maggie said, handing Diana one of the lanterns.

It seemed easier to go along with the plan than to argue. Diana had just gotten close enough to a wall of brass plaques to pick out the name Abraham Northcote when she heard Maggie's scurrying footsteps on the stairs.

"Enjoy your visit!" she called as she dashed outside. An instant later, the door thudded closed with ominous finality.

Too stunned to do more than stare at the blocked exit, Diana grappled with the horrifying fact that Maggie had imprisoned her in the family crypt.

A shudder raced through her. Then, with a strangled cry, she ran up the steps and flung herself against the barrier. "Maggie!" she shouted. "Come back here and let me out!"

There was no answer.

She could hear nothing from the outside.

Diana called for help. She used every trick she'd learned in the theater to project her voice, only to have it bounce back at her off the solid walls of the vault. With a sense of growing horror, Diana realized the place was probably soundproof. She was on the verge of full-scale panic, certain she was going to die in this terrible place, when the door swung open.

Aaron Northcote stood on the other side.

Diana didn't know whether to be relieved or more frightened than before, but she managed to put up a brave front. "Thank heavens you heard me calling."

"Oh, but I didn't. The walls are far too thick. But I did see Mother lead you down the garden path. When she passed by again alone, I decided to look for you."

"Thank you, Mr. Northcote."

He stepped back, a bemused expression on his face. "It must be the full moon," he said.

"But the moon is not at the full," Diana murmured, still unable to believe that Ben's mother had deliberately imprisoned her. She looked back as she emerged from her underground prison and shuddered.

"You must forgive Mother," Aaron said. "She has an odd sense of humor."

Diana did not find anything to laugh about in what had just been done to her. This was not the action of a sane person. Her earlier suspicion that Ben had been visiting madhouses for Maggie's sake seemed confirmed. What if Aaron hadn't come? How long would she have been trapped? The crypt was isolated from the rest of the buildings. It might have been days before anyone thought to look for her there.

"Come along, Mrs. Spaulding," Aaron said in a bracing voice. "You look as if you could do with a nip of brandy. I have some in the carriage house."

She followed him meekly. A few minutes later, she stood in his studio, holding a brandy snifter in one hand. At a loss for sensible conversation, she said the first thing that came into her mind. "I thought Maine was a dry state."

Aaron laughed. Too heartily, Diana thought. She supposed he felt as awkward as she did.

"The law is more often honored in the breach than in the practice," he told her. "Here in Bangor, groggeries openly operate all along what's called Peppermint Row and in the Devil's Half Acre on the other side of Kenduskeag Stream. Never any trouble getting beer or rum, which they call White Eye. That's what the tigers drink."

"The woodsmen?"

He nodded and sipped his own drink, comfortably sprawled in the studio's one overstuffed chair. "When a man's been far from civilization all winter long, it isn't wise to deny him anything. In some ways we're a frontier town here, for all that we're located on the civilized east coast."

Like Denver, Diana thought, or Leadville. But for all their gamblers and whores, neither of those cities tolerated lunatics. Or sorcerers.

Into which category, she wondered, did Aaron Northcote fit?

The contents of his studio provided no answer to that question but they did distract Diana from pondering it further. The smells associated with a working artist filled the air—linseed oil and turpentine and drying paint. A small pedestal stood in the very center of the large room, upon it a bentwood chair, unoccupied at present. The work-in-progress visible on a nearby easel showed Diana a woman straddling that same chair, her hands folded under her chin and her elbows propped on the curved back. Although only stocking-clad ankles peeped out from beneath the hem of her long skirt, the pose was undeniably risqué, and when Diana looked more closely, she saw that the bodice of the dress was nearly transparent, all but baring the model's bosom.

Glass clinked against crystal as Aaron refilled his snifter with brandy. "Go ahead, Mrs. Spaulding," he urged her. "Look around."

Against the darkness of the day, the gas in the studio had been turned up, filling the room with a curious blend of light and shadow. Diana moved slowly from canvas to canvas. There were stacks of them, some freshly stretched and blank, others completely covered in Aaron's own brand of art. Most contained scantily-clad females. More than one was represented as a mermaid.

"Be my guest," he invited when she stopped in front of the largest of the oils. "Review it."

"I do not presume to judge painters. Only writers and actors."

"I've been accused of being obscene."

"Obscenity, like beauty, is in the eye of the beholder. I saw one of your paintings in New York."

"I know."

"Did Ben tell you?"

When she got no answer, she turned to look at her host. Aaron was slouched in his chair, staring bleakly at the amber liquid in his snifter. No one seeing Aaron and Ben together would ever doubt they were related, but there was a certain vitality to Ben that was missing in the younger man.

"You have an . . . unusual style." She glanced at the huge canvas again, searching her mind for a more positive word to use. "It has an unearthly beauty." It was also strangely disturbing.

"My paintings sold well in New York."

"I'm glad."

"Still, I could have handled my own business. There was no need for Ben to collect the bank draft."

So that was what he'd been doing in the gallery. "Since he was going to be there on other business, he could save you the long trip."

"Oh, I went anyway. That put big brother's nose out of joint."
Aaron laughed and downed the rest of his brandy in one gulp.

Diana faced him fully, wondering when he had been in New
York. And where else had he been?

"We have something in common, Mrs. Spaulding," Aaron said.
"Mother doesn't like either of us."

"Why do you say that, Mr. Northcote?"

"She hovered after Ben left." He sounded petulant, like a small
boy. "Gave me no peace. I couldn't stand it. Sometimes I felt she
was bearing down on me like a hound in pursuit of a fox and I'd
have to burrow into the ground to get away from her."

He poured more brandy and downed half of it without coming
up for air.

Diana began to edge towards the door, uncomfortably aware
that Aaron might well be as "eccentric" as Maggie. Being alone
with him suddenly made her very nervous.

With an abrupt movement and a grunt, he sat up straight,
staring glassy-eyed into the middle distance. "Yes," he whispered.
"Yes, of course."

"Aaron? Are you all right?"

"I will be." His gaze fixed on her, sharp and intense. "You must
be my model, Diana. I don't know why I didn't realize before."

"I don't think so, Aaron." She was poised for a rapid retreat
when he spoke again but his words froze her in place.

"I misunderstood when I saw you in New York."

The lump in her throat made it difficult for Diana to speak.
He'd seen her? In New York? She managed only one word.
"Where?"

"At the hall where Ben spoke. I followed you home." A wicked
grin flashed across Aaron's features at her start of surprise. "You
never even noticed me. I thought you were a threat, but I was
wrong. I see that now."

Appalled, Diana tried to sift through all the unexpected
revelations he'd thrown at her. "Were you the man Ben accosted

in Union Square Park?"

"Heard about that, did you? Big brother read me the riot act for being there. Then he gave me train fare home."

As fast as one mystery was solved, more questions cropped up. Retreat forgotten, Diana approached the overstuffed chair. "Aaron, did you leave New York after Ben gave you money?"

Before he could answer, even supposing he intended to, the door of the studio opened and Ben strode through it. In one glance, he absorbed Diana's presence, the nearly empty bottle, and the equally empty glass in his brother's lax hand.

"You know brandy aggravates your gout," he said.

"Always the physician, Leave me be, Brother. I am attempting to commune with my muse."

"Go back to the house, Diana."

"No. You can't have her. I understand now. She's perfect."

Diana resisted Ben's effort to take her arm, wrinkling her nose at the smell of the carbolic he'd washed with after seeing his last patient.

"She must pose for me, Brother." Aaron sounded buoyantly cheerful.

"Over my dead body," Ben declared, and tried again to tow Diana away. She resisted.

In spite of the fact that she'd longed to be rescued only moments earlier, it galled her to be treated like some recalcitrant child. Ben Northcote had no right to dictate to her. Besides, the fact that he hadn't bothered to mention his brother's presence in Manhattan left her out of charity with him.

Diana's tone was just as forceful as the one he'd used to his brother. "I am capable of making my own decisions."

"Take a good look at these paintings, Diana."

"They are extraordinary."

"Are you saying you're willing to take your clothes off for him?"

"I never—"

"What did you think you'd be wearing? He doesn't make a

habit of painting women in more than their skin."

"You're making a great deal of fuss over nothing." She glared at him but in spite of her irritation, she found this show of temper enlightening. He would never make such a fuss if he didn't care about her.

"Shall we discuss this in private?" He indicated Aaron, grinning at them from his chair. "I did intend that we talk."

"There are a number of things I have to say to you, too, Ben Northcote." She didn't budge. "To start with, I want to know why you lied to me."

"About what?"

"You didn't tell me Aaron was in New York. You never mentioned that Maggie is—" She broke off, uncertain how to tell a man she thought his mother was mad. If she was wrong . . . . She drew in a deep breath and started again, her words clipped. "Aaron rescued me after Maggie locked me in your family vault."

"Mother is a tad eccentric." He sounded more amused than apologetic and not at all surprised.

Eccentric? Diana was beginning to dislike that word. Where, she wondered, did Ben draw the line between eccentric and insane?

"I believe," she said aloud, "that I deserve a better explanation than that for what she did."

"All right." His tension was less obvious now but he kept glancing at his brother, obviously wishing Diana would agree to leave Aaron's studio.

She gave Ben's hand, still clamped around her upper arm, a pointed look. After a long, fulminating stare of his own, he released her. Ostentatiously rubbing what she expected was going to be a spectacular bruise, she turned away from Ben to address his brother.

"I'm flattered, Aaron. No one's ever wanted to paint me before. But surely a professional would be better."

"Oh, yes. Plenty of them around. They're all whores, un-fortunately. But there's something special about you, Diana . . . ." Under the intensity of his brother's scowl, Aaron's voice trailed off. His mouth shaped itself into a pout.

Diana had never seen a grown man sulk, but there was no other word for Aaron's attitude.

"Oh, go away," he muttered. "Both of you."

Before his brother could change his mind, Ben whisked Diana out of the studio.

"Where are we going?" Digging her heels into the mud didn't slow him down in the least.

"Back to the house."

"I'd rather go back to the hotel. I don't feel . . . safe here." And she was heartily sick of being dragged hither and yon by members of the Northcote family.

Ben came to an abrupt halt in the shade of the porte-cochere. "There are perfectly logical explanations for everything," he said.

"For keeping the gate locked? Am I a prisoner here?"

"You can leave any time you want, but I'd hoped you'd want to stay."

It was difficult to resist that look, that tone of voice, but Diana made the effort. "Ben, your mother locked me in a crypt." she couldn't help wondering if Maggie was mad, and Aaron, too. And if they were insane, then what about Ben? A Dr. Jekyll, after all?

She wasn't certain how many of her thoughts he read in her expression, but what she saw in the depths of his dark brown eyes was tenderness. And love? She dared hope that was what it was.

With a gentle touch, he tucked a strand of hair behind her ear. She hadn't even realized it had come loose. "You've had a difficult morning," he murmured.

She longed to throw herself into his arms and accept the comfort of his embrace. She backed away instead. "Why are the gates kept locked?"

"Aaron," he said simply. "He wouldn't harm anyone, but he has . . . spells. He goes off on his own if he isn't watched. It's for his protection that we don't leave the gates open."

"He was in New York."

"Yes. He's perfectly capable of taking a train by himself. But he doesn't always behave rationally. It's worse when he's among strangers. And when he's been drinking. I'm afraid his luck will run out one of these days and he'll be arrested and confined in an institution. It happens, you know."

Diana nodded. That was how Nellie Bly had gotten her sensational story. It had been frighteningly easy to end up committed to a madhouse.

"Did he reach Bangor before the blizzard?" she asked.

Ben gave her a sharp look, as if he guessed what she might really be asking, but neither of them voiced the possibility that Aaron could have been the one who'd attacked her in that alley.

"No. And the telegram I got in New Haven advised me of that fact. That's why I couldn't stay longer, and why I didn't invite you to come with me. I expected to have to track him down. There's a place in Boston he goes sometimes. I meant to try there first."

"Ben—"

"He's harmless, Diana. I swear it." He managed a self-deprecating smile. "But I still don't want you posing for him."

"And your mother? Is she harmless?"

"Ah, well. Mother. She's an entirely different case. I think that, rather than speculate, we'd better discuss what happened today with her."

A few minutes later, Ben ushered Diana into Maggie Northcote's inner sanctum, a sumptuous boudoir decorated in the Oriental style. Diana's jaw dropped at the sight of Moorish banners hanging from the ceiling and walls covered with lattice-work screens, all except the one filled with Moorish cabinets loaded down with bric-a-brac. A divan, broad, low, and deeply cushioned, was draped with a heavy rug and heaped with fluffy pillows. Several larger pillows created a "cozy corner" on the floor.

"Oh, you're free," Maggie said, sounding surprised but not particularly disappointed. "Come in and have a seat." She indicated the divan. "The trick is to curl one foot underneath yourself, lean back, then build a wall of cushions at shoulder-level. Wonderfully relaxing after hours sitting upright in a hard chair."

Diana surveyed the obstacle course between the door and the divan. The entire area was littered with inlaid Damascus tables and Cairene folding stands which held assorted statuary and delicate porcelain vases.

"I don't dare move. I'm afraid I'll knock something over."

"Perhaps you'd be more comfortable in here."

Grinning, Maggie opened a narrow door at a right angle to the hall entrance, revealing a room no bigger than a built-in closet. The small cell was furnished with only two pieces of furniture—a library table and a lattice-back chair.

"Here I write," Maggie said. "The outer room is for dreaming."

"Why did you lock Diana in the crypt?" Ben asked, cutting short the tour.

"Research."

"I beg your pardon?"

"You remind me of my current heroine," Maggie informed Diana. "It was very helpful to me to see how you took various statements I made to you earlier. That's when I conceived the idea of locking you in the vault to find out how you'd deal with being shut up with all those dead bodies. I would have released you after a few hours."

"Mother," Ben objected, "it would have been one thing to ask for her help, but—"

"If she'd known there was no danger, she'd not have acted the same way."

Having voiced this irrefutable logic, Maggie turned her attention back to Diana. Her eerily cat-like eyes gleamed. "Did you scream? Did your breathing change?"

As Maggie peppered her with questions, Diana found she could no longer doubt the other woman's motive, even if she didn't approve of what she'd done. She supposed a good deal could be excused on the grounds of excessive zeal. Certainly there was genuine enthusiasm in the way the older woman talked about her work in progress. The writer in Diana responded to that. She did not entirely abandon her doubts about Maggie's sanity, but she did end up cooperating.

"Wouldn't it have been easier to lock yourself in?" she asked, interrupting the flow of questions.

"I tried that. It didn't help. I suppose I was already too familiar with the place."

"You'd spent time in the crypt before?"

"Only once. That was a great disappointment, too. At the end of October, just before Ben left on tour, I was in there for hours one night, trying to evoke a spirit. Of course, I left the door open. I wanted the effect of the wind, but I quite lost my temper when my candles kept blowing out."

"Do you often rely upon real experiences?"

"Oh, dear me, no! I use legend and history for my inspiration. And I have an excellent imagination." Maggie tapped the side of her head. "On the other hand, I am not one to overlook the opportunity for first-hand observation when it walks in my door."

Diana's uneasiness returned. "I see."

Maggie's laugh had a surprisingly girlish lilt. "And I do love dreaming up new ways to kill people, and clever places to hide the bodies."

CHAPTER FOURTEEN

❧

Ben had come home for luncheon. Belatedly, he and Diana sat down to a rushed meal. "I have to leave again soon. I have patients scheduled."

Diana barely listened to the excuse. She felt more comfortable about Maggie now, but she'd remembered an unsettling contradiction to do with Aaron. "Is Ernest gatekeeper?" she asked. "Does he stand by to open and close it?"

"Why do you ask?"

"Because he locked it after you brought me in, and he was nowhere in sight when I wanted to get out."

Ben finished his soup before he replied. "The day you arrived, Ernest's very presence meant Aaron had already returned. I told him to wait by the gate and lock up after everyone was in for the night." He glanced at his pocket watch and rose in haste. "I'm late. I have to go."

"Take me back with you. I'd like to see your office."

He shook his head, a rueful expression on his face. "This morning a lake is covering the pavement from Center Street to Essex Street. The snow machines have been out scraping the roads where there's just ice, but mud and water are another matter. Wait until tomorrow. I'd like you to see the city when she glistens like the queen she is."

"Logic works better than sorcery," she remarked.

His puzzled look made her wonder if he realized just how potent his brand of charm could be. Did he know women saw him on first acquaintance as an engaging rogue, even without the dark and mysterious aura he'd had as Damon Bathory?

She could only hope that the man she was now coming to know was the genuine Ben Northcote and not just another creation of a clever charlatan. That she'd once fallen for the false front presented by Evan Spaulding gave her reason to fear she might still be vulnerable to such tricks.

"I'll try to be back early," he said, stopping to kiss her cheek on his way out.

She caught his arm and tugged. When he halted, she reached up with both hands, seized his beard, and tugged until his lips were level with hers. Her kiss was a lover's, meant to last him through the afternoon and speed his journey back to her.

Once Ben had gone, Diana spent the rest of the afternoon working on her story for Horatio Foxe. At four, she gathered up a half-dozen sheets of foolscap covered with small, neat handwriting. To her surprise, writing the piece on Damon Bathory had gone well.

Because it was an account of an interview with a writer, she realized, not an exposé. It was, in fact, exactly the sort of thing she'd told Foxe she wanted to write. Had it only been two weeks since that meeting in his office? Diana shook her head in amazement. So much had happened. There were times lately when her life in Manhattan seemed a distant memory.

"Diana? Are you there?" Maggie rapped loudly on Diana's door. Without waiting for an invitation, she invaded the bedroom, carrying Cedric the cat draped like a black shawl over one arm and a sheaf of papers in the other hand.

"Well," said Diana a half hour later. Words failed her. "Well."

Maggie had written a story about a runaway camel. She'd added vice and skullduggery and a touch of her trademark horror. It was a compelling, startling piece. Diana knew she could not have produced its like, not in a single day. Not, most likely, in a lifetime.

"You write well, too," Maggie told her, turning the last page of Diana's article. She had made herself comfortable on the bed, lying on her stomach, her chin propped on her fists and the cat curled up beside her. "I suppose this means you will be leaving us soon."

"I do have a job to go back to."

Maggie gave a short bark of laughter. "You might sound more enthusiastic about it!"

"The truth is that I do not like what my column has become."

"Then write something else."

"Easier said than done. There are nearly forty women who supply stories to New York newspapers. Only four—Fannie Merrill, Viola Roseboro, Nell Nelson, and most recently and notably, Nellie Bly—do anything but the women's pages and reviews, except for Middy Morgan, who writes livestock reports for the *New York Times.*"

"Stunt girls," Maggie said with distaste.

"Yes. The four I mentioned are all employed by the *World* and all four take dangerous risks to get their stories. You may have heard of Nellie Bly's adventures. She had herself committed to a mental institution in order to land her present position." Diana shuddered at the thought. At the other extreme was Elizabeth Bisland, also employed by the *World.* Miss Bisland, a young woman who'd left impeccable social connections behind in New Orleans, seemed content to write nothing but book reviews.

Diana and Maggie talked shop through supper. They had plenty of time for it. Once again Ben did not come home. Maggie received a message saying that he had another medical crisis but he sent no private word to Diana.

The evening passed with interminable slowness. Maggie had invited several friends to call. Diana supposed she meant to reveal her secret to them. She could not say for certain, since she was not asked to join them. She went to bed early and slept until the sound of a door closing woke her.

Ben. She was certain of it. His room was located just down the hall from her own. Feeling greatly daring, she got up and lit a lamp.

As penance for locking Diana in the crypt, Maggie had sent to town for a dressmaker. She'd taken measurements for new clothes and provided ready-made undergarments and a new nightgown to augment what Diana had purchased in New Haven. A scandalous amount of flesh showed through the filmy fabric.

Catching sight of herself in the mirror, Diana hesitated. She was wavering between reaching for the doorknob and returning to her bed when she heard a soft rapping sound. Curious, she pulled on a newly-acquired warm wool robe, opened her door a crack, and peered out into the hall.

Old Ernest stood in front of Ben's room. His whisper sounded eerie in the still darkness. "Miss Jenny's sent for you."

"Wake Joseph," Ben ordered.

"Already there," Ernest said.

"Is something wrong?" Clutching the lapels of the robe tighter, Diana stepped boldly out into the hall.

"Nothing that need concern you," Ben said bluntly. "It's after midnight. Go back to bed."

She stiffened. He ought to know by now that she did not take orders well. Since he was exerting not an iota of charm, she found it easy to defy him.

Unaware of her chagrin, or ignoring it, Ben hurried towards the stairwell. Maggie's door opened just after he'd passed by. Clad in a startling red-velvet wrapper that had been fashioned to resemble a monk's robe, she noted her son's rapid retreat, then turned to Diana. "Another emergency?"

"Something about a Miss Jenny?"

"Hmmm," said Maggie.

"Who is Miss Jenny?"

"Are you sure you want to know?" Maggie studied Diana's face so intently that the younger woman felt herself flush. "Well, why not? You're already privy to most of the rest of our secrets. When Ernest comes back inside, tell him I said to take you there." She retreated into her room.

Uncertainly, Diana stared at Maggie Northcote's closed door. No one in this family seemed capable of giving a direct answer to a simple question.

Maggie poked her head back out. "I've rung for Annie. She'll help you dress and go with you."

Prodded into action, Diana went in search of clothing. It was possible Maggie was using her for "research" again, but that concern was overshadowed by her own curiosity. What was Ben up to? She hadn't a doubt in the world that he was trying to hide something from her. Better to discover the worst, she decided, before she became any more involved with the man.

A short time later, Old Ernest settled Diana and Annie under a fur lap robe in the buggy. Blinking sleepily, Annie looked wary. When questioned, she claimed she had no idea who the mysterious "Miss Jenny" might be.

Ernest drove straight into Bangor, never slowing until he brought the horse to a halt in front of a large, white corner house set on a bank in a narrow lot. The pale beams of a gaslight showed Diana that it had a long ell connecting it to a shed and barn, outside of which sat a buckboard.

"That belongs to the Northcotes," Annie said.

Ernest spoke in a laconic drawl, the most garrulous Diana had ever heard him. "Miss Jenny's place. Second best whorehouse in Bangor."

"We shouldn't be here!" Annie grasped Diana's arm and tried to tug her back into the buggy.

Diana shook free. "Come along, Annie," she ordered. "Obviously, Ben does not intend to stay here long. If he did, he'd not have left the horses hitched to the wagon."

Hoping she was right, she marched up a long set of steps leading to a big front door and boldly used the knocker.

The woman who let them in was small and graceful, her hair coiled high on top of her head and a pair of gold bobs in her ears. Instead of the daring, garish costume Diana had expected to see, she wore a simple, tasteful evening gown. Before either of them could speak, a horrendous crash sounded overhead, followed by a shout of anger. The woman turned and ran towards the sound, leaving Diana and Annie to follow.

In spite of her concern for Ben, Diana could not help but be curious about the establishment. The first thing she noticed was that her surroundings were rather shabby. The second was the pervasive smell. Cigar smoke mingled with a variety of strong, clashing perfumes.

Diana passed an empty parlor on the left and a closed door to the right before getting a glimpse of the dining room. Each chair grouped around the table appeared to have a woman's name lettered across the back.

On the upper floor, where the stench of perfume was even stronger, one narrow hallway ran the length of the house. Six doors opened off it on each side. Diana found both Northcote brothers in the second room on the left.

"Joseph!" Annie gasped, just as Ben broke the hold Aaron had on a young man's throat. A woman dressed in nothing but her corset and drawers crouched in a corner, arms held protectively over her head. She was weeping piteously.

"Lord save us!" Annie ran to the gasping Joseph, adding to the confusion by flinging herself into his embrace.

Aaron stood still as a statue, a bewildered look on his face. Slowly, he turned to look at the crying woman. As if in sympathy, tears began to stream down his face. His sobs were more wrenching than hers.

Ben stared at Annie, then caught sight of Diana hovering in

the doorway. "Clear everyone out, Jenny," he ordered in a chilling voice. "Everyone."

"Excitement's over," said the woman who'd admitted them. Her voice was pleasant but firm, and for such a dainty, diminutive person she had an air of command nearly as forceful as Ben's.

Diana took a closer look at her. Jenny was older than she'd first appeared, nearly Maggie's age. In a matter of minutes, she'd herded everyone but Ben and Aaron downstairs and into the kitchen.

"Coffee, Clarissa," Jenny said to a stout woman already there. Then the madam was gone again, taking the sobbing, half-dressed girl with her.

Diana accepted a cup of the hot, strong brew and studied Clarissa over its rim while Annie took Joseph off to the washroom in the adjoining ell to tend to his minor cuts and scrapes. The cook? Another prostitute? Both? "Does Dr. Northcote come here often?" she asked.

Clarissa's amused smile did not reassure Diana in the least. "Seen a lot of him over the years."

Trying not to stare, Diana studied the woman's profile. She had the oddest feeling that she'd met Clarissa before. Now past her prime, Clarissa must once have had a buxom sort of beauty. Suddenly Diana's impression of familiarity jelled. She had seen that face before, or rather a younger version of it. Clarissa had posed for one of Aaron Northcote's paintings.

"You know Aaron, too," she said as Jenny returned to the kitchen. "Will you tell me—"

Jenny cut her off in mid-question. "We don't discuss our gentlemen callers here. Not ever."

Annie reappeared, with Joseph behind her, just in time to hear this exchange. Indignant, she marched right up to the madam and stared her down. "That gentleman caller is mad as a March hare and ought to be locked up before he kills somebody."

"What are you talking about, Annie?" Diana demanded.

"Mr. Aaron's a madman. Everyone knows it."

"Sometimes he hears voices that ain't there," Clarissa said matter-of-factly. "They tell him to do things."

"Lord help us!" Annie gave a squeal. "He's possessed!"

"He's *sick*." As Diana stressed the word, she felt her stomach clench. She'd seen for herself that Aaron not only heard voices but answered them.

What Ben had told her in New York came back to her with haunting poignancy. Those who heard voices, he'd said, were locked up, kept away from all contact with sanity. That, he'd claimed, was the real path to madness, and he'd argued that physicians must search for a better solution, even for those individuals too deranged to be let loose on an unsuspecting community.

"He's dangerous," Annie insisted. "Why else would Dr. Northcote have Joseph watching him?"

"Is that your job, Joseph?" Diana asked the young man. He was a tall, lean, well-muscled fellow with a shock of yellow hair.

"Mostly, mum. At least since Mr. Aaron came back from Philadelphia."

"Don't you mean New York?"

"No, mum. That was later. It was last fall that Mr. Aaron followed his brother to Philadelphia. He got away from me twice after that, too, while Dr. Northcote was away. Gives his old mother fits, he does, him always flitting off somewhere on his own. But it wasn't till he jumped me and tied me up so he could go meet you at the Bangor House that Dr. Northcote insisted on keeping the gate locked."

Diana's heart sank. Something else Ben had kept from her. Aaron had not only been in New York, but Philadelphia, too. Where else? "Was he missing in January?"

"Yes, mum. Don't know where he got to that time. Dr. Northcote never saw him."

"He was in San Francisco," Diana said.

"He never was!" Everyone turned to look at Clarissa, who had uttered the protest.

"How can you be so sure of that?" Diana asked.

Looking as if she regretted the outburst, Clarissa refused to meet Diana's eyes. "Don't like to say how I know, but you take my word for it—Aaron Northcote weren't nowhere near San Francisco anytime in January."

A confused and uneasy silence settled over them all. Before it could be broken, they were joined by the girl from the upstairs room, her tears dried and her lush curves hidden by a loose pink wrapper. "I was wanting a cup of tea," she said in a shy whisper.

"Dr. Northcote needs your help, Joseph." Jenny announced as she followed the young woman into the kitchen. "He's sedated Mr. Aaron and is ready to load him into the wagon." She gave Diana a pointed look. "You'll want to be leaving too, ma'am, if you value your reputation."

Diana and Annie were in the buggy in time to watch Ben settle his brother in the back of the buckboard, then return to the front door where Jenny stood waiting and pass over a handful of bills. As nonchalantly as if she were in her own bedroom, the madam pulled up her skirt and added the money to the sizeable roll already tucked into her garter.

"Take us home, Ernest," Diana ordered.

Once there, she built up the fire in the front parlor and settled in to wait. It was nearly dawn before she heard heavy footsteps in the hallway. With equal parts reluctance and impatience, Diana waylaid Ben at the foot of the stairs. "How is Aaron?"

"I don't know." The agonized expression in his eyes and the defeated slump to his broad shoulders told their own story.

Diana's heart went out to him. "Please, Ben. Talk to me. I want to understand."

"So you can write about it?"

"That was uncalled for. Besides, there was a time when you wanted the plight of the insane publicized."

He stared at her long and hard before he spoke. "You're right. I'm sorry. It's not you I'm angry with but all the so-called experts." He sagged against the carved newel post. "Not one of them understands exactly what it is that causes a person to hear voices, or prevents him from knowing right from wrong. Most doctors simply lock troubled patients away and abandon all hope of a cure."

Diana moved closer in the dimly-lit hallway. They were not quite touching, but their images shared the frame in the mirror that hung at the foot of the staircase. "Most doctors, but not you."

"I don't know what to do for him either. Nothing I've tried yet has helped." His fists clenched at his sides. "But I wouldn't commit an animal to any insane hospital, let alone my own brother. The one here in Maine has 578 patients. There are three physicians to care for them. They desperately need a fourth, and a new building to ease overcrowding, but above all they need to do more than confine victims. You've seen Aaron's paintings, Diana. No matter what anyone thinks of the subject matter, he's a talented artist. Can you imagine what being locked up in an institution would do to him?"

"So you try to keep him a prisoner in his own home."

Watching his face as intently as she was, Diana saw Ben's torment clearly. "It isn't always necessary. There are long periods when he's as normal as anyone . . . any creative artist, anyway." He managed a faint smile. "And even when he's been listening to those damned voices, he's rarely out of control. If he hadn't gotten drunk and decided he had to explain to his last model what her shortcomings were, there'd have been no trouble." He dragged his hands over a face pale with worry. "I shouldn't have brought you here, Diana."

She thought of the crying girl. "You think he's a threat to me?"

"No. He's not a danger to anyone. Not really."

But she could see he was no longer certain of it. "You've wondered if he was the one who attacked me in New York."

"I . . . I've wondered, yes. It doesn't seem likely, and yet . . . ."

She waited, hoping he'd confide in her. She couldn't help him if he didn't trust her with his fears.

"There is a chance my brother was the man in the alley. He might still have been in New York Saturday night, even though I put him on a train north on Friday afternoon."

"Have you asked him when he left New York?"

"He says he can't remember. Then he babbles about his voices and says he just does as they command." Ben hesitated, then added, "He was in Philadelphia when that woman was murdered."

She heard the torment in his voice, but she knew something he did not. "Aaron wasn't in San Francisco when the other woman died."

"How can you possibly know that?"

She told him what Clarissa had said.

"The word of a whore?"

"She had no reason to lie. I don't believe Aaron is a murderer, Ben, or that he's any threat to me." She managed a crooked smile. "Not even you can think of a way he could have been stranded on the train with us and contrived to push me off."

"I should not have brought you here," he said again.

She glared at him, wondering why he had, especially since he'd avoided her once she'd moved into his house. After all, she was not some simpering virgin whose virtue had to be guarded. She was a widow. She'd expected him to visit her bedroom, at least to talk. She'd not have been averse to more. She opened her mouth to demand answers, then closed it again. Ben was swaying with exhaustion. This was not the time to take him to task for behaving like a gentleman towards a guest in his home.

"You need sleep."

He blinked and managed to focus on her face. "So do you."

♋

He'd handled things badly, Ben thought for the hundredth time as he sat by the window in his bedroom and watched dawn break. He hadn't slept.

What if it turned out that Aaron had killed those women? What if he'd killed others? What if he tried again? What if he tried to kill Diana?

Ben had been the one who'd prevented the authorities from locking his brother away. He'd been certain he knew the worst that Aaron was capable of when he was not in his right mind. But what if he was wrong?

Too restless to stay still, he began to pace. He needed sleep, but there was no sense in lying down. His racing mind would keep him awake.

When Diana had believed he had a darker side to his personality, a side which wrote horror stories, she'd shied away from him. Ben found it far too easy to imagine her disgust if she learned the terrible secret he was still keeping from her.

He scrubbed his hands over his face, despair adding to his burdens. The truth haunted him every time he looked into his brother's eyes, but he could not share it with anyone, not even Diana. Not now. Maybe not ever.

And if it turned out that Aaron was a murderer, he could not expect her to forgive him.

෨෬

It was late morning before Diana woke. No one was in the breakfast room. She assumed Maggie was writing and Ben had gone to his office. With a sigh, she picked up the newspaper.

She'd just turned to the ads, noting with amazement that oranges all the way from Florida were available at Thompson and Kellogg's in West Market Square, when Ben appeared in the doorway. From his haggard look, she guessed he'd slept as badly as she had. Or perhaps he had not slept at all.

"Do you still want to go into town?"

She forced a smile. "I'd like to send a wire to Horatio Foxe before he decides I've been kidnapped."

As he served himself ham from the sideboard, she could not help noticing that he seemed bigger. Bulkier. "What on earth are you wearing?"

"I have a pair of chamois skin drawers under my trousers for extra protection from the cold. When I got up, I planned to walk to my office. I keep a sleigh in town. That will leave the buggy for you. To take you to a hotel. Or to the train station." He kept his back to her. "I don't want you to go, but—"

"I'm not going anywhere. Not yet." Bad as the night had been, this was a new day. With the sunrise, Diana's natural optimism had returned. She'd fallen in love with this man and she believed he loved her in return. There had to be a way to find happiness together.

Neither of them said anything for a few minutes. He brought his plate to the table and began to eat. She sipped her coffee and thought about a dozen things at once. No topic seemed safe to broach.

"How is Aaron this morning?"

"Chipper." Ben's clipped reply discouraged discussion but Diana persisted.

"Back to himself, you mean?"

"Whatever that is, yes."

"Well enough for you to leave his side, obviously." There was a hint of asperity in her tone, too.

"I do have other patients. A good many of them seem to have put off seeing a doctor until I returned from my travels."

"I've noticed how busy you've been."

He paused in the act of slicing ham to give her a sharp look. "Did you think I was avoiding you?"

"The idea occurred to me, but I dismissed it. Right now I suspect you're baiting me, hoping I'll give up and go away. I don't intend to. Not until I can send my piece on Damon Bathory to Horatio Foxe."

She knew at once that had been the wrong thing to say. Ben's face closed up, shielding his thoughts. He put down his coffee cup with a thump and stood.

"I need to get to the office."

"I'll go with you. Who knows? Perhaps I can be of some help to you."

His laugh was deliberately rude. "I doubt you're cut out to be a nurse, Diana. Medicine is not a pretty profession, and when I have to go out to see patients, it's no pleasant sleigh ride."

"I'll have you know that one of my distant ancestors, back in England in the sixteenth century, was a healer as well as a famous herbalist. She wrote a book to warn housewives which plants could be poisonous if eaten."

"Herbalist? Or witch?" The sardonic tone was back, the one she'd heard him use in New York. "Perhaps she knew the Blood Countess," he added. "Elizabeth Bathory lived in the sixteenth century, too."

"Not unless your famous ancestor visited England. And the proper term for an herbalist who also heals is 'cunning woman.'"

"Ah. Well, you are that, Diana."

Apparently resigned to her company, Ben waited while Diana got her coat, then escorted her to what he called "the doctor's wagon," a four-wheeled buggy painted black with green trim and silver markings. It had a folding top that offered some small protection from the biting cold. In the back a special compartment held medical supplies, with room for Ben's brown leather satchel.

"You carry that doctor's bag everywhere," Diana remarked. "What's inside?"

"Splints and forceps, rolls of homemade bandages, a large piece of rubber sheeting, and a pair of white muslin obstetrical pants to use during deliveries, among other things."

"Who wears the pants," she asked, "the doctor or the patient?"

He laughed, as she'd hoped he would, and relaxed a little. "The mother-to-be."

"And what's in this box?" She indicated a black case in the back.

"See for yourself." He flipped it open, revealing rows of small, corked bottles, all carefully labeled. They contained medications as diverse as quinine and ipecac, digitalis and spirits of ammonia, ground *cannabis sativa* and calomel.

Diana picked one at random. "What is betony used for?"

"It is a popular cure-all." He clucked to the horse. "It's even said to cure insanity if boiled in a quart of strong ale and drunk."

His words came out as huge white puffs, quick-frozen in the frigid air. Diana shivered and tugged the fur collar of her coat up to shield her cold cheeks. For once even Ben wore a hat—a fur cap with earflaps—together with a heavy wolfskin coat and fleece-lined gloves.

When they reached the downtown area, Ben abandoned talk of a medical nature to take on the role of tour guide. "Over there is C. L. Dakin's art store." He pointed to the oversized oil painting in the window. "That's supposed to show the 1605 discovery of Monhegan."

"Does Aaron show his work locally?"

Ben nodded. "The Bangor Art Association has a gallery. They also sponsor lectures at the Bangor Opera House." He nodded towards that impressive-looking building. "Six years ago, Oscar Wilde visited Bangor at their invitation. Before he spoke, he visited the gallery and singled out one of Aaron's paintings for praise."

Diana did not doubt Ben's word, but she found it difficult to imagine the effete Oscar Wilde, that self-styled "apostle of aestheticism," prancing along Bangor's elm-lined streets in his customary black velvet knickers and silk stockings, his trademark lily in one hand and an oversized boutonniere in his lapel. "Did he scandalize the sober residents of Bangor?" she asked.

"They thought him a trifle eccentric."

They made one stop before Ben's office, to send Diana's telegram to Horatio Foxe. Diana had only to put him off until Monday, when Maggie planned to travel to Boston in order to tell her publisher face to face that she was going to announce her identity as Damon Bathory. When she'd broken the news to a few close friends, in confidence, she'd been gratified by their response. Although they'd been shocked, she'd told Diana, they'd not been appalled.

The message Diana sent was brief: "B NOT MAN IN ALLEY. PLEASE APPROVE EXPENSE OF EXCLUSIVE." She signed it and included her current address, in care of Dr. Benjamin Northcote.

Ben pointed out more landmarks when they resumed their journey. Just north of Norumbega Hall and the Windsor Hotel, he turned right into Spring Street and brought the buggy to a halt in front of a small, plain wooden house. His office was in a neighborhood that contained a mixture of boarding houses, stores, homes, and restaurants. It was also quite close to Miss Jenny's establishment.

They needed to talk about Miss Jenny, among other things, but once again Diana bit back confrontational questions. The truce between them was fragile this morning. She felt as if she were treading on eggshells.

Ben escorted Diana through a door marked "Office" and into a simply furnished waiting room. It was empty when they arrived but did not remain so long. They hadn't even reached the adjoining surgery before a man rushed in carrying a young girl in his arms. The child was whimpering pitifully and the cause was obvious— her left arm was swollen to twice its normal size.

"In here," Ben instructed, indicating the surgery.

Diana followed them. The girl was a toddler no more than

two years old. Although Diana was sure her pain had not decreased, her cries grew weaker as her strength, perhaps even her will to live, was drained away by prolonged suffering.

Ben stripped off his coat and hat, tossing them into a corner as he bent to examine the arm. "An abscess. It will have to be lanced at once."

The child's father went white. Diana took his arm and steered him firmly back to the outer room. "Wait here," she ordered and returned to the surgery, shedding her own outerwear as she went.

Ben was already administering anesthetic. Diana wrinkled her nose as she caught a whiff of the pungent vapor.

"You'd better leave. There's worse to come."

Diana braced herself. As soon as the child was asleep, he made the first incision. When pus shot up in an arc, foul looking and noisome, Diana found a clean cloth and wiped up the mess, but she soon realized that it was the infected area that most needed attention. Ben had to stop after each discharge to clean the incision so that he could see what he was doing. Without a word, Diana took over that part of the job. Through seemingly endless repetitions of the task, she persevered, until at last the operation was over.

Ben regarded her with an unfathomable expression as he secured the bandages.

"Did I do something wrong?" she asked.

He cleared his throat and the warmth that came into his eyes made her knees weak. "No. Some professional nurses would have been too queasy to assist me in a case like this one. You did well."

"I'm only squeamish when it comes to reading horror stories," she quipped.

Ben's voice was gruff. "Go out and tell that father his little girl will recover. And since you're here, you may as well see what the next emergency is."

CHAPTER FIFTEEN

ℰᏩᏣ

Ben had locked himself in his basement laboratory by the time Diana came down to breakfast on Saturday. He'd instructed the servants that he was not to be disturbed.

"He does this now and again." Maggie pursed her lips. "Gives me an idea. What if a mad scientist . . . ." Her voice trailed off and a moment later she departed for her inner sanctum.

Diana ate, then ventured outside. The dry, chilly air invigorated her. It was a perfect day to walk and her first stop was the carriage house.

"He's painting, mum," Joseph told her when she asked after Aaron. "He won't like it if he's disturbed."

"He's himself again, then?"

"Oh, yes, mum. Right as rain."

After a moment's consideration, Diana decided to walk into town. Grudgingly, Ernest relinquished a spare key to the gate, so she could let herself out and in again.

Her main purpose was to find out if Horatio Foxe had replied to her telegram, but she stopped first at the Bangor House for lunch. The place was crowded. As she waited to be seated, a handsome lithographic folder caught her eye, a familiar flyer used for advertising purposes.

With a sense of inevitability, Diana took a closer look. She had not been mistaken. A portrait of Nathan Todd in his role in *The Duchess of Calabria* graced the front. Inside were views of the principal scenes from the play. Todd's Touring Thespians were coming to Bangor.

Belatedly, Diana realized she'd known that. Jerusha had mentioned it on the train. With all that had happened after, it had completely slipped her mind. The company, she now saw, would give six performances at the Bangor Opera House, starting on Monday night. That meant they'd probably arrive sometime on Sunday—tomorrow.

Her first instinct was to be pleased that she'd soon see old friends again. Her next thought was that explaining her presence would involve revealing the truth about Damon Bathory. Their timing could not have been worse. Maggie could not go to Boston to meet with her publisher until Monday. If the news leaked . . .

She'd have to avoid the actors, Diana decided. At least until after her story broke.

When she'd enjoyed a fine meal and done a bit of window shopping, Diana went at last to the Western Union office. The reply she'd expected had arrived, but Foxe's message stunned her. A third female reporter had been murdered in an alley, this time in Los Angeles. Another critic, like the first two, and like them she'd been killed on the same Saturday night Damon Bathory concluded his visit to her city.

Diana gave no credence to the idea that Ben had murdered any of those women, although it was obvious Foxe still thought so. However, the news did send her scurrying back to the Northcote mansion. Now that there were three cases, coincidence could no longer explain them away. It seemed likely that the killer was a member of some touring theatrical troupe or act, and that the same person might, after all, have been responsible for the attack on her in New York.

As she trudged up and down the hilly landscape of Bangor, her mind raced. Fragmented memories chased after her—a sound behind her, a tug on the back of Ben's cloak, a blow to the head. If her fall from the train had been no accident, then it followed that the troupe in question was Toddy's. That meant someone she knew had killed those three reviewers and had tried, twice, to kill her.

She wanted Ben, wanted him to hold her close and tell her that it would all be all right, that he'd keep her safe. Ben, however, did not emerge from his lab for supper. Likewise, Maggie was too absorbed in her new project to stop and eat. Diana dined in solitary splendor and went to bed that night in a troubled frame of mind. First thing in the morning, she promised herself, she would insist on talking to Ben. If he put her off again, she'd do the sensible thing and take the first train back to New York.

Diana awoke some time later to the groggy notion that Cedric the cat was perched on the end of her bed, his furry bulk pressing against her feet. Only gradually did she realize that the steady breathing was that of a much larger creature.

Still only half awake, she tried to convince herself that the distinctive odor tickling her nostrils was carbolic, the scent of the doctor, but it was not. The smell, unmistakably, was turpentine, the hallmark of the painter.

"I know you're awake," Aaron said. "You might as well talk to me."

"What do you want me to say?" She hugged the covers tightly to her chest as she sat up and reached for the oil lamp on the bedside table.

The first flicker of light, from the match she struck to ignite the wick, showed her that Aaron's face wore a broad, satisfied smile. In fact, he looked like a delighted little boy who'd just gotten away with something. Or a child who'd made a magnificent discovery all by himself. His words, even when spoken in a decidedly adult male voice, reinforced the juvenile image.

"I've had a marvelous idea." He slid up the bed until his hips were aligned with hers and they were sitting face to face. He seemed very large, very solid. If he chose to attack, she'd have little chance of warding him off.

"What idea?" In spite of her best effort, her voice shook a little. "What is it that couldn't wait until morning?"

Puzzlement flickered briefly across his features, as if he had not realized the time. He didn't seem to understand the implications of being in her bedroom, nor did he appear to be affected by glimpses of her in her nightdress.

"What idea?" Diana repeated.

The childlike delight returned as he seized both her hands. "I know what's been missing from my paintings. I understand at last. I must paint you."

"Aaron, we've discussed this before—"

"No. You don't understand. From now on I must paint only one woman. Only you, Diana. You will be more than my model, you will be my inspiration."

His intensity rattled her. For a moment all she could think of was that Ben would be upset. "I won't take my clothes off for you," she blurted.

"No need. It is your face that haunts me. Imagination will provide the rest of the body. A mermaid's tail, and—" He broke off at a faint noise just outside her door.

"Joseph is trying to sneak up on us." Aaron giggled, a high, outlandish sound Diana found disconcerting. Without another word, he left the room. A moment later Diana heard two sets of footsteps moving away.

℘℘℘

Good morning, my dear," Maggie greeted Diana at breakfast. From her cheery demeanor, the new story had progressed. "Ben was called out again last night, shortly after you retired, I believe. I expect he went straight to the office afterward. Sunday is a doctor's busiest day. Patients come into town for church and stop to have their minor ailments tended before they return home. Saves them an extra trip, you see."

All Diana saw was that, once again, she'd missed her chance to talk to Ben. He was busy, that was true, but he also seemed to go out of his way to avoid her. She buttered a roll and chewed thoughtfully. Should she board that train to New York?

"What church do you attend?" she asked her hostess.

"Witches," Maggie declared in lofty tones, "do not belong to any organized religion."

"Ah." Diana buttered a second roll, lowering her head over the task to hide her smile.

There were times when Maggie's eccentricities did amuse her. Diana longed to accept Ben's contention that his mother was harmless. *Have a care,* she cautioned herself, and deliberately called up memories of Evan Spaulding. Being wrong had consequences. She must take her time and ask the right questions.

"I suppose you want to attend services at some house of worship," Maggie said. "It is Palm Sunday, after all. Well, you have your pick of churches in Bangor. There's First Methodist just off Essex Street, First Baptist on Harlow, Episcopal on French Street, and Hammond Street Congregational." Maggie toyed with the eggs on her plate. The runny yellow yolks looked garish against the delicate blue and white willow pattern. "Annie has already left for St. John's. A pity you were not up early enough to go with her."

"I'm not Catholic."

Years on the road with Todd's Touring Thespians had weaned Diana away from regular worship services. Actors customarily slept late on Sundays or were traveling to the next stand on that day. The pretext of going to church, however, would give her an hour or two of freedom to do as she wished.

"I believe," she said, "that I will go to the Baptist church." The location was admirably suited to her real plan.

A short time later, Ernest dropped her off in front of a sturdy brick structure. "I'll walk to Dr. Northcote's office after services," she told him, then watched the buggy drive away. As soon as it was out of sight, she set out in the same direction on foot, moving at a brisk pace in spite of the hilly terrain. She darted past the turn to Ben's office. The house she sought was not far beyond.

She knocked at the kitchen door this time, although she suspected that all the gossiping old biddies who might spread word of a "lady" visiting Miss Jenny's place would be in church at this hour. "Are you alone?" she asked when Clarissa opened it. "I need to speak with you. In private."

"Ask questions, you mean." Clarissa's face wore a sly look as she motioned Diana through the door. "I hear tell you work for one of them big New York newspapers."

"That's true." Diana wondered how she'd found out. Aaron, she supposed. "I had to earn my own living after my husband died."

"Same as me," Clarissa said.

Diana did not correct any assumptions Clarissa might be making. She wanted the older woman's cooperation. "Can we talk here? I don't want to get you in trouble with Miss Jenny."

"She's gone for her usual Sunday drive, but you're right. She'd turn me out if she caught me telling tales out of school. Real particular, Miss Jenny is, about keeping information on her clients what you might call confidential. She says we're bound to respect their privacy, just like their doctors and their lawyers."

"An admirable philosophy." Diana's tone was dry. "How long do we have before she comes back?"

"Tell you what. If she turns up while you're still here, we'll just let her think you're here for the same reason other respectable women come. Got a dollar?"

Puzzled but game, Diana produced four quarters. Foxe had been generous. She'd reimbursed Ben, and paid Maggie's dressmaker for all but the one gown Maggie insisted was a gift, and still had more than enough money for a train ticket back to New York.

Clarissa handed over a small package wrapped in brown paper. Anxious to get on with her questioning, Diana tucked it into her bag and began, "You've known Mr. Aaron a long time, haven't you, Clarissa? He even put you in one of his paintings."

With a glance down at her substantial body, Clarissa placed one hand under each breast and hefted them. "Got these immortalized in their prime," she said with considerable pride. "Mr. Aaron gave me a sketch to keep for myself, too."

"So you two were . . . friends?"

Clarissa regarded her with suspicion. "You won't do nothing to hurt Mr. Aaron?"

"I have only his best interests at heart. I think he may have a great future as an artist, if he's allowed to continue to paint."

"Sit down," Clarissa invited, reaching for the coffee pot keeping warm on the back of the woodstove. "Take off your coat. If you promise me you won't let on to Miss Jenny who told you any of this, I'll answer your questions."

"Fair enough. When did you first meet Aaron?"

"Must have been seven or eight years ago now," Clarissa said. "I was just a skinny young thing then, new to the game. The way I heard it, old Mr. Northcote, Mr. Ben and Mr. Aaron's father, brought both them boys here when they was barely into long pants, but that was a long time afore I come here."

Diana sipped her coffee, telling herself that she shouldn't be shocked. But this was Ben Clarissa was talking about. She didn't like to think of him gaining his first experience of women in Jenny's whorehouse. "Let's focus on Aaron," she said. "Tell me what you know first-hand about him."

"Well, he's always been a strange one," Clarissa admitted. "Has these funny spells when he'll start to talk to thin air. Communin' with his muse, he calls it. Sometimes. Others he just acts like he's forgot where he is. One time he walked right out on me, like he didn't see me there on the bed, all ready and waiting."

"What happened the other night?"

"I expect he's got a new model." Clarissa met Diana's eyes across the kitchen table. "Seen it happen before. First he flatters a girl into posing for him. Then he remembers she's a whore. You probably think whores don't have feelings, but we do. Poor Flora was in tears because of what he said to her and she wasn't the first he made cry."

"Did he ever strike one of you? Pull a knife?"

"Oh, no! He's not violent."

"But the other night—"

"Mr. Aaron never hurts any of the girls." Clarissa cut in. "Never said he didn't break a few bits of crockery. When he gets going, he shouts, too. What with Flora carrying on, making a fuss because Mr. Aaron told her she was too ugly to model for him anymore— ugly inside, he told her—Miss Jenny sent for Dr. Northcote."

"Does that happen often? Mr. Aaron coming here and getting upset, I mean. And does Dr. Northcote always come rescue his brother?"

"The last time Mr. Aaron caused a row, last summer that was, a neighbor sent for the marshal, and he told Dr. Northcote that he'd lock Mr. Aaron up if he disturbed the peace again. So Dr Northcote, he asked Miss Jenny special to send for him first. Then he went away, a'course. But we scarce saw Mr. Aaron all the while Dr. Northcote was gone, so it didn't matter."

Clarissa stared out the window, watching a robin in the back yard. Diana waited, hoping she'd volunteer more. After a moment her patience was rewarded.

"He looks out for his own, Dr. Northcote does, no matter what. Why, I remember hearing how once, back when Dr. Northcote was first setting up his practice, before I knew either of them, that it was him Mr. Aaron was calling names. They had one bang-up fist fight, right here in this house. Ended up with Mr. Aaron knocked out cold. Dr. Northcote was some broke up about that. Never meant to hit him so hard, he said."

The idea that Ben, not Aaron, had been the violent one gave Diana pause.

"Dr. Northcote thinks Aaron might have followed him when he left Bangor last fall, and caused some trouble in some of the places he visited. Aaron won't say where he was. He claims he can't remember. You said he couldn't have been in San Francisco in January. How can you be so sure of that, Clarissa? If would mean a lot to Dr. Northcote to have proof his brother was right here in Bangor."

"You promise you won't let on to Miss Jenny it was me that told you?"

"I swear it."

Clarissa finished her coffee, plainly troubled by the prospect of incurring her employer's wrath. At last, however, she lowered the cup and gave Diana a conspiratorial wink. "He was at the doctor's office. Upstairs over the surgery. All through the middle part of January."

"You're certain?"

"Course I'm certain. Sometimes he has these spells where he can't abide other people at all. That Mrs. Northcote, Mr. Aaron's mother, she's not the easiest person to live with."

Although Diana took Clarissa's point, she couldn't help wondering how the woman had learned of Aaron's whereabouts. "If he didn't want company—"

"I do the housekeeping at Dr. Northcote's office, so I have a key. I went around there, on the eighth of January it was. I remember, because it was Madam Yvonne's birthday on the seventh. She's one of Miss Jenny's competitors and she always throws herself a big party, just to pull customers away from us. Anyway, there was Mr. Aaron, holed up in the little room under the eaves."

"Painting?"

"Not that I saw. Just hiding out. Anyway, he made me promise him that I wouldn't tell anyone where he was, and I've kept that promise. Until now."

If Aaron had been in Bangor on the eighth, there was no way he could have reached San Francisco by the ninth.

Clarissa's face wore an indulgent smile. "Once I knew he was there, I made sure he ate right. He didn't like me fussing, but I just ignored his complaints. Men need looking after, you know. They just hate like the dickens to admit it."

When Diana left Miss Jenny's she had only a short distance to walk to reach Ben's office. Ernest was waiting for her there. "Dr. Northcote's been called out again," he told her. "Said I was to take you home."

"The man is entirely too dedicated to his patients," Diana muttered.

Ernest took offense. "Lot of 'em waited till he come back for doctoring. Didn't trust the young whippersnapper he asked to cover his practice for him."

Without giving her time to reply, Ernest went to hitch the horse to the buggy. Left alone, Diana studied the neat, orderly room in which those patients waited for Ben to see them. It was impeccably clean, speaking well of Clarissa's abilities as a housekeeper.

Belatedly, she remembered the small packet Clarissa had sold her, and a suspicion of what it held sent heat rushing into her face. First checking to make sure no one would walk in while she examined it, she tore the paper and looked inside. As she'd guessed, it contained a sponge and a slip of paper with instructions for using it to prevent pregnancy. Hastily rewrapping the contents, she stuffed the packet back into her bag.

Diana intended to go straight to her own room when she

returned to the house, but as soon as she entered, she heard voices in the front parlor. Both were familiar. With a sinking heart, she went to join Maggie and her guest.

"Why look, Mrs. Northcote!" Nathan Todd exclaimed when Diana appeared at the door. "It is that famous New York reviewer, the one who so dislikes your stories."

Toddy knew Maggie had written them? Astonished, Diana struggled to make sense of this new development. When they'd been stranded on the train, Ben had been posing as Damon Bathory. How could Toddy have discovered his real name, let alone un-masked Maggie as the true author of Damon Bathory's terrifying tales?

"How long have you known?" she demanded.

His burst of good-natured laughter surprised her. "Half an hour," he said. He glanced at his pocket watch and grinned. "Give or take a few minutes."

"The better question is *how* he knew." Maggie occupied the rococo sofa, Cedric ensconced on her lap. "It seems the word is out. Your friend arrived on the morning train and heard all about me at the depot."

On leaden feet, Diana came the rest of the way into the room. "What, precisely, did you hear?"

"Two men talking about the identity of Damon Bathory. Their source seemed to be Mrs. Northcote herself."

"Some of my friends appear to lack a certain discretion," Maggie said with an apologetic smile, but she didn't seem unduly concerned that the cat was out of the bag.

Silently, Diana swore. She'd have to send her story about Maggie to New York this afternoon and pray some other newspaper had not already got wind of the news. It would be touch and go whether Maggie had time to warn her publisher before the item was picked up by the Boston papers.

"How did you know I was here?" Diana asked Toddy.

"Oh, I told him about you," Maggie admitted. "Why not? It

was obvious he knew you and equally clear he's a fine fellow. After all, he came here to offer me a splendid business opportunity."

"Business?" With every bit of new information she gained, Diana grew more confused. She sank wearily into a chair and waited for the next revelation.

"Congratulate me, Diana," Toddy said. "I am to dramatize the works of Damon Bathory."

"I should congratulate Mrs. Northcote." Diana turned her head to address Ben's mother. "You are fortunate Mr. Todd bothered to ask permission, Maggie. It's all too common a theatrical practice to take plot, characters, even dialogue, directly from a novel without troubling to get the permission of the novelist."

"I had no idea." Maggie's sharp eyes, as they pinioned Toddy, said differently. All at once, Diana saw this development as Maggie must. Ben's mother had been worried that her upcoming meeting with her publisher would not go well. Here, presented on a silver platter, was an alternate means of reaching an audience.

"It's all the fuss over that unauthorized dramatization of H. Rider Haggard's *She,*" Toddy complained. "It has turned into a major plagiarism case in the courts. Smart money says unscrupulous playwrights are due for a reckoning. They're going to be brought to account for their sins." He shrugged. "I thought it wise to avoid litigation."

Maggie nodded sagely. "I knew you were trustworthy. I have a sense about people." She stroked Cedric lovingly. "Cats have the same ability. Those they like are invariably worthy of their affection. I was a cat myself in another life." She paused to let that statement garner its proper reaction, then spoke to Diana. "I am sure you two have things to say to each other. Do not go upsetting this lovely man, my dear. I envision a brilliant future on the stage for my characters."

With Cedric draped over one shoulder, she exited the parlor. Toddy rose politely and stood staring after her, mustaches quivering as he tried to quell his laughter, but all trace of amusement vanished when he shifted his attention to Diana.

"Well, my dear, I have a bone to pick with you." He stalked towards her, a determined gleam in his eyes.

For one disconcerting moment, Diana imagined that she was back in that alley in New York. She laughed nervously when Toddy, seeing her reaction, backed off, giving her a puzzled look. "Why are you cowering? You never cower."

Stiffening her spine, she sat up straight. It had not been Nathan Todd who attacked her. He was too heavy-set. Charles Underly? Perhaps. Or Billy Sims. But not Toddy. Besides, he had no motive. She had never criticized his acting in print.

"What bone do you have to pick?" She was pleased to discover her voice was steady.

"It's about what you wrote in last Wednesday's column."

"What are you talking about? I haven't written a word for 'Today's Tidbits' since I left New York."

"Someone has."

"Horatio Foxe." She should have known.

"Your editor?"

"Yes. The same one who added gossip to my column once before."

"Confound it, Diana! We thought you'd returned to New York after the storm. Do you mean to tell me you've been here all along?"

"I've been working on a story about Damon Bathory."

"But . . . but everyone thinks you've continued to write your reviews." He grimaced. "Well, that explains one thing. Last Wednesday's column was a selection of comments from previous pieces . . . the worst of the worst, including your comments about the quality of the acting in *The Duchess of Calabria.*"

"I'm sorry, Toddy. I'd have stopped him if I'd known."

"Lavinia was very upset."

"I imagine she was." And if Lavinia had been upset, so had Toddy.

"You can make it up to her. All you have to do is write a new, favorable review and get it into the local paper."

"But, Toddy," she said gently, "I expressed my honest opinion about her acting in the first place. I can hardly reverse myself without lying."

"What's wrong with lying?"

Diana thought about his words for a moment. If she was right, if someone in Toddy's company was a killer, then she might be able to provoke him into another attack by writing a new review. She hoped she could. Finding the real killer was the only way to be sure Horatio Foxe did not make accusations against Ben.

"Miss Ross's interpretations of her roles are startling," she said, composing aloud. If she did write a new review, she could make amends to Lavinia at the same time. "One cannot help but compare her performance to those of some of the greatest actresses of our time. How's that?" As long as she did not say just how badly Lavinia's performance would compare, she was not lying, and the ingenue could take the words any way she liked.

Toddy beamed at her. "Excellent. Can you write something similar about Charles?"

"No."

In fact, she intended to be even more brutally critical of his performance and that of Billy Sims. They were now her primary suspects. Remembering the evil look Underly had given her on the train, she shivered. If his eyes had shot real daggers, she'd be dead right now.

"You know, Toddy," she ventured, "it would be no great loss to the company if you dispensed with Charles Underly's services."

"I'd sooner let Sims go," Toddy said. "You were right in your assessment of his acting ability. A cigar store Indian displays more emotion on the stage. Tell you what. Don't mention Sims at all in your new review. Just add a few lines of praise for Underly and we'll call it square."

"I cannot make the entire cast sound like geniuses on the stage. Bangor may not be New York, but the theatergoers here aren't stupid." She grinned suddenly. "They have seen all kinds of performers at their Opera House, even Oscar Wilde."

೮೧೪

Ben came home tired. He listened without comment to Diana's account of what she and his mother had been up to since he'd last seen them. All the while emotions roiled and bubbled inside him like volcanic lava about to erupt.

"I don't know which infuriates me more," he said in a voice as tight as the knot inside his chest, "Mother blithely handing over stage rights to her stories, or you spending time alone with a man you've now decided could have murdered three women and attempted to dispose of you."

"I don't think Toddy killed anyone. He was not the man in the alley."

All that prevented Ben from exploding was his mother's arrival on the scene.

"What are the two of you talking about?" she asked from the doorway. "I really think, Ben dear, that one of you had best tell me what's been going on. I haven't signed anything yet, you know. I can change my mind if this Todd fellow is unreliable."

She'd clearly overheard too much to be put off with less than the truth. Resigned, Ben gave her a terse summary of the few facts they knew about three murders in Philadelphia, Los Angeles, and San Francisco. Then he told her about the attack on Diana and her "accident" on the train. Finally he explained Horatio Foxe's theory and offered up Diana's alternative—that someone from Todd's Touring Thespians was a murderer.

"To prevent my editor from accusing Ben of the crimes, I propose to find evidence against Charles Underly," Diana said, when Ben stopped speaking. "I am certain he's the guilty one. Unless it's Billy Sims."

"My son was gone on all three of those dates, and while you

were in New York City." The color had drained out of Maggie Northcote's face. Belatedly, she had realized what Aaron's absences could signify.

"No." Diana gave the other woman's forearm a comforting squeeze. "Aaron was in Bangor when the women in California were killed. I talked to someone who saw him here in January."

Her expression cleared. "Well, then, there's nothing to worry about." With a lightning-swift shift of mood, she turned to Ben. "Do you think having a suspected murderer in a lead role of a dramatization of one of my stories would attract a bigger audience?"

"If someone in Todd's troupe is guilty," Ben snapped, "then Diana is in mortal danger." Their apparent unconcern drove him over the edge. He grasped Diana by the shoulders and fixed her with a hard stare, wishing he did have the skill to hypnotize her into obedience. "Go back to New York. Take your story on Damon Bathory to Foxe in person."

"I sent in my story about an hour after Toddy left, and told Foxe that a bigger story will follow after I trick the killer into confessing."

"Damnation, Diana!"

"We could lock him in the crypt till he talks," Maggie suggested. "The moon will be at the full two days from now. That should help."

They both ignored her. Frustrated, Ben read Diana's determination in her eyes. She meant to go on as she'd begun. "What mad plan have you concocted?"

"It is perfectly logical," she assured him. "I've asked Horatio Foxe to print a piece advising readers that I am close to tracking down a murderer. I've told him exactly what to say. He'll follow my instructions, if only because he knows some other newspaper will pick up the story off the Associated Press wire if he doesn't. As soon as a copy of the *Intelligencer* reaches Bangor—Wednesday by my reckoning—I'll make sure it is delivered to the hotel where the company is staying. They'll all read it, and the killer will conclude that I'm staying on in Bangor in order to accuse him. He'll think I know he is a member of Todd's company."

The flaw in her logic seemed glaring to Ben. "And why, precisely, does he think you've delayed going to the authorities? What kind of fool uncovers a killer's identity and doesn't go straight to the police?"

Diana huffed at him. "He'll think I'm waiting for Foxe, or some other editor, to agree to my price for the story." She sent him a brilliant smile. "Trust me, Ben. Our killer already has a low opinion of women who review plays for a living. He'll have no difficulty believing I'm motivated by greed."

"Damnation, Diana! I should have kept you locked up."

"How else can he be caught?" Ben's mother asked in what, for her, was a reasonable tone. "And how else can we prevent a scandal?"

"You thrive on scandal, Mother."

"Yes, but you would not."

"So you expect me to let Diana offer herself as bait?"

"Family loyalty demands it, Ben," his mother said, and swept out of the room.

"Diana, think!" Ben pleaded.

"I have. This will work. I'll be in no danger. Come and have supper, Ben. You'll feel better when you've eaten something." In a fair imitation of Maggie Northcote at her most flamboyant, Diana followed after the older woman.

Food, however, did not improve Ben's mood. No matter how he argued against Diana's plan, she would not change her mind. She informed him it was too late to stop it now, then abruptly changed the subject. "I had a visit from Aaron last night."

That succeeded in distracting him. Her casual announcement nearly had him bolting from his chair to confront his brother. The red haze before his eyes cleared only when Diana and his mother both grabbed hold of him.

Speaking quickly, lest he break away, Diana recounted everything that had passed between herself and Aaron.

"Joseph is next to useless," Ben muttered.

"Say rather that Aaron is clever." Diana loosened her grip, then smoothed her fingers over the back of his hand.

How clever? Ben wondered. Clever enough to have killed three women without getting caught? As much as he wanted to believe Diana's theory, in spite of the danger she'd be in if she were right, he thought it just as likely that Aaron was guilty. Clarissa would not hesitate to lie for him.

And if his brother had murdered those women? What then?

Family loyalty, as his mother had reminded him, made demands. In this case the demand seemed to be that he choose between his brother's welfare and that of the woman he loved.

CHAPTER SIXTEEN

∞⟩⟨∞

On Monday, shortly after Ben left the house to take Maggie to the depot to catch the Maine Central's morning train to Boston, Diana received a note from Jerusha Fildale.

This was exactly what she needed, Diana decided, and called for Annie. "Is there a pair of ice skates in the house?" she asked when the maid appeared. "This is an invitation to go skating on the river." She paused to glance out the window. The weather appeared to be warmer than it had been. It looked quite pleasant. *"The Whig and Courier* says the river is open below Orrington, but I don't know where Orrington is."

"To the south, mum. Some places downriver, the tidewaters keep the channel open all winter. But the ice should hold solid enough here. They wager on it, you see, and most folks are sayin' how it'll be weeks yet till ice out."

"And skates?" Jerusha had her own. She brought them with her on winter tours.

"Mrs. Northcote has a pair. Very fine they are, too, with ankle supports and shiny buckles and nickel-plated steel runners. I'll fetch them."

While she waited for Annie to return, Diana tapped the note

against her chin. This outing would give her the chance to take Jerusha into her confidence. The actress might have noticed something useful about her colleagues' behavior. More than that, she might be able to see Diana's situation more clearly. Jerusha had never hesitated to offer romantic advice before. Diana doubted that she would this time. And if Jerusha thought Diana should get away from the Northcotes, she would help her do so.

When Diana set out a short time later she was not surprised to find the gates locked. Using the extra key Old Ernest had given her, she let herself through and set off at a brisk pace towards downtown Bangor. Before meeting Jerusha, she made one stop, at the new Western Union Telegraph Company office, located directly below the old one. By now the employees knew her on sight.

"Fine place, is it not, Mrs. Spaulding?" one of them greeted her from behind a gleaming walnut counter. It divided the business room, where completed telegram blanks were received from customers, from the operating room. In the latter, banks of instrument tables were loaded down with quadruplex repeaters, typewriters, and other equipment.

"Indeed it is, Henry."

Spacious and well lit, the office had sufficient staff to keep it humming twenty-four hours a day, seven days a week. Each telegrapher worked in his or her own cubicle among the tables, separated by a foot-high, sound-deadening glass and wood partition. At the moment, only a few were busy. One woman who was not, worked at her knitting while she waited to send or receive Morse Code. George, the press operator, played solitaire.

"Any new messages for me?"

"Nothing yet today, Mrs. Spaulding. If something comes in we can send it out to Dr. Northcote's house. Save you coming into town."

Diana hesitated, but only for a moment. "An excellent idea, George. Thank you."

With a lighter heart, Diana continued on her way to the section of the river that citizens of Bangor used for skating. She had no difficulty locating it. Several wooden chairs had been set up on shore so ladies could sit comfortably while they clamped blades to boots. Convenient logs served the same purpose for gentlemen.

A cheerful fire burned on the bank to warm those who came as spectators as well as those who'd ventured out onto the ice. Diana noticed at once that most of the skaters wore ear protectors. The bright circles of cloth were held together by a metal band that slipped over the head and underneath a regular hat, a clever invention that went a long way towards preventing frostbitten ears.

Since it appeared she'd arrived ahead of Jerusha, Diana debated waiting to skate until her friend arrived, but the ice looked much too tempting. A few minutes later, she was wobbling her way around the circle, part of a large and congenial group of women and young children. Their older brothers and sisters were back in school after a two-week holiday.

It had been more than a year since Diana had put on a pair of ice skates, but once she got her balance back, she began to enjoy herself. When she'd first settled in New York she'd skated once or twice on the lake in Central Park, at the north end reserved for ladies in order to spare them having to endure the more boisterous activities of men and boys. A red ball, she recalled, was hoisted at the bell tower on Vista Rock to signal when the ice was thick enough to be safe. She did not see any such indicator here.

Although Diana thoroughly enjoyed the skating, by the time half an hour passed she began to feel uneasy about Jerusha's absence. For what seemed the hundredth time, she looked around for her friend. At first no one looked familiar. Then she thought she recognized Ben's dark mane above the caps and hats. Wishful thinking, she decided when the man came no nearer. After all, Ben's intention had been to go directly to his office after seeing Maggie off. Diana suppressed a sigh. She imagined that skating with Ben Northcote would be as romantic as dancing with him. She wondered if she would ever be privileged to do either.

She made one more circle of the skating area. This time, when she approached the gathering place on shore, Jerusha was there. So were half of Toddy's company—Lavinia, Toddy himself, Patsy, Billy Sims, and Charles Underly. Jerusha and Toddy appeared to be arguing. Lavinia waved gaily at Diana, then headed for the chairs. Diana continued on towards the bonfire. She was warming her hands when Lavinia came up beside her.

"I read this morning's *Whig and Courier*," Lavinia said. "I am so glad Toddy could persuade you to see the error of your ways." She preened a bit.

Diana was not sure what to say to the woman. It hardly flattered Lavinia if the only way she could get a good review was to have her lover intervene with the critic.

"A week ago I was ready to spit in your face if I ever saw you again," Lavinia continued, "but Toddy says you've been here all along."

"I came to Bangor directly from New Haven," Diana assured her. "I had nothing to do with the columns printed in the *Intelligencer* in my absence. Blame them on the same man who blackened your name in print the last time. My editor likes scandal, Lavinia. I do not."

"Hmmm."

Several local residents, who were sharing the warmth of the fire with Lavinia and Diana, seemed to be taking an interest in their discussion. By mutual agreement the two women took to the ice before they continued the conversation.

"Toddy told us how grateful we must be to you. After all, you led him to Damon Bathory. I am quite looking forward to starring in an adaptation of one of those stories. I'm told they are very popular."

"What role has Toddy assigned to you?"

"The greatest part since Lady Macbeth—Hannah Sussep."

Diana bit back a groan. That explained why Toddy and Jerusha were at odds. At best, Lavinia would play Maggie's Indian witch as melodramatic and stagy. "I am sure you will be unforgettable in the role."

"A half-mad heroine out to take revenge on her enemies." Lavinia's eyes glittered. "I relish the challenge."

In other hands, Diana thought, Jerusha's perhaps, the part might become a character of heroic proportions. Lavinia would never reach that level. She'd equate shrieking and thrashing about with madness. Or incoherent babbling.

Just then Charles Underly skated past, calling out to Lavinia to come and be his partner. He sent Diana a fulminating look.

"Go," Diana urged, reminded that she wanted to ask Jerusha about Underly and Sims.

Jerusha was still with Toddy and neither of them was paying the least bit of attention to anyone else. Diana looked for Billy Sims but found no sign of him. Patsy was just putting on her skates.

Keeping one eye on Jerusha, so she'd know when the other woman was free to talk, Diana made a wide circle on the ice, grateful that her ankle had healed so quickly and so well. She kept her distance from Underly and, when she finally caught sight of him, Billy Sims as well.

Another ten minutes passed and Diana had just begun another loop when she heard a cry of panic behind her. She turned in time to see Lavinia land ignominiously on her backside. Charles Underly reached her first and attempted to assist her to her feet, but her skates kept slipping out from under her and threatened to bring both of them down in a heap.

"Lend us a hand, Diana," Underly called.

Obligingly, Diana skated towards them, taking the most direct route. She had gone no more than a few feet when she heard an ominous cracking sound. Before she had time to react, the surface beneath her feet shifted, throwing her off balance. She landed hard on her right side and, horrified, felt herself slide out of control. Sheer momentum carried her farther from shore and directly towards a steadily widening crevice at mid-river. One foot, then the other, plunged into the frigid waters of the Penobscot.

Diana screamed, scrabbling at breaking ice in a futile attempt to halt her descent. She found a handhold in time to prevent total submersion, but it was not sufficient to save her from a thorough dunking. Cold water splashed into her nose and mouth, choking her, while the strong river current tugged at her nether limbs.

Frantic, Diana tried to tread water. More by luck than design, the full skirt of the gray traveling suit she'd worn as a skating costume aided her efforts to keep afloat. The ballooning fabric held trapped air beneath it, but Diana knew the garment would soon become waterlogged. Once that happened, the weight would be one more force dragging her down. Her limbs were already almost too numb to control.

Her only hope of survival was to crawl back out onto ice that was still solid, but every time she clutched at the edge of the fissure with any force, in an attempt to pull herself up and out, more bits broke away and more cold water sloshed over her, freezing on her face and drenching her hair.

"Grab hold!" someone shouted. A rope snaked across the surface of the river and slapped against her cheek.

Nearly too weak to obey the command, Diana reached for it, wrapping her frozen fingers around the lifeline. An instant later, she was jerked forward, until the upper half of her body flopped onto the ice like a landed fish. Strong hands grasped her wrists, drawing her the rest of the way out of the water.

Someone turned her over. She supposed she was lying flat on her back on the ice but she couldn't feel it beneath her. A terrible numbness had overtaken every part of her body. It took tremendous effort for Diana to open her eyes and stare up at a very blue sky. She thought it was the prettiest sight she'd ever seen.

"Bring her close to the fire."

Obeying Jerusha's order, someone lifted her and carried her at a run. Then more hands seized her and she was propped up next to the crackling blaze. She knew it must be hot, since other people were sweating, but she felt nothing but an icy cold. Then, slowly, warmth started to penetrate her soaked clothing, making it steam. The smell of wet wool rose with the vapor and Diana began to shiver uncontrollably.

Men and women alike milled around her, talking, maybe even shouting at her, but she could not understand a single thing they said through the buzzing in her head. Languid, her eyes drifted closed and she gave in to an overwhelming desire to sleep.

When Ben arrived on the scene, Charles Underly was holding Diana's limp body in his lap. Ben shoved him aside and bent over the still, pale form. At least someone had shown the good sense to wrap a blanket around her.

Devastating fear had clawed at Ben from the moment a runner brought word to his office that Diana had fallen into the river. It eased slightly when he saw her chest rise and fall. Her breathing was shallow, but at least she did breathe.

"Was she unconscious when she was pulled out?"

"No," Jerusha told him. "She's not drowned, just cold. And this time she does not seem to have sprained or strained anything."

Ben shot her a quick, censorious glance, but the misplaced levity did not come from a lack of caring. She was as shaken as he by Diana's condition. "She'll be all right, Jerusha. She just needs warming up."

"Someone moved the warning sign," one of the local men said. "The one that said, 'THIN ICE?'"

"Ayuh. My boy found it in the bushes on the far shore."

"Dangerous prank," another man opined.

"Or deliberate maliciousness," Ben said. He looked for Charles Underly, but the actor had already left the riverbank. Billy Sims, he noted, was still there, along with Nathan Todd, Patsy Jenkins, and Jerusha.

For the moment, getting Diana warm again was uppermost in his mind. He sent word ahead for Annie to heat water for a bath and carried Diana, well wrapped, to a waiting wagon. By the time they reached the Northcote house, a tub steamed in front of a blazing hearth in Diana's bedroom.

"Help me get her out of these wet clothes," he barked at Annie. Diana, now half awake, was too drowsy to undress herself, but she was easier for him to manage than when she'd been unconscious and a dead weight.

The dull thud of something heavy hitting the carpet distracted Ben as he stripped off Diana's skirt. A key gleamed in the light streaming in through the bedroom window.

"Unlocks the front gate, sir," Annie said, glancing at it. "Old Ernest gave it to her." Then she gasped, for they were down to Diana's undergarments. Soaked, they clung to her like a second skin. "Ain't proper for you to be here, sir, you bein' a man and all."

"I'm a doctor, Annie."

And, at first, looking after Diana's health kept his focus on that. But when she was in the water, its warmth turning her icy skin pink once more, he could no longer ignore the fact that he was also "a man and all."

He'd almost lost her. Ben's hands trembled as he balanced her while Annie quickly washed her hair, then bundled it into a thick towel to dry. The realization that she'd come close to death today left him feeling empty inside. When he'd contemplated sending her away, he'd consoled himself by thinking that he'd always know where she was, that he could visualize her, happy and content, even if it was somewhere else. Now he understood just how meaningless his own life would be if she was not part of it. He was no longer certain he could give her up, not even if doing so was best for her.

When she was warmed and dried and dressed in a clean nightgown, he tucked her into bed and sent Annie away. At first he sat on the bed, holding her hand in his, watching over her. But when she started to shiver again, he hesitated only a moment before throwing off his outer clothing and climbing under the covers with her. Body heat was the best thing for hypothermia, he told himself. He tucked her in close to his own warmth and wrapped his arms around her.

୫୦୬

A long time later, Diana stirred. Her hand caressed the forearm crossed beneath her breasts. "Am I dreaming?" she murmured.

Gently, Ben disentangled himself. It was not fair to tempt them both when he still did not see how he could offer her a future. "A nightmare, perhaps," he said as he went to stir the embers.

He thought she'd fallen asleep again. Then her soft voice reached him over the crackle of the fire in the hearth. "Ben?"

"Here, Diana." He returned to her bedside and lit a candle. She was still pale, but her eyes were clear.

"What happened?" Almost as soon as the question was out, she gasped, remembering on her own. "I was skating. I fell through the ice."

"You were pulled out quickly, but it was a near thing." He tried to suppress the emotion in his voice but didn't think he succeeded.

"I should have been more careful. It was a foolish accident." She forced a smile. "Why, it could as easily have been Lavinia who fell through. She was headed towards the thin ice when she took a tumble."

Let her believe that, Ben decided. It might even be true. He intended to find out at his first opportunity.

"You need rest," he said aloud. And he needed to think. "Can you sleep some more?"

Diana considered his question for a moment. "I think I need food first."

"I'll fix you a tray."

In the kitchen, as he warmed leftover soup and sliced bread

and ham, Ben attempted to think logically about the THIN ICE sign. It could be that some child, playing, had tipped it over and failed to put it upright again. Deliberately removing it seemed an unreliable way to kill someone. There had been a great many people around. Any one of them could have broken through that thin patch. Maybe what happened to Diana had been an accident after all.

Diana had propped herself up against the pillows by the time Ben brought her the tray. "Did you rescue me?" she asked.

"I arrived on the scene after you were already out of the water."

Diana blinked at him in confusion. "But I was sure I saw you in the crowd earlier. Few dark-haired men are so tall or tend to go about without a hat."

"Only one other I can think of." But why would Aaron harm Diana? And how could he have left the estate without Joseph or Old Ernest knowing?

Spoon poised over her soup, Diana studied his face. She had no difficulty guessing his thoughts. "It might have been Aaron, I suppose. There is a strong resemblance between you. It hardly matters."

Unless Aaron had moved that sign. Ben hid his concern from Diana, distracting her with anecdotes about his patients, but he could not stop his racing thoughts. Aaron might have moved it if his voices had told him to.

When Diana had polished off every item on the tray and drifted back into a healing sleep, Ben woke Annie to sit with her. Then he made his way to the carriage house. His questions would not wait until morning.

One was answered at once. Joseph was deeply asleep. On the table by his bed was a glass. Ben sniffed the dregs and grimaced as he recognized a sleeping potion he'd concocted in his own laboratory. It was the draught he'd intended Aaron to take, harmless enough but powerful. Ben had no way of telling how long ago Joseph had been drugged, nor could he guess how much longer the fellow would sleep.

He found his brother in the studio with all the lights blazing. Aaron scowled when he caught sight of Ben. "I am working, Brother. Go away."

"Where were you earlier?"

"Where else should I be? Here. Working. Go away, I tell you." When Ben made a move to look at the work in progress, Aaron turned the easel away from him and hunched protectively over the canvas.

"Don't give any more of your medicine to Joseph," Ben warned him.

"Then don't try to foist that horrible-tasting stuff off on me. I prefer brandy." Aaron resumed his painting. After a moment, he no longer seemed aware that Ben was still in the studio.

When Ben left, he locked the door behind him. He was about to pocket the key when he realized that it was a duplicate of the one for the padlock on the front gate . . . and likely every other lock on the property.

He tested it on his laboratory and was not surprised to hear a click. No wonder Aaron got in and out of the gate at will. Ben pushed the door open and entered the long, narrow room, his thoughts still circling the central problem. Could Aaron have hurt Diana?

Even if Ben consigned what had happened on the river today to sheer bad luck, he knew he had no right to keep Diana here, no right to dream of a future for them. And yet she was everywhere he looked, even among the glass beakers and bottles and distilling equipment.

∽∾

By the time Maggie returned, early on Tuesday afternoon, with the news that her publisher had reluctantly agreed to continue to publish Damon Bathory even though "his" identity would no longer be a secret, Diana felt fully recovered from her ordeal in the cold water. She'd gotten dressed as soon as Ben had left for his office that morning.

"So, one matter settled," Maggie declared as she wrapped up her account.

"Now on to the second," Diana said. "The newspaper story on my discovery of a killer's identity."

"I've had an idea about that," Maggie said. "I want to invite the entire theatrical troupe to supper here after Wednesday night's show. If you're right, one of them will be looking for an opportunity to act. What better place to catch him?"

"I may be wrong." Diana glanced at the flowers Charles Underly had sent. There were other bouquets, from Toddy, from Jerusha, but Underly's was the largest and most fragrant.

"So much the better," Maggie said. "If there is no killer among them, then I'll have had the chance to meet the actors who will be playing characters I created."

What she said made sense, and Diana still wanted an opportunity to talk to Jerusha. "Very well. I'll issue the invitation in person. The company is staying at the Windsor Hotel."

A short time later, she rapped on the door of the room Jerusha shared with Patsy. They'd scarcely had time to say hello before there was another knock.

"Toddy," Jerusha predicted. "He's worried about you."

"Because of that fall through the ice? I am completely recovered."

"Not because of that," Toddy said when they let him in.

Diana wondered if he was about to bring up the murders, though she could not conceive of his knowing anything about them unless he'd been involved.

"It's that man you're living with," Toddy said instead. "What do you really know about him?"

"He's a respected physician." Defensive, she gave him a narrow-eyed look. "You were willing to leave me at his mercy in New Haven when you thought he was a writer of horror stories. Why are you so concerned about him now?"

"Didn't leave you at his mercy." Toddy looked offended. "Had a little talk with him before I left. And Jerusha gave you money so you didn't have to be kept by him."

"So he told me." Diana rewarded Toddy with a quick peck on the cheek. "I'm able to look out for myself, you know."

"Are you, Diana? You made a bad choice when you married Evan. There's no denying that."

"Toddy," Jerusha warned.

"No, it's time she knew. He wasn't much of a husband to her, or much of a man, either." He sent a sheepish look in Jerusha's direction. "I know I'm not one who should throw stones, but Evan Spaulding was a bounder, Diana. He—"

"I know most of what he did, Toddy. And I know how he died. I was there, remember?"

Clearing his throat, Toddy looked as ill-at-ease as Diana had ever seen him. "Should have done something sooner," he said. "Should have looked out for you, not let him go off on his own with you."

"You couldn't have stopped him, Toddy. Or me, either. I pledged myself to him, no matter that he took his wedding vows lightly. But that's over and done now. And Ben is nothing like Evan."

"I'm very much afraid he's something worse. I've heard stories since I've been in this town. Wild tales about what goes on in that house. Nice remote setting. A brother no one ever sees, kept in the carriage house. A secret laboratory in the basement. Shades of Dr. Frankenstein! Or Dr. Jekyll. And that mother of his! Do you know, just before you came home, she was regaling me with a lurid account of a witches' sabbat she claims she attended."

"Toddy, she has an active imagination. That's all."

"How do you explain her eyes? Color of a new penny, they

are," he said to Jerusha, who had not met Maggie.

"And Dr. Northcote's, as I recall, are a deep, soulful brown with amber flakes." Jerusha grinned at Diana, further infuriating Toddy.

"You've not met her."

"She will," Diana interrupted, and extended the invitation Maggie had sent.

"I'm not sure I want to get any closer to someone who indulges in that sort of thing," Toddy muttered. "More dangerous than directing the scene of the three witches in that cursed Scottish play."

"Yet you want to adapt her stories," Diana reminded him.

"That's just good business, but the woman herself . . . well, she's strange, Diana. Confounded me two or three times just in the short while I was with her."

"She excels at that," Diana admitted, and was surprised to hear herself add, "There's no real harm in her."

"I for one am dying to meet the woman," Jerusha said. "And what actor ever turns down a free meal?"

Toddy ignored her to take Diana's hands in his. "Is it possible he's used animal magnetism to make you obey his will? That's what Lavinia thinks, and she was once a magician's assistant, you know."

Diana jerked her hands free. "Nonsense."

Toddy huffed. "Well one hears of such things, you know. And him a doctor, with such a mother, and madness in the family. Well!"

His concern touched her, even as it made her want to defend Ben and his family. "Come to supper tomorrow night. You'll see for yourself that all is well, and that any danger I may be in has nothing to do with Ben."

His gaze sharpened. "What's going on, Diana? It hasn't escaped my notice that since you met this man you've been uncommonly accident-prone."

"That has nothing to do with Ben." She patted his cheek. "Read tomorrow's papers, and then come to supper. Will you do that for me, Toddy? And bring all the company with you?"

"Are you going to tell me what's going on?" Jerusha asked when Toddy finally left her hotel room.

Diana thought about it, then shook her head and changed her mind about questioning Jerusha. Her friend might let something slip to the others. And if, by chance, Diana was right about Charles Underly, then too much knowledge could put Jerusha in danger. "Come to supper tomorrow night. You can decide for yourself who is and isn't fit for bedlam."

"Be careful, Diana."

"You, too? I thought you liked Ben!"

"I wouldn't kick him out of my bed, but that doesn't mean I'd turn my back on him, either. Unless you're very sure of him, don't be too quick to trust again."

Unspoken, the words *remember Evan* hung between them.

Diana returned to the Northcote house in a thoughtful mood. She'd wondered about Ben's laboratory herself. When Annie informed her that he was down there again, she gathered her courage and rapped on the door.

"It's open!" He looked up from a microscope when she entered. "I thought it might be you." He glowered at her, but the look softened as she came closer. "Mother had to muster a powerful argument to keep me from rushing after you to the hotel. How could you take such a risk?"

"If Charles Underly is the sort of man who kills women in dark alleys, he's not likely to attack one in broad daylight."

"He could be the sort who arranges accidents."

She did not want to think about that. Not now. Instead she surveyed her surroundings. There was scientific equipment everywhere—mortars and pestles, alembics, bottles full of medicine, and jars containing specimens she wasn't sure she wanted to identify. "No cadavers?" she asked.

"Not today."

"Maggie told me you're a city coroner."

"I also make some of my own medicines. Any good physician knows how to roll pills."

The width of a counter separated them, but she felt the sensual tug of his presence. He'd slept in her bed last night. She wanted him there again, this time when they were both awake.

"You must know a great deal about cures," she said, with studied casualness. "And preventives."

Misunderstanding, he began to talk about herbal remedies for madness. "I've done a good deal of research on the subject just recently. Most of it is foolishness, of course. One old recipe instructs the physician to wrap a frog's liver in colewort leaves and burn it, then give the patient the ashes to drink in wine."

She made a face.

"Another goes into great detail and takes into account the phases of the moon." His forehead wrinkled as he struggled to call up the precise names for the ingredients. Diana had the feeling they were as strange to him as they sounded to her. "Six ounces of diasabestian mixed with twelve grains of diagrydian dissolved in a draught of clear posset ale in the morning after fasting. Then fast four hours. Then drink a draught of thin broth. And the next day the patient is bled—three ounces from the head vein."

"Charming. Perhaps you should share that one with Maggie. She can use it in one of her stories."

"That's not all of it." Ben's smile had a wry twist. "After the bleeding, morning and night until four days before the full moon, the patient must take a walnut-sized portion of a digestial cordial to settle vapors."

Her uneasiness returned. "The moon is full tonight."

"Diana, it's all nonsense." He came around the table and, at last, gathered her into his arms. "It would be as much use to wrap the red stone found in the belly of a sparrow—what the ancients called chelidonius—in a cloth, and tie it to someone's right arm. That is also supposed to cure lunatics and make them amiable and merry."

"Amiable and merry," she repeated against his chest. "A desirable state." She sighed. "You seem to have lost interest in making merry, Ben Northcote. You seem to have lost interest in me."

He bent his head and kissed her lightly on the lips. "Does this feel like lack of interest?"

But when evening came, he was called away by another medical emergency. Or so he said.

CHAPTER SEVENTEEN

❧☙

On Wednesday, according to plan, copies of Monday's *Independent Intelligencer* arrived in Bangor. It was all there. Diana's regular column revealed the true identity of Damon Bathory. Then, in a feature story, readers found the bombshell—she promised to unmask a killer in time for the Sunday edition. Foxe hadn't changed a word she'd sent. The piece included just enough information to make the guilty party think he'd been discovered. The hints and innuendo the article contained were designed to convince the murderer that if he acted quickly enough he could still prevent Diana from revealing his name.

Diana's suspects had a performance that night, after which they came to a late supper at the Northcote mansion. In anticipation of an attempt to kill her, Joseph and Ernest were stationed right outside the dining room door.

The first appearance of a threat came from Nathan Todd. A murderous look in his eyes, he launched a verbal attack the moment he was relieved of his mackintosh and galoshes.

"You lied to me, Diana," he bellowed. "You are still writing 'Today's Tidbits' for the *Intelligencer.*"

Stepping around Ben, who had placed himself in front of her

at the first sign of potential danger, Diana glided up to her old friend and patted his arm. "It's a long story, Toddy," she said in a soothing voice. "Come have supper with us and I'll try to explain, but to tell too much, I fear, would give the game away."

"Now, don't you be criticizing this young woman, Mr. Todd," Maggie admonished him, taking his free arm and steering him towards the parlor.

"Oh, la! Such a fuss." Jerusha swept in, shedding umbrella and gossamer.

Lavinia Ross arrived on Charles Underly's arm. Diana wondered if she was trying to make Toddy jealous. If so, she was going about it the wrong way. A quick glance at Jerusha told Diana that her old friend was in fine fettle. Now that Diana thought about it, her interaction with Toddy seemed to have an added zest to it.

"I assure you that she cannot be cowed," Maggie was telling Nathan Todd when Diana followed them into the parlor. With fine actor's instincts herself, Ben's mother waited until everyone was within hearing distance before she added, "I've tested her mettle for myself."

"And how, madam, did you do that?"

"Why, I locked her in the family crypt, just to see how she'd react."

An appalled silence fell only to be broken when Lavinia Ross burst into delighted laughter. "I'd like to have seen your face when you realized you were trapped," she said to Diana. "That must have been a sight."

"You have a low kind of humor, Lavinia," Billy Sims informed her. He stepped closer to Diana, oozing charm and consolation. "It must have been terrifying."

"Yes. The whole incident made me wonder if Maggie had followed Ben on tour in order to deal with critics."

Maggie attempted to look innocent and missed by a mile. It did not take much encouragement to get her to provide details of her "experiment" with Diana in the family vault. "Of course, I

never tried to kill Diana. There appears to be someone else trying
to do that."

"You were attacked?" Jerusha turned to stare at Diana. "That
article—your article—only mentioned critics in Philadelphia and
. . . where was it?"

"Los Angeles and San Francisco. All places popular with
theatrical and lecture tours. Yes, there was an attempt to harm me.
I took it as a sign I was on the right track."

She let that suggestion hang in the air for a long moment. On
cue, Ernest announced that it was time to go into supper. Amid
the clamor of voices demanding more details, Diana alone remained
quiet, refusing to say any more.

"But your column's been implying that Damon Bathory had
deep dark secrets," Patsy blurted. Then, realizing whose guest she
was, she turned bright pink and fell silent.

"You know she hasn't been writing the column since the storm,"
Toddy reminded them.

"So she says." Lavinia sent a suspicious look in Diana's direction.
"Her byline was there, just as it was in the paper we saw today."

"But what about the murders?" Jerusha took the chair next to
Toddy. Maggie was at his other hand. Lavinia pretended not to
notice.

"You will have to wait to read all about it with everyone else,"
Diana told them.

"Why?" Todd demanded. "If you know who—"

"I do." Diana let her gaze rove over the entire assembled
company, resting briefly on each of the troupe's members but a
little longer on Underly and Sims. "But, you see, Toddy, as long as
no one else has the same information, that news is valuable.
Congratulate me, my dear friends. I am about to make a 'killing'
of my own. When my editor meets my price, I will tell him who
murdered those women and tried to stop me from investigating.
The revelation should be worth a tidy sum."

"Oh, la!" Jerusha declared. "How mercenary! But how clever

of you, too."

The meal served, they all began to eat, but their attention remained fixed on Diana. Sims's cuff dipped in the gravy because he could not seem to take his eyes off her.

Patsy kept fanning herself and at last burst out with an admonition. "While you delay, someone else could be murdered!"

Todd made a strangled sound, then chuckled. "What a great gag!"

"Gag?" Caught off guard by the comment, Diana gaped at him.

"Going to name the killer on Sunday, right?"

She nodded.

"What day is Sunday?" Toddy asked the company at large.

"Easter," said Ben in a repressive tone.

Toddy chuckled. "Sunday is also the first day of April. April Fool's Day. Good one, Diana."

"But it isn't . . . I don't—"

"I should have known," Jerusha said, laughing with the rest. "Why, otherwise, I'd think you might mean to accuse one of us."

"Why would she do that?" Underly demanded.

"Because some of us were in all those places where the women were murdered, and at just the right times."

"You really had us going." Toddy slapped the table with glee. "Why, I even started to wonder if your fall on the train might have been some nefarious attempt to bury you permanently in that snowbank." Still chucking, he had to use his napkin to wipe the tears from his eyes.

"If that's the case, then the culprit must be Mrs. Wainflete." Billy Sims chortled in delight at the idea. "An obvious suspect now that I think about it."

Diana blinked, darting a quick look at Ben. All their guests now seemed to think the entire story nothing but an elaborate April Fool's Day hoax.

Worse, no one looked the least bit guilty.

୫୦୯୬

Following the meal, the men adjourned to the library for cigars and brandy. Ben considered the company, careful to keep his face expressionless. Either these people were more accomplished actors than he thought, or he and Diana were wrong. Could it be that the killer was not a member of Todd's Touring Thespians?

No one seemed to be other than he was. It was hard to conceive that any of them, even while talking of the last stand, the current one, and the journey ahead, might be plotting to silence Diana before she revealed his identity.

Underly was sour by nature but no more irritable than usual.

Todd was jovial and entertaining.

Sims was making serious inroads into Ben's brandy.

The others were of no importance. According to what Jerusha had told Diana, none of them had been in Philadelphia when the first victim died.

"Shall we return to the ladies?" Todd made the suggestion at the earliest possible moment. "I'd like to continue my discussion with Mrs. Northcote. I've great plans for making plays out of her stories."

Ben didn't care to know the details. After all, he'd seen this company perform.

The usual entertainments filled out the rest of the evening. Billy Sims played the piano and sang a few songs, apparently oblivious to the fact that the instrument was out of tune. He had a good voice, making Ben wonder if he might do better as a singer than an actor. Lavinia rendered a tune, as well, with considerably less talent.

By the time she sat down at the keyboard, it was well past midnight. The moment she paused for breath after the first song, Todd decreed that they must be on their way back to the hotel. "Even actors need a bit of sleep," he said with a genial laugh.

Ben waved goodbye with Diana standing on one side of him

and his mother on the other, to all appearances a normal family who'd just entertained a few friends.

The image gave him pause.

"A triumph," his mother declared, as Ernest closed the door and went behind the departing guests to lock the gate. "And that young woman may do quite well in the roles of Hannah Sussep and the Blood Countess. At least in some scenes. I talked to her a bit earlier. She has an instinctive understanding of the classic principles of revenge tragedy."

Ben thought Lavinia Ross would be a disaster in either role but he did not say so. Let Mother keep her illusions, at least until she'd seen the actress on stage. "So, you deem the evening a success?"

"A social triumph." She stopped at the foot of the stairs and ran one hand over the griffin on the newel post, a pleased smile on her face. "What other Bangor hostess can boast of having had the entire cast of a play to sup? But even more glorious are the ideas I've gotten for new characters after listening to that lot." Chuckling to herself, she toddled off to bed.

Ben and Diana retired to the parlor, where he poured them each a brandy.

"Could it be that my conclusions were all wrong?" Diana asked. "There are still three dead women in cities the members of Todd's Touring Thespians visited."

Taking back the glasses, Ben set them on a table and gathered Diana into his arms. "There's nothing we can do about them tonight."

"No."

"Have you been sleeping as badly as I have?"

"Worse."

Ben's lips had barely touched Diana's when the shouting began. A moment later, Joseph burst in on them. One hand was pressed against his bleeding head. In the other he clutched a copy of the *Independent Intelligencer*.

"He's gone, Dr. Northcote!" Joseph cried. "Your brother's run off again!"

"Damnation! I thought he was locked in!"

"He was, but when I went back to check on him, he was gone."

Ben examined Joseph's injury. "Nothing serious. Aaron didn't strike you, then?"

"No, sir. I fell on my way to tell you he'd escaped."

"Go," Diana said when Ben hesitated and looked at her. "I'm safe in the house."

"Stay with her," Ben told Joseph.

He went first to the carriage house. There was no sign of Aaron, but the portraits he'd just completed were now on display. Ben cursed under his breath. They were all half-naked mermaids. And they all had Diana's face.

With Ernest's help, Ben searched the grounds, aided by a moon just past the full, but there was no getting around the hard truth—Aaron was long gone. He could have slipped out at any time after he read that newspaper.

Ben didn't care for the implications. Had Aaron taken Diana's promise to reveal the name of a murderer as a threat to him? He'd always claimed he couldn't recall some of the things that had happened to him on his visits to Philadelphia and New York, but had he remembered now? Or had he jumped to the conclusion, reinforced by the kinds of questions Ben had asked him, that he might be a killer and not realize it?

There was no way to know until Aaron was found. Haunted by the possibilities, worried about what his brother might do if he believed his voices had led him to commit a crime for which he could be locked up, Ben returned to the house to tell Diana he was going off the grounds to search for his brother.

"If I can't find him, I may have to call in the marshals. I can't take any more risks."

"He cannot believe I was about to accuse him! He could not

have killed those women. Remember what Clarissa said."

"She's a whore, Diana. She'll say anything for money. And if she did lie, Aaron could be guilty." The idea sickened him. "Have you a better explanation? No one confessed at your little supper party."

"And Aaron has not confessed, either."

"He ran away. That's proof he—"

"That's proof he's scared. Confused. Not that he killed anyone. He told you he couldn't remember."

"I can't take any chances. Do you know what I found in his studio? New paintings. At least a half dozen of them. All of you. He's obsessed with you."

"That has nothing to do with anything."

"It has everything to do with it!" He seized her by the shoulders. He'd break his vow never to send Aaron to an institution rather than risk this woman's life again. "You're . . . important to me, Diana."

"You're important to me, too, Ben. You're the finest man I've ever known."

Their lips met, hard. Only by holding her close could Ben momentarily assuage his pain. She clung to him with a fervor that nearly undid him, but after a moment, he found the strength to release her.

"I must go. I must find him."

It was only after Ben left that Diana thought of Maggie, who had somehow managed to sleep through the ruckus.

Maggie was Aaron's mother. She had to be told what was happening. And she might just know something that would help.

The older woman wasn't pleased to be roused from sleep, but when she heard what Diana had to say, she bundled herself into her red monk's robe, ordered coffee, and then demanded to know everything. For once there was no artifice in her manner. Maggie was genuinely worried about her son.

"There's always been something a little odd about the boy," she admitted when Diana had summarized the bare facts—her own encounters with Aaron, including what she'd seen at Miss Jenny's, and the search for him after Joseph ran in. "The Bathory blood, I suppose." At the expression on Diana's face, she shrugged. "I don't make everything up. The Blood Countess was real. So was my great-uncle Anton who died raving."

"That may be, and Aaron may be . . . ill . . . but that does not make him a killer. Have you ever seen him lift his hand to anyone? Do anything more violent than shout?"

"Joseph?"

"Only when he thought Joseph was attacking him."

Maggie nodded. "Aaron doesn't hurt people unless they threaten him."

"Why did your son go to Philadelphia?" Diana asked.

Maggie started to answer, then frowned. "I suppose there was more than one reason. He said he needed to get away from me. We quarreled and he left. He'd never gone on such a long trip alone before, but there was no real reason why he shouldn't. He'd often been to Boston on his own."

"Why did you quarrel?"

"He was upset because I asked Ben to impersonate Damon Bathory. I don't think he really wanted to do it himself. He just wanted to be asked."

"He was jealous of his brother?"

"So I thought. And, of course, he had a reason of his own to go to Philadelphia. He had some paintings in a gallery there." She grimaced. "After what happened in Philadelphia, Ben took over handling his business affairs. Aaron is much too emotional to deal with selling his work."

"What happened in Philadelphia?" Diana asked, feeling as if she had to pull teeth to get any information out of Maggie.

"Aaron became convinced that the price on one of his paintings wasn't high enough and insisted it be doubled. The gallery manager refused. The next thing he knew, Aaron had given the piece away." She threw up her hands in despair. "When he got back home, I insisted he authorize Ben to deal with the galleries. There aren't that many. Just Philadelphia, Boston, and New York. Only New York on what was left of the tour."

"So he had no reason to go to San Francisco or Los Angeles. And in fact, he did not."

"Ben doubts the word of that . . . woman."

"I think I can prove she knew what she was talking about." Belatedly, she'd grasped the significance of where Clarissa had seen Aaron.

෨෬

It was mid-day on Thursday before Ben returned. He didn't give Diana a chance to say anything before he started to speak.

"I can't put this off any longer, Diana," he said in a rush. "There is something I haven't told you about Aaron. What's wrong with him is my fault. It's because of me that he's the way he is."

"How can that be?"

"It's something that happened between Aaron and me a long time ago." Ben stared straight ahead at the cabbage roses on the parlor wallpaper. "It was just after I returned to Bangor with my medical degree. I'd bought out another doctor's practice and taken over his patients, including the girls at Jenny's place. I was called out to treat one of them after a customer beat her up. Aaron was there when I arrived. He was, I soon learned, a regular client."

When he hesitated, Diana edged closer, placing her hand on his arm. Her closeness, the sense of unspoken support, seemed to give him the courage to go on with this difficult confession.

"Aaron and I were always scrapping as boys. We were different enough in temperament that we were frequently impatient with each other. Father taught us to box at an early age, and sometimes

I think he actually encouraged our aggression towards each other. That night, Aaron had been drinking and he started going on about how the girl who'd been beaten up had deserved what she got. I told him to shut up, but he just became more insulting. He had a few choice names for me, too. I tried to ignore him, and for a while I succeeded, but after I'd checked on my patient, he accosted me in the hallway. He was still spewing abuse and I lost my temper. I struck him and he hit back. We fought there on the landing. He stumbled, his balance impaired by the drink, and I hit him again, harder than I'd intended. He fell the entire length of the stairs and cracked his skull on the newel post."

Ben's hand went to his stomach, as if the memory made him sick.

"I didn't kill Aaron, but what I did to him was worse."

"Go on, Ben." Diana kept her voice soft and made sure it held no recrimination.

"Aaron fell and struck his head," he repeated. "He was unconscious for several hours before he finally came around. At first I thought there was no lasting damage. The next day he seemed completely normal, but it wasn't long before I became aware of . . . oddities. He'd stand with his head to one side, carrying on conversations when there was no one else around. His painting became undisciplined, more disturbing in its effect. He lost his temper more often. I wasn't the only one to notice the changes. People began to hint that he should be institutionalized."

"Are you telling me you've blamed yourself all this time for Aaron's condition?"

"I've sought other reasons. There are many theories. Some say insanity is inherited, but other experts think that a man's mind can be affected by a blow to the head. If I hadn't struck him—"

"Ben, you're wrong!"

"I'm a doctor, Diana, and I know what I did."

She moved directly in front of him, taking both his hands in hers. "Look at me," she commanded. "Do you remember what you yourself once said? That even doctors, even in this modern age, still know very little about the mind?"

He tried to pull away, but she wasn't having any of that.

"Look at me! Maggie says she had an uncle who went mad. You know insanity can be inherited. Aaron talked to imaginary muses before that night, Ben. Ask Clarissa."

"Clarissa!" He tensed.

"She told me that even before she first knew him, even before you set up your practice, well before your fight, people talked about how Aaron heard voices. That wasn't because of anything you did. He was already ill."

Hope blossomed in Ben's dark eyes. Diana caught his face between her hands, forcing him to meet her steady gaze.

"You never noticed Aaron's problems before you went away to school because you were accustomed to his behavior. Only after you returned did the symptoms stand out. And because noticing followed hard upon those fisticuffs between you, you blamed yourself."

"Could it really be so simple?"

"What I'm telling you makes sense." The diagnosis of inherited madness was not one she wanted to accept, but better that than to let Ben go on suffering from unmerited guilt.

"Whatever caused his condition, he still may be a danger to others. To you."

Diana watched him carefully. As a physician, if not as a brother, he believed he'd failed Aaron.

"I must find him."

"I know where he is, Ben," Diana said quietly. "He's gone to the same place he hid back in January. He's in the rooms above your office."

CHAPTER EIGHTEEN

❧◊❧

Several hours later, after they had brought Aaron home and convinced him that no one suspected him of murder, Diana pirouetted before her mirror in a new evening gown. It was a splendid creation of blue velvet with a vest of straw-colored satin embroidered and trimmed with black Chantilly lace. It had a long, square train and a small satin collar and epaulets that were composed of double frills of lace held by richly beaded passementerie that fell in tassels.

"Suitable for a night at the theater?" she asked Ben, who watched her from the doorway. She rather liked the hungry look in his eyes.

Diana had returned to the house to discover that Maggie's dressmaker had delivered the creation in their absence.

"You want to go out? Tonight?"

"Maggie would like to see Toddy's troupe in action. Surely you don't want her to go alone."

"Can you bear *The Duchess of Calabria* again?"

"I shall enjoy Maggie's reactions to it."

Diana had all but decided she was wrong about Charles Underly. In any case, if something was going to happen, it seemed likely it would be after Saturday's performance, not tonight. All the murders, and the attempt on her in New York, had followed the same pattern.

She smiled confidently at her image in the mirror and winked at Ben's scowling countenance reflected behind her. The common thread, if there was one, was the day of the week and the imminent departure of Todd's Touring Thespians from their current stand.

"I do not like seeing you use yourself as bait, Diana. I want you safe."

She did not argue, merely turned and extended her hand. "Maggie's waiting for us. Do you want to change into more formal apparel or go as you are?"

He took his time studying her gown. "I'll change," he said in a voice that was very nearly a growl. "Don't take one step out of the house without me."

A short time later they were on their way to the Bangor Opera House. "You'll find it a very modern structure," Maggie said. "There are enough fixed folding chairs for an audience of 700. A marked improvement over the moveable benches used elsewhere in the city."

When she saw the interior, Diana had to agree. On stage a painted curtain decorated with castles and snow-capped peaks formed the backdrop for a spacious stage.

"When Oscar Wilde was here," Ben said, "they hung tapestries that made it look like an elegant parlor."

As the play began, Maggie fell silent and said not a single word as the drama unfolded. Diana did not attempt to speak either. She studied the actors from a new perspective and came away thinking that, on stage at least, neither Toddy nor Charles Underly were convincing murderers.

At the interval a note was delivered to Diana. "From Lavinia Ross," she murmured in a bemused voice. "An invitation to come backstage after the play." It was the last thing she'd expected. It reminded her that she'd received a similar invitation on a certain Saturday night in New York.

An hour later, they descended the flight of stairs that led from the stage to the dressing rooms, which were situated directly beneath the auditorium. The one Lavinia shared with Patsy and Jerusha was heated with steam and fitted out with a large mirror. Gas brackets on each side provided light to apply grease paint, and there were plenty of hooks for clothing. A marble wash bowl added the final elegant touch. Someone who cared about the needs of theatrical people had designed this theater.

"I have been considering what you told us at supper last night," Lavinia said after she and Diana had greeted each other with false affection and even more exaggerated compliments, on Diana's part, about Lavinia's performance. "Your promise to reveal the identity of a murderer was not intended as a joke, was it?"

"No," Diana admitted.

"And your fall on the train? That was no accident? Nor was the incident on the ice?" In spite of Lavinia's breathy voice, her words conveyed the seriousness of the questions.

"I don't know. And I don't know who the murderer is, either. It was just a bluff."

Lavinia turned away to rub rouge off her cheeks, but the mirror reflected the wicked glee in her eyes. "I do. Send for the constable, Diana. Tell him to arrest Charles Underly."

Jerusha gasped. Patsy's hands stilled in the act of removing her greasepaint.

"The law demands proof," Ben said in a mild voice. "I have no difficulty believing Underly guilty, but the city marshals and the county sheriff may need convincing."

"I can testify that I caught him creeping about in the drawing-room car that night on the train," Lavinia said. "It was just before you were found in the snow, Diana. Charles tried to convince me he was waiting for me. That he had a romantic interest in me.

That is why I didn't mention the incident before. Toddy is so terribly jealous." She ignored Jerusha's snort of disbelief. "It did not seem suspicious at the time."

"Did no one notice that he'd slipped out of the parlor car? He'd have had no business in the drawing-room car."

"Mrs. Wainflete had already retired for the night," said Jerusha. "No one else would have cared."

"Except Toddy." Lavinia's squawk of protest had no effect on her rival.

"If anyone had seen him," Jerusha mused, "they'd have assumed he was on his way to the men's washroom. The door to the gents was right next to the exit."

"It doesn't matter what anyone thought at the time," Lavinia sputtered. "We all know how upset Charles was by his reviews. Now we know what he did about it."

"His behavior that night does sound suspicious," Diana agreed, "but being in the drawing-room car is not enough, of itself, to condemn him."

"There's more." Lavinia's eyes gleamed with malice. "He deliberately caused me to fall on the ice, then called to you for help in order to lure you across the thin part. And those three women were stabbed, were they not?" She did not wait for confirmation before she pounded the final nail into Charles Underly's coffin. "Surely you have noticed how he clings to his cane."

"His cane? But—"

Lavinia laughed. "Didn't you realize it's a sword stick? One twist of the handle and he can unsheathe a length of the finest Toledo steel. Perfect for dealing with intrusive members of the press."

Ben had heard enough. He slipped out of the dressing room and sent for both the marshal and the county sheriff's deputies. When they arrived, they took Charles Underly into custody, ignoring his loud protests.

"I am innocent, I tell you!" he shouted.

"What if he's telling the truth?" Diana whispered. She and Ben stood beside Maggie and the three actresses at the entrance to their dressing room.

"He'd be a fool to admit to the charges."

Underly sent a last, pleading glance over his shoulder. It contained none of his usual arrogance, or even resentment, only panic and confusion. "Help me, for God's sake! Find the real killer."

"I didn't think he was that good an actor," Diana murmured.

Nathan Todd, watching from the other side of the small lobby that separated the dressing rooms, wore a stricken expression. Ben wasn't sure what upset the actor/manager more, the accusation that Underly was a murderer or the news that Lavinia had been keeping secrets from him. Todd rounded on the young woman as soon as the prisoner was out of sight. "If you thought he was trying to seduce you, you should have said something."

Jaw set, back ramrod straight, Lavinia stormed into Todd's dressing room. He followed, slamming the door behind him.

"Oh, la," Jerusha said.

"Maybe he'll finally realize what a shrew that girl is," Patsy remarked as sounds of an escalating quarrel reached them. She handed Jerusha her wrap, preparatory to returning to the hotel.

"Will the next two performances be canceled?" Maggie asked.

"Oh, I doubt it." Jerusha managed a bright smile. "Toddy was saying just this morning that he'd found a likely young actor right here in Bangor. I expect he'll take him on to replace Charles."

"Unless Charles Underly is set free."

Ben turned to stare at Diana. She almost sounded as if she felt some sympathy for the fellow.

෨෬

Time hung heavily on Diana's hands after Ben escorted her and

Maggie home. He let them out in the porte-cochere and turned the buggy back towards town. He told them he meant to sit in on the prisoner's interrogation, that he wanted to be there when Underly broke down and confessed.

Maggie went off to bed. Nothing seemed to affect her ability to get a good night's sleep. But Diana could not settle down. At length she decided that she needed a bit of fresh air to help her relax. The day, like its weather, had contained high points and low points—rain in the forenoon had cleared off, then it had clouded up, then the skies had cleared again. Although overall it had been a mild day and tomorrow was supposed to be even more balmy, Diana added a heavy cloak on top of her new gown before she ventured out.

Taking her time, she made her way along the short stretch of path from the main house to the darkened carriage house. No lights burned, suggesting that Aaron was sound asleep. Joseph, she remembered, had his own snug little room on the lower level, tucked in between the bays where sleigh, buggy, and buckboard were kept.

She continued along the path, hoping the exercise would soon tire her out sufficiently to allow her to sleep through the night. Instead, she appeared to be waking up and thinking more clearly. Her uncertainty about Charles Underly's guilt increased. What evidence was there against him? Only what Lavinia had said. That information did seem incriminating, but what had impelled the young actress to come forward? Why, when everyone else thought Diana's threats were a joke, had she taken them seriously? Something, somewhere, did not make sense.

Guided by moonlight, Diana walked on until she came to the stand of ash that surrounded the crypt. The trees would leaf out soon. She wondered if she would be here to see them. There were times she thought Ben loved her and meant to propose marriage. Others when she was sure he saw no future for them.

If insanity could be inherited, then he might one day go mad.

So could any children he fathered. She exhaled a gusty sigh. There were ways to prevent conception—witness the sponge from Miss Jenny's, which she'd hidden in her armoire. But was she willing to take a risk on Ben himself?

Diana stopped at the sound of a soft footfall behind her. She looked back but saw only shadows and moonlight. Utter silence surrounded her. No creature seemed to be stirring and yet she suddenly had the uneasy feeling she was not alone.

There should be small sounds, she realized. Wildlife. Birds. Animals were only quiet when they sensed danger.

The bushes off to her right rustled. Cedric, she thought, out hunting mice. Or some other nocturnal creature. Then a shadow moved and fear stabbed through her. Whatever she'd just seen was as tall as she was. It had left waist-high branches swaying in its wake.

The blow came just as she bolted for the house, striking behind her right ear. Diana reeled as pain exploded. Colored stars flared before her eyes. In the second before everything went black, she knew they'd made a huge mistake. Charles Underly was not guilty.

The real killer was here.

When she came to her senses, she was lying on cold, smooth stone. Her head throbbed unmercifully. An involuntary moan escaped her.

"About time," a familiar voice said. "A crypt is not a comfortable place in which to wait."

Reluctantly, Diana lifted eyelids that felt weighted with cement. "You couldn't have killed those three women," she whispered.

"Why not?" Lavinia Ross demanded.

Diana's captor stood with her back braced against the heavy door of the Northcote family vault, blocking the exit. A flickering lantern cast eerie shadows over her facial features, but Diana could see her eyes plainly. There was no mistaking the hatred that glittered in them.

"The person who attacked me in New York—that was a man. I saw him. Felt his grip on me."

Lavinia laughed. "You must have more than one enemy, Diana. I had nothing to do with any attack in New York."

Foxe. It had been Foxe's man all along.

Diana cursed him silently for throwing her off Lavinia's trail.

Careful not to move too swiftly, lest she make the pain in her head worse, Diana eased herself upright. The beautiful velvet and satin gown felt cold against her body. The heavy cloak she wore did nothing to ward off the chill settling into her bones.

She had no idea how long she'd been unconscious, but she knew it was unlikely that anyone had seen them enter the vault. No one was going to rescue her this time. She had only her own wits to rely on.

At least Lavinia hadn't stabbed her on the spot. But a closer look at the object in the other woman's hand, the object she'd probably used to clout her victim on the head, sent Diana's optimism plunging. It was a deadly-looking pistol.

"I wanted to kill you in New York." Lavinia's words made Diana shiver in a reaction that had nothing to do with the temperature in the crypt. "I contrived to have Toddy invite you backstage, but you didn't come."

"Is that how you enticed those other women?"

Lavinia laughed again. This time the sound had a wildness about it, as if her control had slipped. Or her sanity. "Toddy has been useful," she admitted. "The fool was so blinded by love that he'd do anything I asked."

Had Toddy been her accomplice? Or an unwitting dupe?

"You were performing in Philadelphia in November as a magician's assistant," Diana said. "Dolly Dare must have seen that performance."

"She deserved to die! They all did! They said terrible things about me!"

The shrill voice made Diana flinch, but what terrified her was the look in Lavinia's eyes.

"Stay where you are!" Lavinia cocked the pistol for emphasis.

Diana gave up a reckless attempt to scramble to her feet and run. She swallowed convulsively and tried to reason with her captor. "With Charles in custody it will be difficult to blame my death on him. And shouldn't you stab me? The gun is all wrong."

With a visible effort, Lavinia got herself under control. She smiled sweetly and spoke in her little-girl voice. "Shall I shoot you? Or leave you here to die of starvation and cold? Or stab you to death? I didn't use Charles's sword-stick, you know. I have my own knife."

Diana didn't care much for any of those choices and liked Lavinia's erratic behavior even less.

"As it happens, I've already decided. I had time to think while you napped." Her tone sounded rational. Her words were not. "You will stay here long enough to contemplate all your sins against me. The others had only a moment to regret what they had done, but your crime is far greater. You betrayed your own kind. You thought you were clever, didn't you? You critics are all alike. You don't care who you hurt."

Diana stared at her as she muttered invective against her victims, quoting bits of bad reviews, clearly irrational on the subject. In her heart, Diana knew that nothing she'd written had been terrible enough to warrant such a reaction. She was not responsible for Lavinia's madness. And yet a sense of guilt pressed down on her, almost paralyzing in its intensity. Was this, she wondered, how Ben felt about Aaron's condition?

Abruptly, Lavinia began to shout. "You made a fatal mistake when you panned my performance, and another by not remembering that a woman can desire revenge as intensely as a man."

This was what Maggie had seen in Lavinia, Diana thought. The reason she'd imagined the actress capable of portraying Hannah

Sussep and the Blood Countess.

"I always meant to kill you, Diana." Lavinia fumbled behind her back with her free hand and opened the door. "You were doomed from the moment you first blackened my name in print."

"You cannot possibly hope to get away with this."

"Brave words," Lavinia sneered. "But I will, you see, and shift the blame to Charles Underly, too. Charles is sure to be released from jail. There's no real evidence against him. If worse comes to worst, I'll break him out. I learned how to pick locks in my previous career."

Diana eased to her feet as Lavinia backed out of the crypt, but the gun trained on her chest discouraged her from trying to rush the other woman.

"Why should Charles listen to you?" Did he know Lavinia was responsible for his arrest? Diana wasn't sure.

"He'll listen. I've never met a man yet I couldn't persuade to believe me. And afterward, dear Diana, I'll come back here and kill you and make it look as if Charles did you in."

"You're insane!"

"Am I? I prefer to think of myself as very, very clever." With a jaunty salute, she slipped through the opening and locked the vault behind her.

Alone in the crypt, Diana fought against incipient panic. Lavinia had left her in the vault alive. That meant there was at least a chance she might escape. Diana clung to that faint hope.

The temperature was above freezing, but it was still terribly cold. The flickering lantern provided no heat at all. Diana stopped and stared at it. When it ran out of oil, she'd be left in the dark. Hurriedly, she collected the other lanterns from their niches. Then she paced, since the only way to stay warm was to keep moving.

In a melodrama, she thought, the heroine locked in a tomb would be rescued in the nick of time by the hero, but this story wasn't following any script that Diana had ever read.

Ben would come home. Perhaps he had already returned. But

he'd assume she was asleep. No one would wonder where she was until at least late morning, and if Maggie went straight to work on her current project and Ben had to be in his office early, it might be evening before she was missed.

How long would it take Lavinia to carry out her plan? Hours? All day? Diana continued to prowl the confines of her prison like a caged beast. That there were glaring holes in Lavinia's logic, flaws that could lead to her capture, did little to cheer her. If Lavinia did not return, Diana might well freeze to death, or die of starvation.

It was only when she stopped pacing that she became aware of a current of colder air. Puzzled, she sought the source and located a grate high above her head. She'd assumed that the crypt was soundproof and had made no attempt to call for help, but where air could come in, perhaps sound could get out.

Diana shouted for all she was worth and did not stop until her throat was raw and her voice raspy.

Nothing! Frustration turned to anger. If she did not survive this ordeal, at the least she must find a way to implicate Lavinia in her death. Picking up the lantern, she studied the vaulted chamber. It was all but bare, since the Northcotes sealed up their deceased kinfolk. Lacking any other source of inspiration, Diana began to read inscriptions.

Abraham Northcote, Ben and Aaron's father, had died eight years earlier. To his right was a space for Maggie. "Magda Bathory Northcote, Beloved Wife of Abraham Northcote," the brass plate said. It gave her birth date—1837—but left the space for date of death blank.

To the left of Abraham Northcote was another brass plate. Diana leaned closer, expecting to find the name of a sister, or perhaps some member of the previous generation. Instead, like Maggie's inscription, the plaque said "Beloved Wife of Abraham Northcote."

Miriam Graham, Beloved Wife of Abraham Northcote, 1830-1856.

Ben's father had married twice. His first wife had died thirty-two years ago. Diana chewed thoughtfully on her lower lip, wondering how old Ben was. She'd never been any good at guessing ages.

Aaron, she mused, had inherited his mother's eyes.

Had Ben?

The lantern sputtered. Before it could go out, Diana lit a second one, glad she'd had the presence of mind to plan ahead. The conclusion she'd just drawn cheered her considerably, but she still had no idea how to go about leaving a clue.

ℰↄ◯ଢ଼

Underly's questioning went on for some time. He repeatedly claimed he was innocent of any wrongdoing. "I was sound asleep in the parlor car the night Diana fell," he insisted. "And I never had any intention of seducing Lavinia Ross."

Ben frowned. A sudden, clear memory surfaced—Underly snoring as Ben was attempting to doze off. It must have been about the time Diana left the parlor car, and Underly had an annoying, distinctive snore. The racket had continued, uninterrupted, right up until Jerusha noticed Diana in the snowbank and screamed for help.

Leaving Underly in custody—it was still possible that he was the killer, and that Diana had fallen by accident—Ben made his way to the Windsor Hotel. The night clerk knew him on sight and gave him no trouble about room numbers. He even provided a master key.

A few minutes later, Ben knocked politely at Lavinia Ross's door. The woman had lied about Underly being in the drawing-room car. He wanted to know why.

When he got no answer, Ben pounded on the wooden panels. There was no response from Lavinia, but the noise brought Patsy, rubbing sleep out of her eyes, to the door of the adjacent room. Ben spared her only a glance before he let himself into Lavinia's room. "Empty!"

"Try Toddy's," Patsy suggested. But Lavinia was not there either. Nor was Nathan Todd.

Under overcast skies, Ben drove home at a fast clip, only to discover that Diana was also missing.

ഇാൽ

Diana had no idea how much time passed while she waited, huddled on the landing in the crypt, trying in vain to contain her almost constant trembling. Did the moon still light the sky outside? Or was it day already? She fought tiredness, knowing that if she slept she'd have no warning at all when Lavinia returned for her.

She'd sacrificed her gown to leave a clue. Fumbling beneath the warm cloak, reluctant to remove it if she didn't have to, she'd torn at the frills of lace on her shoulders. They'd come off more easily than she'd expected. In a corner of the vault, out of easy sight of the door, she'd arranged bits of fabric on the flagstones to form Lavinia Ross's initials. As final messages went, it wasn't much, but she felt better for knowing Lavinia would not get away with her crimes.

Even though she'd been expecting it, the sudden sound of the door opening startled Diana. She scrambled awkwardly to her feet, hastily removing her cloak and bracing herself to throw it over Lavinia's head. She froze as the lantern she'd set on the floor caught the ominous glint of metal. Lavinia held an unsheathed blade in one hand and her gun in the other.

Risking a moment of exposure, Diana tossed the heavy fabric and rushed out after it. She pushed Lavinia aside and bolted through the door, shouting for help and praying someone would hear.

Lavinia let out an infuriated shriek. "I'll kill you!" she shouted. One corner of the cloak slipped, allowing her to wrench a hand free. As she lunged after Diana, she dropped the knife but managed to catch hold of the back of Diana's skirt with enough strength to throw them both off balance.

As she fell, Diana rolled towards the protective shelter of the trees and away from the lantern's beams. Murky clouds filled the sky and low-lying ground fog eddied around her. There was a chance she could hide.

Lavinia wrenched free of the cloak. She still had possession of the gun. Lifting it, she took aim.

Diana squeezed her eyes shut . . . .

She opened them again at the sound of a grunt. A man had tackled Lavinia. Together they writhed in a tangle of limbs on the frozen ground, now visible, now concealed by the swirling mist.

"You'll not harm her!" Diana's rescuer declared.

"Ben?" The voice was muffled and all she could see of him was dark hair and broad shoulders beneath a white shirt that reflected the lantern light . . . and the gun caught between the combatants, primed and ready to fire.

Diana stumbled to her feet.

A single shot exploded, drowning out her cries for help. The man's heavier body carried the woman's to the ground and pinned it. Then both figures lay ominously still.

Feeling as if her heart had just been rent in two, Diana tried to run to them. Her legs refused to cooperate. She collapsed, tears veiling the terrible sight of a dark stain spreading across the white fabric of the shirt.

A crashing sounded in the shrubbery. Suddenly the small clearing was filled with sound and confusion.

"Too late," Diana moaned, covering her face with her hands. He was dead. Dead trying to save her.

"Diana? Are you hurt?" Strong arms seized her, hauling her unceremoniously into an embrace.

"Ben?" His dear face was close to her own. There was no mistake. "I thought it was you—"

He followed the direction of her gaze and froze. His breath

hitched. "Aaron."

Leaving Diana's side, Ben knelt next to his brother's motionless form. As he pulled Aaron off Lavinia, the actress tried to crawl away.

Aaron. Not Ben. Still numb with shock and horror, Diana watched two men wearing badges take Lavinia into custody. She did not go without a struggle. She was still shrieking curses when they dragged her away.

Ignoring the commotion, Ben gently lifted his brother and carried him towards the carriage house. "He's alive," he said as he passed Diana. "but just barely."

Diana struggled to her feet, meaning to follow, but someone stepped in front of her, blocking the way. She blinked, at first unable to believe her eyes. The cigar clamped between his teeth bobbled as Horatio Foxe scowled down at her.

"Been busy stirring up trouble again, I see."

Less than an hour later, sitting across from Foxe in the breakfast room, Diana sipped coffee and attempted to sort out what he'd just told her. She only picked at the food on her plate, her appetite dulled by her concern for Ben and his brother.

Foxe, who had no trouble putting away a hearty breakfast, had arrived on the 5:30 AM train from the west. By that time, Ben had returned home, gone to Diana's room, and discovered she was missing. Meanwhile, Charles Underly had been released for lack of evidence.

"Where did Underly go when they set him free?" Diana asked, remembering Lavinia's plan to convince him to flee.

"He'd just turned up in the lobby of the Windsor when Dr. Northcote returned there after finding you gone. It seems Underly thought better of following advice from the very person whose accusations had made him seem guilty."

"Where was Toddy? Didn't he notice Lavinia's wanderings?"

"Gone back to Miss Fildale. Dr. Northcote rousted them out of her hotel room and called in the local constabulary. He recruited every able-bodied man he could find to search for you." Foxe dragged on his cigar and rubbed his hands in glee. "What a story! What a scandal! You'll have to write it up from your own perspective, but I was here at the end. I can add my bit."

"Why did you come?" Diana asked, sipping more coffee. It didn't seem to help. Her mind remained wrapped in fuzz and she still felt half frozen.

She glanced up in time to see Horatio Foxe turn an interesting shade of red. "Well, er . . . confound it, Diana! What would I tell m'sister, eh, if anything happened to you?"

They sat in silence for a few minutes before another question occurred to Diana. "How did Ben guess I'd be in the crypt?"

"It was that young actor, Billy Sims. He told Northcote how Lavinia Ross had gone on and on about Mrs. Northcote's story of locking you in that place once before. Northcote's got good instincts. Guessed right away that Lavinia might stash you there. Then, of course, the minute we set foot on the property we heard you screaming."

Her heart went cold at the thought of how close Ben had come to being the first man on the scene. Then she immediately felt guilty. Aaron had been horribly wounded saving her. For all Diana knew, he was even now at death's door. Ben hadn't let anyone into the carriage house but Maggie, and neither of them had come out again.

"Well, Diana," said Foxe, finishing off the last of the sausages. "How soon can you be ready for the trip back to New York?" He took out his pocket watch and contemplated its face. "It's too late for the 7:15 for Boston but if you hurry up and pack we can catch the Flying Yankee."

"I can't leave now!"

"Of course you can. Nothing to hold you here. Is there?"

When she didn't answer, he looked alarmed.

"Well, now. I guess that means you want me to sweeten the pot." He cleared his throat. "Meant to, anyway. M' sister has been saying for months that I don't make the best use of your talents. How does the police beat sound? No more scandal. Just murders and other juicy crimes."

Not very long ago, reporting the news had been Diana's fondest dream. She told herself she'd be a fool to turn down Foxe's offer. And yet she hesitated.

"Confound it, Diana! What's the matter with you?"

"Maybe she doesn't like the way you do business, Foxe." From the doorway, Ben fixed the editor with a hard, cold stare. "You hired an out-of-work actor to attack Mrs. Spaulding, just to persuade her that I was a viable suspect in two murders that had nothing to do with me."

"They were connected." Foxe puffed himself up and glared back.

"If not for you, Diana would never have been mixed up in this and my brother wouldn't be fighting for his life."

"He's still alive?" Tears of relief sprang into Diana's eyes.

"For now. The bullet struck near the heart and he's lost a lot of blood."

"How can I help? You said once that I'd make a good nurse."

Horatio Foxe bounced up and down in agitation. "You work for me, Diana."

Both Diana and Ben ignored him. "That's not necessary, Diana," Ben said. "I have Mother's help. And Joseph's."

Foxe sputtered indignantly and went so far as to employ the word "raise."

"Do you want to go back to New York?" Ben asked.

"I do have to earn a living."

"Stay here and write for the *Whig and Courier.*" The heat of his gaze was so intense that if she'd been a candle she'd have melted into a puddle of wax.

"If not for me, Aaron would never have risked his life," Diana whispered.

"What happened to Aaron wasn't your fault. In fact, having seen his paintings, I'd say he acted to save his muse—an idealized concept, not a flesh and blood woman. Because of you, even if he doesn't pull through, he'll have left a legacy in those portraits and seascapes."

"Nevertheless, I should leave." She didn't want to go, but so much was unsettled here. Her presence would only add to the turmoil. "You need to focus on helping Aaron recover. You don't need the added burden of—"

"I need you."

"Do you want a wife, or just a shoulder to cry on?" Foxe interrupted.

His bluntness grated on Diana, but Ben didn't seem to mind the plain speaking.

"I want a wife," he said.

Those were words she'd longed to hear, and because she wanted so badly to believe he meant them, she knew she must be sensible. "Aaron—"

"If it's the fear of inherited madness that's holding you back, it need not concern you. Father married Maggie when I was two. I don't remember my real mother and have always called Maggie by that name, but I'm not descended from the Bathorys." He kept his gaze on Diana. "Only Aaron was."

Remembering the inscription in the crypt, she nodded. He'd just confirmed what she'd already worked out for herself.

He drew in a deep breath. "I know Maggie isn't the easiest person to live with. My mother—stepmother—is—"

"Eccentric," she finished for him.

"To say the least. Can you accept her as she is?"

The question was not asked lightly, and Diana took the time to consider. She was no longer afraid of Maggie, but would Aaron's mother want her around if Aaron failed to recover from his wound? Would she hold Diana responsible for his death?

Puffing on his cigar, Foxe looked from one to the other. "Even if she were to marry you at once, she'd still need to return to New York to put her affairs in order."

"That shouldn't take more than a week." Ben crossed the room to go down on one knee beside her chair. When he took both her hands in his, Horatio Foxe slipped past them and left the room, for once respectful of someone else's privacy.

"Ben—"

"Marry me, Diana."

But she shook her head. "We did not even know each other a month ago."

"What difference does that make?"

"I married in haste once, Ben. I don't want to make the same mistake again." A flood of memories from her life with Evan streamed into her mind, none of them happy. And she remembered how Rowena had tried to talk her out of eloping. She hadn't listened to Foxe's sister and she'd lived to regret it.

Ben rose and took a step away from her. For one chilling moment, Diana thought he was about to give in and tell her she should go back to New York with Horatio Foxe.

His hands curled into fists at his sides. "I don't want to live without you. When I thought I'd lost you forever, thought I might never see you again, it was almost more than I could bear."

Diana could read that remembered torment in his eyes, but she had also seen his reaction when he thought his brother was dead. "Evan—"

"I'm not Evan!" His temper flared quickly and was gone again in an instant. He spread his arms wide, inviting her to take a good look at him. "Am I anything like your late husband?"

She shook her head. "But that changes nothing. You need to look after Aaron. I need to be sure what I feel for you is real. We both need time apart. If we rush into marriage, we might be making a terrible mistake, one that could ruin the rest of our lives."

"I won't change my mind about wanting to marry you, Diana, but I understand that you have to be sure how you feel about me.

And about Mother and Aaron. I'll give you another month, the same amount of time we've known each other. If you haven't returned to Bangor by the end of April, I'll come to you and we'll settle this."

He returned to her side and bent to kiss her lips, sealing the bargain, then left the room before she could voice any more objections.

The abrupt departure left her reeling.

Cedric appeared in the empty doorway a moment later. The black cat padded across the carpet, leapt into Diana's lap, and curled himself into a ball. Without thinking, Diana dropped her hand to his back and began to stroke his soft fur. The steady rhythm of the movement and the deep, throaty purr it elicited from the cat soothed her troubled thoughts.

By her silence, she had given tacit agreement to Ben's proposal. Mesmerism? Sorcery? Or love? To her own surprise, Diana realized she was smiling.

"The next time I see Ben Northcote," she told the cat, "I will be the one who tells him what we will do next."

She would go back to New York with Horatio Foxe, Diana decided. She might even try out that new assignment he'd offered her. But first and foremost, she'd use the weeks away from Ben to contemplate her past. That was the only way she'd be able to make sensible decisions about the future.

"April," she said to Cedric, as she scratched him behind one ear and provoked a positive ecstasy of purring. "A month." She nodded. "Yes, that seems an entirely reasonable length of time."

Just look how much had happened to her in March!

Author's Note

ഇറ

Although the characters in *Deadlier than the Pen* are fictional, I've made reference to a number of real historical figures, in particular to Nellie Bly, intrepid reporter for the New York *World,* whose investigation into the treatment of the insane is the basis for what Ben sees and Diana imagines. Both New York City, particularly "the Rialto," and Bangor, Maine are real places. They are presented as accurately as I could manage. Only specific private homes, and one newspaper office, are complete inventions. Real newspapers from 1888 provided a tremendous amount of information about these places and I am grateful to Mantor Library at the University of Maine at Farmington and the Maine State Library for collecting so many of them on microfilm.

I have incorporated a number of incidents that occurred during the Blizzard of '88 into my novel, in particular stories of passengers trapped on trains. The party for Jim the "trick cat" and the camel's escape on Broadway were also real events.

Those readers interested in the sources I've used will find a complete bibliography at my website:

www.kathylynnemerson.com

Look there, too, for information about the next Diana Spaulding mystery.